BRIGHT LIGHTS,
BIG CHRISTMAS

Bright Lights, Big Christmas

A Novel

Mary Kay Andrews

THORNDIKE PRESS
A part of Gale, a Cengage Company

Copyright © 2023 by Whodunnit, Inc.
Thorndike Press, a part of Gale, a Cengage Company.

Thorndike Press® Large Print Dynamic Drama.
The text of this Large Print edition is unabridged.
Other aspects of the book may vary from the original edition.
Set in 16 pt. Plantin.

**LIBRARY OF CONGRESS CIP DATA ON FILE.
CATALOGUING IN PUBLICATION FOR THIS BOOK
IS AVAILABLE FROM THE LIBRARY OF CONGRESS.**

ISBN-13: 979-8-88579-318-6 (hardcover alk. paper)

Published in 2023 by arrangement with St. Martin's Publishing Group

Printed in Mexico
Printed Number: 1   Print Year: 2024

For my niece, Sarah Abigail Murry,
with a heart full of love

CHAPTER 1

Kerry Clare Tolliver couldn't remember a time when the smell of a Fraser fir tree didn't make her smile.

Tollivers had been growing this particular variety of Christmas tree, in this particular patch of farmland in the mountains of western North Carolina, for four generations.

But today, standing in front of the flatbed trailer loaded with hundreds of freshly cut and baled fragrant firs, she wanted to cry.

"Mama, please don't ask me to do this," she whispered.

Her mother wrapped an arm around Kerry's shoulders. "I'm sorry, honey, but there's nobody else. Your daddy is coming home from the hospital tomorrow, and somebody's got to be there to make sure he eats and takes his meds and gets his sorry butt up to do physical therapy. Like it or not, that somebody is me."

"What about his sorry wife? Seems like it shouldn't be his *ex*-wife who has to play nurse."

Birdie — short for Roberta Tolliver — gave a short laugh. "Come on. You know Brenda is the human equivalent of a potted plastic plant. Cute, but useless. Anyway, I'm not supposed to know, and I'm sure as hell not supposed to tell you, but Murphy says she's flown the coop. Moved out right before Halloween. Honestly, I really don't mind. But that means you've got to step up and take Jock's place. We've already missed out on the first week of the selling season. Either you go to New York and run the tree stand with Murphy, or it doesn't happen."

Kerry shrugged. "Would that be such a bad thing? I mean, can't we sell the trees to our local retailers, like always?"

"No."

Kerry turned to see Murphy, her older brother, who'd walked up behind them. He was an imposing figure — six-four, with a beefy build, dark bristly beard, and weather-beaten skin. Dressed in a quilted plaid flannel jacket, jeans, and muddy work boots, with a chain saw slung over his shoulder, he looked like something straight off a wrapper of paper towels.

"That late freeze in May wiped out a

8

quarter of the trees. Locals won't pay the premium prices to make up for the loss. Anyway, the New York trip accounts for seventy-five percent of our revenue, and like Mama said, we're already a week behind."

Murphy stowed the chain saw in the toolbox in the back of his pickup truck and slammed the lid for emphasis.

Now Kerry was eyeing her father's truck — the rusting 1982 Ford F-150 with the vintage fifteen-foot travel trailer hooked up behind it. Like the pickup, the trailer had seen better days. The teardrop-shaped body with faded two-tone turquoise-and-white paint looked like a discarded canned ham.

Spammy, as the Tollivers called the 1963 Shasta trailer, spent most of the year parked in a barn at the tree farm. But every November, for nearly four decades, on the day after Thanksgiving, the trailer got hitched to the truck and then driven the seven hundred miles to New York City, where the Tollivers set up their Christmas tree stand in the West Village. This year, Jock's heart attack and hospitalization had delayed the trip by a week.

"I can't believe you expect me to live in this hunk of junk," Kerry said, walking around the trailer and peering in through the door, which was draped with spider-webs.

"Have a little respect," Birdie said, patting the trailer's mud-splattered door. "Spammy is practically a family heirloom."

Kerry pointed at the curtained-off cubicle that contained the dreaded chemical toilet. "There's no way I'm using that gross thing."

"It don't work anyway," Murphy said.

"Then where . . . ?"

"We use the bathroom at the café, or at the deli on the corner," her brother said. "Neighbors let us use their showers."

He grabbed a broom and thrust it at her. "Might want to sweep it out before you hit the road. I think there's a squirrel's nest in the bunk where you'll be sleeping." He looked at his watch. "I'm leaving outta here five minutes from now, which should put me in the city by tomorrow, noon, at the latest. I need to know now, right now, whether you're coming. Otherwise, the trip's off. We can't afford to hire help this year."

Birdie's calm gray eyes seemed to bore into Kerry's soul. Birdie had been only seventeen when she had Murphy, twenty-one when she had Kerry. She and Jock had split up when Kerry was seven. Murphy had stayed on the farm with Jock, and Birdie

10

and Kerry had moved into a small cottage in town. The two were more like sisters than mother and daughter. Kerry knew Birdie would never *order* her to make this trip. Not in so many words. She'd kill her with that pleading look, slay her with silence. Birdie Tolliver was a ninja master at guilt.

"It's not that I don't want to go. I do. I'm willing to help. But I'm terrified of towing the trailer."

"Don't be such a scaredy-cat," Birdie said. "You used to tow the boat to the lake every summer, growing up. And what about all those years you towed the horse trailer when you were show jumping?"

Kerry sighed. She knew she was beaten. "Okay. I'll do it."

Birdie beamed. "It'll be almost like old times. You used to love it when the four of us would live in Spammy in the city. You thought it was like living in a dollhouse." A dreamy look crossed Kerry's mother's face.

"New York at Christmas is magical. Walking down Fifth Avenue to see all the store windows decorated. Getting hot chocolate at the market at Union Square . . ."

"Won't be time for any of that with just the two of us working the tree stand this year," Murphy said bluntly.

He pointed at Kerry, taking in her fashion-

11

able slim jeans, lightweight sweater, and suede flats.

"Hope you got warmer clothes than that. We got a space heater in the trailer, but it gets cold on that street corner, with the wind whipping down from those apartment buildings. Call me when you're an hour out from the city and I'll put out the traffic cones to block off our parking spot."

Murphy climbed up into the cab of his own truck, where his English setter Queenie was patiently waiting in the passenger seat, fired up the diesel engine, and slowly drove away.

Kerry watched as the trailer loaded with trees moved down the farm's rocky driveway. It was sunny and in the mid-sixties, but she shivered, already anticipating the month she was about to spend living in that cramped trailer, coexisting with a brother she hardly knew.

"You'll be fine," Birdie said, reading her mind. "He's kinda rough around the edges, but Murphy's a good man. And I think it'll be good for you to get back to a big city again. You can't keep hiding out here in the boondocks forever, you know."

CHAPTER 2

Murphy had been wrong about the squirrel's nest in the bunk. It had actually been mice that had taken up residence in the crumbling slab of foam mattress. One of the tiny residents went scurrying across the floor as soon as she set foot in the trailer.

Kerry screeched loudly, caught the mouse with her broom, swept it out the open trailer door, then picked up the mattress and flung it outside. She spent the next three hours sweeping and scrubbing and sanitizing the trailer.

It was obvious that no woman had slept a single night here since her parents had divorced.

Jock's string of girlfriends — and his most recent wife, Brenda — had shown no interest in accompanying their man on the annual trip to New York.

And as for Murphy? He'd lived alone, since high school graduation, in a sharecropper's cabin on the farm that he'd painstakingly restored. Kerry knew, from the gossip around Tarburton, that her resolutely reclusive brother dated — and was what she might call a serial monogamist — but he'd never introduced any of his lady friends to her or Birdie.

Murphy was thirty-nine, she was thirty-four, and although they were brother and sister, the two hadn't lived under the same roof in decades. He was a stranger to her.

But then, Kerry mused, as she peered into a tiny mirror tacked outside the unused bathroom cubicle, that cut both ways. What did Murphy, or anyone else in the family, really, know about her?

When she'd moved back home to Tarburton three months earlier, she'd been deliberately vague about what she called a "temporary" relocation. She hadn't mentioned the fact that the advertising agency in Charlotte where she worked as an art director had merged with another, larger agency in Atlanta, thus rendering her what the firm's human resources department liked to call "redundant."

Kerry had been working nonstop since graduation from art school in Savannah, until she was suddenly . . . not. She'd managed to live on her separation pay for the first three months, but the rent on the Charlotte loft was ridiculously expensive, and every day, as she stared at the online account of her dwindling savings, she'd asked herself why.

She'd built a life around her work. Her boyfriend, Blake, was an account executive at the ad agency. Most of her friends either worked there or were people she'd met through networking. Once she was out of work, she realized, with more than a trace of bitterness, she was also out of mind.

Blake hadn't actually ghosted her. He'd just . . . gradually shifted his interest, until the only souvenirs she had of their two-year relationship were a tennis racket he'd left in her hall closet, along with a windbreaker and a tube of the expensive toothpaste he bought online.

There was nothing keeping her in Charlotte. It was time to face facts. It was time to go home — to her childhood bedroom at Birdie's cottage a few blocks from the square in Tarburton.

She took on some freelance graphic design assignments, mostly website work that she could probably do in her sleep. Aside from taking an occasional walk around the square, Kerry rarely strayed far from the house.

15

"You're getting to be a hermit, just like Murphy," Birdie observed one sunny autumn Saturday morning, as she headed out with a basket over her arm to meet up with old friends at the weekly farmers' market on the square.

Kerry looked up from the novel she was rereading. "I'm fine. Okay?"

Birdie shrugged. "I just think it's a shame to stay inside on a gorgeous day like this. Winter will be here before you know it."

"I happen to like winter," Kerry told Birdie.

"I'll remind you of that in January, when the roads up here are iced over and we haven't seen sunshine in days and everything is gray and gloomy," her mother retorted.

The truth was, Kerry rarely ventured into her hometown because she felt so out of place there — like an alien, beamed down to the wrong planet. During the last few months she'd lived in Charlotte, she'd felt aimless and adrift there, too. Maybe, she thought, experiencing a fleeting moment of optimism, a month away from both places, in New York, was what she needed, to reset her equilibrium.

Birdie hefted a cooler onto the front seat of

the pickup truck. "There's sandwiches here so you don't have to stop to eat." She placed a plaid thermos in the truck's cup holder. "Here's your coffee. Your daddy said to tell you there's a good rest stop outside Winchester, Virginia, where he and Murphy always pull over. Clean bathrooms and plenty of room to park. Make sure you lock the doors and get a couple hours of sleep before you get back on the road."

"Okay," Kerry said. She drummed her fingers on the steering wheel. The sun was rising, peeking through the fog-shrouded mountains. Nervous energy fizzled in her veins. She hadn't slept much the night before, worrying about the trip, towing the trailer while braving New York City traffic, and yes, the prospect of living in a mouse-infested claustrophobic canned ham for the next three weeks.

"I better get going," she said, gunning the engine. "I don't wanna piss Murphy off by being late."

"Have you got your phone? And your charger? Plenty of wool socks? Extra underwear? God knows when you'll get to do laundry."

"Yes, yes, yes, and yes," Kerry said. "I'm a grown-ass woman, Mom. Not an eight-year-old going to summer camp."

"I know," Birdie said, leaning in and kissing Kerry on the cheek. "And I know you'll be working, selling trees. But don't forget what I said about the magic of New York at Christmas. Don't forget to stop and have fun."

"You mean, don't forget to stop and sniff the subway platform?"

"Don't be like that," Birdie chastised.

"Fun. Right." Kerry rolled her eyes.

She took a deep breath, looked both ways, and slowly pulled out onto the county road. "As if."

18

CHAPTER 3

Google Maps told her she should reach New York in nearly ten hours, which would have put her in the city by around five o'clock Saturday.

But those maps didn't account for an aging truck with a top speed of fifty miles per hour, towing a fifteen-foot trailer. It didn't account for the construction delays on the interstate, snarled traffic around multiple wrecks, and it definitely didn't take into consideration the frequent stops necessitated by a white-knuckle driver amped up by too much caffeine.

It was already past three when Kerry pulled into the rest stop outside Winchester. She found a parking spot at the back of the lot, locked the door, and, despite all the coffee, instantly dozed off.

It was nearing dark when her phone buzzed her back to consciousness. She yawned and reached for the phone, gasping when she saw the time — 5:30 — and the caller — Murphy Tolliver.

"Are you getting close?" Her brother never wasted time on niceties.

"Not exactly. This damn truck won't go over fifty, and with all the construction on the interstate . . ."

"Okay, where are you? Jersey?"

"More like Virginia."

"Jesus, Kerry! You're still hours away. At the rate you're going it'll be close to midnight. I haven't slept in two days and I'm freezing my ass off in this truck waiting around on you."

"Then get a hotel room," she snapped. "I'm doing the best I can."

"We can't afford a hotel in the city. Just call me when you're an hour out. And hurry up. We need to be ready to start selling trees first thing in the morning."

He disconnected and Kerry scowled down at the phone. "Gonna be a fun few weeks, for sure."

By the time she'd navigated the Lincoln Tunnel and emerged onto West Thirty-Eighth Street, Kerry's hands were slippery with sweat and her pulse rate was sky high. If her GPS was correct, she was thirty minutes away from the corner in the West

Village where Murphy had erected the tree stand.

She tapped his name on her call list and he picked up on the first ring. "Hey. You getting close?"

"According to my phone, I'm five miles away." Her eyes burned with fatigue and her stomach roiled from the stress of the day.

"Well, I've got bad news. Some a-hole in a gray Mercedes parked in front of the stand. Pisses me off. Everybody in the neighborhood knows we park the trailer here this time of year. If it's not moved, you'll have to park down the block. I'll put out some cones to try to block it off till you get here."

"Okay. Whatever." She wanted to ask Murphy why he hadn't blocked off the spot in front of the tree stand *before* the rich a-hole parked there, but arguing with her brother was like howling into a hurricane. A waste of time.

As she got closer to Greenwich Village she held her breath and slowed her roll. She was terrified she'd sideswipe cars parked on both sides of the already narrow streets. As she passed street signs, old memories from those long-ago family trips to the city bubbled to the surface. Morton Street.

She'd Rollerbladed down this block on a quiet Sunday, hanging on to a rope being towed behind Murphy on his bike. And yes, Christopher Street. There was a street vendor on this corner who sold roasted chestnuts, and wasn't that the deli with the black-and-white cookies she'd never seen any place but New York?

The buzz of her phone yanked her back to reality.

"Look up ahead. I'm waving at you from the right side of the street."

Sure enough, there was Murphy, who'd stepped off the curb at the next intersection and was waving both arms over his head.

At the same time she spotted the sign. TOLLIVER FAMILY CHRISTMAS TREES: FARM FRESH SINCE 1954, painted in Birdie's neat hand-lettering. The tree stand was wrapped around the corner of Hudson and Twelfth, and the trees themselves were stacked upright against the rough-cut two-by-four fencing that Murphy had erected.

And just as he'd warned, a gleaming charcoal-gray Mercedes sedan was parked in front of the stand, squarely in the middle of two parking spaces and directly in front of Murphy's pickup.

"A-hole," Kerry muttered.

Her brother jogged over to where she was

idling. "Slide over and I'll get it parked across the street." Murphy's breath formed puffs in the cold night air. He pointed to a space on the cross street, several yards down, where he'd placed four traffic cones between two construction dumpsters.

"What? You don't think a girl can park this trailer?" Kerry shot back. "Dad taught me how to back a trailer onto the boat ramp at the lake when I was fifteen. And I parked a horse trailer at shows all over the state for years."

"Not on a street like this, with city traffic and cars parked on both sides of the street you didn't," Murphy said. "This ain't about you being a girl. You're not used to parking this trailer, and I am. Now shove over and let's get this done, dammit."

Instead, Kerry opened the door and jumped down onto the pavement. "Go ahead, Murphy. Mansplain to me how it's done."

The cold air hit her like a blast. When she'd dressed that morning, she'd dressed for North Carolina cold, with temperatures in the fifties. But this was New York City cold; temperatures were hovering in the high twenties. She was already regretting her windbreaker, jeans, and tennis shoes.

She ran across the street, dodging oncoming cars, and stood in front of the first dumpster. Murphy waited until the light changed, and while Kerry picked up the traffic cones to make room, he made a wide left turn onto the cross street, pulled the nose of the Ford in front of where she stood, and with no back and forth at all, nimbly slotted the truck and the trailer between the dumpsters.

Kerry stood, chagrined, with her mouth hanging open. Her brother got out of the truck cab and went around to the rear of the trailer, inspecting his parking job. She walked around and met him at the door to Spammy.

"Okay, you win," she admitted. "That was amazing."

Murphy grunted and opened the door of the trailer, ducking as he stepped inside with flashlight in hand. "Let's hit the rack. Gonna be a busy day tomorrow."

She watched as her brother pulled a sleeping bag from the cupboard beneath the kitchen dining booth. He lowered the pads from the benches on either side of the Formica-topped table so that they formed a mattress, then removed his jacket and balled it up to use as a pillow. Finally, he unlaced his boots, shoved them beneath the bunk, and stretched out, pulling the sleeping bag up until it reached his chin. He whistled, and Queenie joined him on the bunk.

"That's it? You're just gonna go to sleep?" Kerry stood looking down at Murphy. "It's freezing cold in here. Where am I supposed to pee?"

He rolled on his side to face her but didn't open his eyes. "We can't hook up the electricity or the space heater until we move this thing over to the spot in front of the tree stand. There's another sleeping bag and a couple extra blankets in the cupboard above your bunk. Me and Dad just use an old coffee can, but if you're gonna be a priss-ass, go to Lombardi's, the café across the street. You can use their bathroom, and if you're hungry, ask Claudia for something to eat. Tell her you're my sister. But go now because they close in thirty minutes."

Murphy rolled over, turning his back to her. She'd been dismissed.

Kerry speed-walked to Lombardi's. The café occupied the ground floor of a six-story brownstone. It was almost midnight, as Murphy had pointed out, and the place was nearly deserted. A server was washing glasses behind the bar that lined the right side of the room, and a curvy blonde stood

25

at the hostess stand, rolling silver in linen napkins.

"Uh, hi," Kerry started. "I'm Murphy Tolliver's sister. I know it's late, but he said you'd let me use your bathroom?"

The woman pointed toward the rear of the dining room. "On the left. Help yourself."

The hostess was still at her post when Kerry emerged from the bathroom. "Thank you so much," she told the woman. "Murphy said I should ask for Claudia?"

"That's me," the woman said. "You hungry, hon? There's some pasta fagioli left from the dinner special. And maybe a glass of wine to warm you up?"

Her stomach rumbled at the mention of food. She looked around the café. A towering Christmas tree with red, white, and green twinkle lights filled the front window. The tables had fresh white linen cloths and drippy wax candles stuck into straw-wrapped chianti bottles. Lombardi's was the classic old-school red-sauce kind of place you didn't find in small Southern towns like Tarburton. "I wouldn't want to keep you . . ."

"You're not," Claudia said. "I've still got to count out the cash register and finish up my side work. Sit over there at the bar and

26

tell Danny what you're drinking. I'll run back to the kitchen for your soup."

She was savoring a generous pour of Valpolicella when Claudia slipped a bowl of steaming soup in front of her, along with a napkin-wrapped basket of breadsticks and a tiny bowl of butter.

"Thank you *so* much," Kerry said, dipping her spoon into the thick meatball-studded broth. "Mmm. This smells divine."

"My grandmother's recipe," Claudia said. She helped herself to a breadstick and nibbled on it. "So you're Murph's sister."

Danny the bartender leaned over and stared at Kerry. "Yeah, I guess I see some family resemblance."

"It's these doggone thick eyebrows," Kerry said, pushing her hair out of her eyes. "The curse of the Tollivers."

"I didn't even know Murph had a sister," Danny volunteered. "I thought he was like, raised by wolves down there in those North Carolina mountains."

Kerry laughed and took another sip of wine. "That's partly true. Our parents split up when I was seven, and Murphy stayed on the farm with our dad. I guess he really took that mountain man image to heart."

"Ya think?" Claudia said. "Speaking of,

when is Jock coming?"

"Murphy didn't tell you? Daddy had a heart attack, followed by quadruple bypass surgery. That's why I came this year."

"Your brother's not exactly forthcoming about stuff like that. I was wondering why you guys weren't here right after Thanksgiving. I'm sorry to hear about your dad. He's a good guy. He always seems so . . ."

"Indestructible?" Kerry suggested. "He certainly thought so. Maybe now he'll finally give up smoking."

"Just as long as he don't give up drinking," Danny interjected.

Kerry kept gazing around the room. "This place seems so familiar to me. Has it always been here?"

"Since 1962," Claudia said. "I'm the third generation to run Lombardi's."

"That explains it," Kerry said. "I have this vague memory of sitting right here, but on a stack of phone books, eating a big bowl of spaghetti. There was a white-haired lady who showed me how to twirl the noodles around my fork."

"That would be my grandma, Anna," Claudia said. "So you used to come to the city too?"

"Yeah. Me and Murphy and my parents. But I stopped coming after the divorce."

28

"Four of you, including two little kids? Living in that thing?" Claudia laughed. "That's taking togetherness to an extreme, if you ask me."

"Can you see the two of us living together in a camper?" Danny asked, poking Claudia's arm.

"Bad enough we have to work together," she said.

"You two are family?"

"First cousins, technically," Danny said.

Kerry scraped the bottom of her bowl to scoop up the last bit of soup. She dabbed her lips with her napkin and reached in the pocket of her jacket to retrieve her billfold.

"No charge," Claudia said quickly. "On the house."

"But . . ."

"We got a deal with your family," Danny explained. "We get the biggest, best Tolliver Christmas tree every year, and you guys get the Lombardi meal plan."

"At least let me pay for the wine," Kerry said.

"No way," Claudia said firmly. "And listen, in the morning, if you need coffee and a bathroom, come over to Anna's, that's our bakery next door. Danny's daughter Lidia will take care of you."

"Really? That would be great," Kerry said,

suppressing a yawn.

Claudia walked to the café's front door, unlocked it, and held it open. "I'm not actually kicking you out, but I kinda am. We know how early your brother gets going in the morning."

"Thanks again," Kerry told her. "I have a feeling tomorrow is going to be a long day."

CHAPTER 4

Kerry tiptoed into the trailer. To her shock, while she was gone, Murphy had made up her bunk. The mattress was thin, the blankets smelled like mildew, and the pillow was rock hard. Still, she was dead asleep within minutes.

In her dream, Murphy hefted his chain saw from his shoulder, yanked the pull-cord, and an ear-splitting buzz filled the morning air. He held the saw against the base of a massive tree's trunk, and the roar grew louder.

Kerry could feel the earth shaking beneath her feet, smell the sharp tang of fresh-cut pine.

She wanted to scream, to stop her brother from felling the tree. She opened her mouth, but no sound emerged.

The saw roared and the ground shook. She sat straight up in bed, gasping, her eyes wide. It was pitch black and her heart was

31

beating a mile a minute. She was awake now, but the rumble did not abate, and in fact, the tiny trailer actually was vibrating.

Kerry reached beneath her pillow, pulled out her phone, and thumbed it to life, passing the flashlight beam around the trailer, pausing when it reached the bunk only a few feet away.

Murphy was asleep on his back, mouth agape, snoring so loudly it surely would have drowned out the sound of any self-respecting chain saw.

According to her phone, it was two o'clock in the morning. She sank back down onto the bunk, pulling the sleeping bag over her head, but nothing could mute her brother's snores. Finally, she tip-toed over to his bunk and with effort, managed to roll him over on his side.

Tomorrow, she promised herself, she'd find a drugstore and some earplugs.

On Sunday morning, armed with a cup of coffee and a still-warm cheese Danish from Anna's, Kerry returned to the pickup, but not before plucking a parking ticket from the truck's windshield.

She winced when she saw the amount of the fine. Then, as per Murphy's instructions, she sat in the cab of the pickup truck, waiting, her eyes trained on the charcoal Mercedes parked in front of the Christmas tree stand.

"The owner's sure to come move it this morning," Murphy said. "As soon as he does, I'll put out the traffic cones to block it off, but you need to be ready to move the trailer over here."

Despite her grumbling, she knew his plan was sound. Every hour, she let the truck idle for a few minutes, enjoying the warmth blasting from the heater before cutting the engine again. Once, around ten o'clock, she saw a tall man dressed in a black puffer jacket approach the Mercedes.

She turned the key in the ignition. But instead of leaving, he opened the trunk, retrieved a small duffel bag, closed the trunk, and walked away, his cell phone pressed to his ear.

Her heart sank as she watched him walk down the street and disappear into a brownstone three doors away from the café.

At noon, she called Murphy and begged him to relieve her while she took a quick bathroom break.

At twelve thirty, the man was back, still on his phone, followed by a little boy who looked to be about six or seven. This time he loaded a laundry bag into the back seat of the car before walking away, trailed by the boy, who was looking longingly at Murphy, who was busily tacking up signs in the Christmas tree stand.

Kerry watched while her brother sold one of the smaller trees to a young couple who tied it on top of a baby stroller. He spent thirty minutes chatting with an older woman in a fur coat, and she was amazed by how animated he seemed, talking to this stranger.

At four, her phone buzzed. "Hey, can you come over and watch the stand for fifteen minutes? I gotta deliver a tree to a customer."

"What if the guy moves the car while you're gone?"

"Then you put out the traffic cones and wave away anybody who tries to park there," Murphy said.

"Prices are color-coded by those ribbons tied on the trees," Murphy instructed. "Red's the most expensive, that's eighteen hundred dollars for a fourteen-footer. Cheapest tree is sixty bucks for one of the tabletop trees. It's all on the signs." He untied the nail apron he was wearing and handed it to her. "You've got enough cash in here to make change. Anybody wants to buy with a credit or debit card, they'll have to wait until I get back, cuz I need to take my phone with me."

"Wait. We have trees that cost nearly two thousand dollars?" Kerry asked.

"Yeah. But there's only four, well, three now, because I sold one earlier and her son's coming back to pick it up this afternoon. Okay, I need to go."

He hefted a six-foot tree onto his shoulder and looped a wreath around his wrist and left.

It felt good to be out of the truck. Kerry made her first sale, a four-foot tree to a thirty-something redheaded woman with a toddler in tow. "Just ask Murphy to bring it up to my place when he gets back. I'm Skylar. He knows where I live."

Twenty minutes later, when her brother returned, the Mercedes still hadn't moved.

"Better grab something to eat now," Murphy said. "Whoever owns that car is gonna have to move it in the next hour, or risk getting a ticket, and that's when you need to be ready."

Kerry was hungrier than she'd realized. But Anna's was closed, so she walked across the corner to a bodega called Happy Days, bought herself a large bag of Fire Doritos and an extra-large cup of burnt-tasting coffee.

She sat behind the steering wheel of the truck, inhaling the chips, staring at the Mercedes, willing it to move.

Minutes ticked by. People strolled by the Christmas tree stand, stopping to pet Queenie, or to examine the trees. The temperature dropped and she started the truck and ran the heater for ten luxurious minutes, anxiously watching the truck's fuel gauge, which showed she only had a quarter of a tank of gas.

Her phone rang. "How's it going?" Birdie asked.

"Swell," Kerry said. "I'm freezing my ass off in the truck, waiting for some dude to move his Mercedes so we can park Spammy by the tree stand and hook up the electricity. In the meantime, I've been inhaling carbs like it's my job, and Murphy's snores kept me awake most of last night."

Her mother laughed. "Just like his father. I'd forgotten how loudly Jock snores. Now I understand why Brenda jumped ship."

"How's Dad feeling?"

"Cranky. I threw away his cigarettes and I've been making him get up and walk around the house every couple of hours. And he's bloated. The pain meds make you constipated —"

"Too much information," Kerry said hastily.

"You did ask."

"Hey, Mom, do you remember Lombardi's?"

"The Italian restaurant on the corner? Of course. We used to eat dinner there every Saturday night. Is it still there?"

"Yeah. The granddaughter runs it with a cousin. Last night, I was sitting at the bar, eating soup, and I had this flashback to when I was a kid, and this nice old lady showed me how to twirl my spaghetti on the back of a spoon."

"Anna. The owner. She spoiled you rotten, stuffing your pockets full of her amaretti cookies. And Matteo, her husband . . ."

Kerry was watching the activity across the street as her mother reminisced. The tall man in the puffer jacket was back.

"Gotta go, Mom," she said, disconnecting.

She sprinted across the street, dodging traffic.

Puffer Coat Man was now sitting in the car, talking on the phone.

"Excuse me," she said, pounding on the driver's side window with her fist. He glanced over at her and raised one finger, like, *Hang on. Unlike you, I'm a super-busy self-important CEO-slash-rock-star-secret-agent man of mystery.*

"Hey!" she hollered. "Are you gonna move this car, or just use it as a phone booth?"

His eyes narrowed and he lowered the phone, and then the window.

"Is there a problem?"

"Hell yeah, there's a problem. I've been waiting for this parking spot since yesterday. I've already gotten two tickets and been propositioned by some skeevy dude who seems to think I'm turning tricks from my trailer. I'm living on stale Doritos and deli coffee, so my blood sugar's low and my bladder is full, and I've really, really gotta pee, so I need you to move this car. Like, now."

Mercedes Man removed his mirrored aviator glasses and looked her up and down.

It wasn't a pretty picture, Kerry knew. Her long brown hair was greasy, so she'd shoved it up under a trucker hat she'd found in the trailer. There were dark circles under her eyes, and she'd been wearing the same grubby clothes — for the past two days.

Naturally, Mercedes Man had blue eyes the color of the Caribbean and the perfect amount of chin stubble and those Bambi eyelashes God always wasted on men who already had too much going in their favor.

"Find another parking spot, why don't you? The city's full of 'em." The window started to slide upward, and he returned to his secret agent phone call with a dismissive nod in her direction.

Kerry was not proud of what happened next. She pounded on the hood of the car with her fists and kicked the tires. "I. Need. This. Space," she shrieked, her fury boiling over like a pent-up stream. She started slapping at the driver's side window, but suddenly, she felt a thick arm wrap around her waist and physically lift her off the pavement.

"Whoa! Whoa, little sis!"

She turned her head. It was Murphy, who'd heard the ruckus.

"Calm down, Kerry," Murphy was saying. He lowered her to the ground. "Get ahold of yourself, will ya?"

Mercedes Man was out of the car now. "Murph, do you know this lunatic?"

"Afraid so," Murphy said. "Patrick McCaleb, meet my little sister, Kerry. She's, uh, worked up because we've been waiting for this spot to open up. You know, because it's where we always set up the trailer, in front of the tree stand."

Patrick looked over at the tree stand, and then at the trailer. He slapped his forehead.

"Oh, man. Sorry. Of course you guys always park here. My bad. I wish you'd said something earlier. I feel awful."

"I didn't realize this car was yours, or I would have," Murphy said. "But, uh, would you mind? We need to park the trailer here so we can run the power line from the café."

"Moving it right now," Patrick said. "And, uh, I do apologize." He held out his hand, gloved in fine leather, to Kerry, whose fingertips were stained orange from the Doritos.

"Yeah, I'm sorry too," Kerry said, wiping her hands on the back of her jeans. "Guess I kind of lost it there. Nice to meet you, Patrick."

"Likewise," Patrick said. He got in the Mercedes, started the engine, and pulled into the street.

CHAPTER 5

Murphy made a fire in a steel drum trash can, feeding it with Christmas tree trimmings and a stash of firewood he'd brought along in his own truck. Kerry stood in front of the fire, extending her hands to the warmth.

"Okay, I'm hitting the sack now," her brother announced. He handed her his phone and the credit card square attached to it. "Anyone wants their tree delivered, take down the address and phone number. Got it?"

Queenie thumped her feathery tail and moved beside Murphy, who held out his hand, palm down. "Stay, girl. Stay with Kerry."

"Wait. You know that guy?"

Murphy yawned. "Which guy?"

"Patrick. Mercedes Man."

"Yeah. He's all right. Lives in the neighborhood. Does something in an office."

"I saw him with a boy earlier. Is that his son?"

"Yeah. Austin. Okay, I'm out. Wake me up at nine and I'll take the night shift."

Murphy clambered into the trailer and closed the door. The snoring commenced.

Business was slow. A skinny redheaded teen rolled up to the stand on his skateboard. He took his time examining the trees, standing each one up, walking around it, humming softly.

"What kinda trees are these?"

"Fraser firs," Kerry said.

The skateboarder held up a three-foot tree with a yellow ribbon tied to a branch.

"How much is this one?"

Kerry pointed to the sign. "Sixty dollars."

"For real? Dude, I can buy a fake one for half that."

"Okay." She went back to her book. "Go buy a fake tree. Dude."

He thrust a crumpled twenty-dollar bill in her face. "Here."

"No," she said. "It's sixty. Not forty, not twenty."

"That's crazy," he countered. "I bet it's not even organic."

She sighed and looked up. "My family grows these trees on a farm in North Carolina. They plant the seedlings and baby them, then transplant them and fertilize and shear them. It takes seven years to grow a tree this size. It's hard work. We had a late-season frost this past May. Lost a lot of trees, which means we lost a lot of money. My brother cut and baled these trees last week, and my brother drove them up here, but my father couldn't come because he recently had a heart attack. If you want a certified organic fake tree made in an overseas sweatshop, go buy one. But in the meantime, you should definitely go away."

"Wow. Harsh!" the kid said, pocketing his money. He kicked the tree he'd been examining and laughed when it fell to the pavement.

Queenie, who'd been lounging at Kerry's feet, stood up and gave a low, menacing growl.

The kid scooted away on his skateboard.

"You're definitely Murphy's sister."

She turned to see Patrick, the Mercedes Man, had walked up during her exchange with the redhead.

"Sorry. I haven't had much sleep, and he was really getting under my skin."

"Hey, is all that stuff you told him about growing Christmas trees really true?" Patrick turned his head and sneezed, then sneezed again.

"Absolutely," Kerry told him. "I mean, it's not like I spend a lot of time on the farm, but it's definitely a labor of love for my dad and brother."

"I'm sorry to hear about Jock," Patrick said. His eyes, she noticed, were red and watering.

"The doctors say he'll be fine. If my mother doesn't kill him while she's nursing him back to health. Speaking of which. Are you okay?"

He sniffled. "It's not a cold, if that's what you're worried about. I'm allergic to pollen. Especially conifer pollen."

"Wow, guess you're in the wrong place."

He smiled and rubbed at his eyes. "Antihistamines usually help." He looked around. "But this is a lot of trees."

"A whole tractor-trailer load," Kerry said. "Dad lost over a hundred good-sized trees when we had that hard freeze back in May."

"You'd think Christmas trees could stand cold weather," Patrick said, looking around at the mini forest surrounding them.

"Normally they can, but when it starts to warm up in the spring, the trees start sending out new growth, and then this hard, prolonged freeze hit, and the cold settled at the fields down at the lowest elevation of the farm. It looked like they'd all burnt up."

"Fascinating," he said.

"Really?" Kerry shrugged. "I've always thought it was sort of boring. We're the largest Christmas-tree-growing county in the state of North Carolina, which is the second-largest grower in the country, behind Oregon."

"I take it you're not into farming?"

"No," she said quickly.

"May I ask what you are into?" He had an old-world politeness that Kerry found touching, coming from a secret-agent rock-star type.

"I'm an art director for an ad agency," she said. "Was an art director. Currently I'm what my dad calls self-unemployed."

"So that's why you've branched out into selling Christmas trees?" He chuckled at his own pun and Kerry couldn't help but smile.

"I'm here because my mother guilt-tripped me into coming along to help Murphy. Mom and I used to come too, until she and Jock split up when I was seven. It takes a minimum of two people to run the stand, and someone had to drive Spammy up. And since my dad is recovering from heart surgery, that left me."

"Your mom is taking care of your dad?"

He raised one eyebrow. "How very civilized."

"You'd have to know Birdie," Kerry said.

"Can't imagine my ex doing that for me," Patrick said.

"How long have you been divorced? If you don't mind my asking," she added hastily.

He shoved his hands in his pockets. "Separated for a year, divorced for a year."

"Sorry."

"We've finally worked things out, I think. At least, as far as Austin is concerned."

"Good for you," Kerry said.

"Pat?" A woman appeared on the sidewalk a few yards away. She had a rolling suitcase in hand. "I'm taking off. I put Austin's clothes in the dryer, but I can't find his library book."

"It's already in his bookbag for tomorrow," Patrick called back.

The woman was petite, with long, dark hair. "You'll feed him dinner, right?"

"Have I ever not fed my son?" he said, sounding offended. "See you Thursday."

"I told you, I'm not back till Friday. It's on your calendar. Don't you ever look at that?"

"Only every day. See you Friday, then."

The woman nodded and walked off down the block, her high-heeled boots clicking on the pavement.

He watched her departure and sighed.

"Your ex?" Kerry guessed.

"Gretchen. The divorce was her idea, but she stays mad at me for reasons only she and her therapist understand."

"But she comes to your place and does his laundry?" Kerry asked.

"Our place." He sniffled. "Or Austin's place, to be more accurate. He's a sensitive kid. After we split up we both agreed it was better for him to stay in the house where he'd always lived. So instead of him shuttling from my place to Gretchen's, he stays put and we rotate in and out. Gretchen travels for work, so this week I'll be here till Friday."

Kerry couldn't help but be curious about such an unusual custody arrangement. "And then what?"

"I've got a little studio apartment in Soho," he said. He glanced at his watch. "I better go up. Our neighbor babysits whenever we need her, but it's getting late." He looked around the Christmas tree stand.

"Austin is fascinated with this place. He thinks it's a magical forest."

"Tell him he's welcome to hang out with us anytime," Kerry said.

"Don't worry. He'll be down here tomorrow, as soon as he gets home from school," Patrick said. "Your brother is his hero."

CHAPTER 6

"Kerry, wake up!"

She opened one eye. Her brother was leaning down, his face inches from hers in the half-dark trailer. He smelled like bacon. And unwashed socks.

"Hmpff?"

He shook her shoulder. "Come on, now. I let you sleep in, but it's way past seven. I gotta get the electricity hooked up this morning, and I can't do nothin' with you in here."

She pushed aside the sleeping bag and blankets, swung her legs over the edge of the bunk, and shivered. Murphy stomped away, his footsteps shaking the trailer. "Let's go," he called over his shoulder.

Quickly, she pulled on three layers of clothes and her boots.

Glancing in the tiny mirror near the bathroom alcove she shuddered at her own image. Somehow, some way, she had to get a shower and wash her hair today.

She knocked on the door at the bakery and a young woman in her twenties let her in. "Murph's sister, right? I'm Lidia and I got coffee going," the girl said. Kerry nodded and kept walking, heading to the bathroom to brush her teeth and wash her face.

A few minutes later, she emerged, breathing in the heavenly coffee fumes.

Lidia handed her a coffee mug and Kerry dumped in a packet of sugar and a splash of cream. She cradled the mug in both hands, letting the warmth seep into her chilled bones.

"Something to eat?" the girl asked.

Kerry eyed the glass display case. "Is that banana bread?" she asked, pointing to the top tray.

"Yep."

"I'll take it."

"Want me to warm it up under the toaster?" Lidia asked.

"I want you to warm *me* up under that toaster," Kerry said.

She sat at a window facing the sidewalk and watched as Murphy and Danny the bartender snaked a thick extension cord from the basement window of Lombardi's café, across the sidewalk, and hooked it up to the outlet on the side of their trailer.

50

Next, Murphy covered the cord with thick reflective silver duct tape. Standing, he gave Danny the thumbs-up sign.

By nine o'clock, Kerry had sold her first tree, a six-footer, to a harried mom with two toddlers crammed into a side-by-side stroller. The woman was squatting down on the sidewalk, inspecting the base of the tree to make sure it was straight when, out of the corner of Kerry's eye, she saw one of the kids, probably just barely two years old, tumble out of the stroller and make a break for the street.

"Hey!" She dropped the tree and went after the kid, yanking him by the hood of his quilted jacket just moments before a yellow cab went barreling past.

"Nooooo!" The kid's face went scarlet with fury and he pounded Kerry's knees with his mittened fists as she herded him back toward the stroller.

The mother scooped the child into her arms. "Oh my God, Oscar," she exclaimed, hugging him tightly to her chest. She looked over at Kerry. "Thank you."

Little Oscar was still crying, tears and snot streaming down his face, as his mother handed Kerry three fifty-dollar bills. "I'll send my husband to pick up the tree after he gets home from work tonight."

"Uh-oh." Kerry pointed at the stroller, where the other little boy had one foot out of the stroller, poised for his escape.

"Elmo!" The woman hurried over and gently pushed the child back inside. "Let's go home now." She plopped Oscar into the top tier, looked over at Kerry, and rolled her eyes.

"Twins, everyone said. It'll be such fun! At forty! Whee!" She turned the stroller around and wheeled it briskly away.

Two hours passed without another sale. Murphy busied himself sweeping up fallen pine needles and sorting the Christmas trees by price. Finally, at eleven, he yawned widely. "I'm hitting the hay," he told Kerry. "You can handle things, right?"

She looked around, feeling panicky. "Now? What if someone has questions, or wants a tree delivered, or . . ."

"Mondays are always slow. Business won't pick up again till late afternoon. Handle it," he said firmly. "I've been up since five, and I need some shut-eye. If you need something to do, you could string Granddad's lights on the outside of Spammy. They're in a bin in the bed of my truck." He gestured at Queenie, who was sitting quietly on the folded-up utility blanket that served as her bed. "And she'll need a walk in an hour or so."

"Who'll watch the stand?"

But Murphy had already retreated into the trailer.

Time dragged. Bored, Kerry fetched a plastic bin from the bed of her brother's pickup truck. She sighed at the sight of the contents — a hopelessly snarled bundle of old-fashioned multicolored C9 Christmas tree lights.

With the aid of a roll of duct tape and a stepladder, she spent the next hour unsnarling and outlining the rounded contours of the travel trailer with the big-bulb lights, not stopping until she'd used all eleven strands. Finally, she stepped back, held her breath, and plugged the last strand into the extension cord's power strip.

"It's the miracle of the lights," she told Queenie, who'd walked over to investigate Kerry's handiwork. "Not a single burnt-out bulb!

"Okay, girl," she agreed, when the dog gently prodded her hand with her snout. "I need to stretch my legs too." She stretched bungee cords across both entrances to the stand, hung up the CLOSED sign, and clipped Queenie's leash to her collar, tying a plastic bag to the leash.

They walked down the street, crossed at the light, and kept walking until she spotted a small enclosed dog park. Queenie efficiently took care of her business. The sun was out and Kerry was glad to have an excuse to explore the neighborhood.

On the way back, she stopped at the bodega across the street from the stand and got a cup of mediocre chicken noodle soup, then returned to the stand to eat her lunch.

People rushed past, barely glancing at the trees. Bored, Kerry went to the truck and fetched a steno pad and pencil she'd noticed tucked up under the passenger-side sun visor.

She began doodling on a blank page, doing a quick pencil study of Queenie, who, true to her name, always managed to look regal, even while resting on a dirty moving blanket on a grubby city street, with her head tucked daintily over her paws.

Kerry studied Queenie, noticing for the first time the heart-shaped patch of brown fur on her nose, and the long tufts of hair protruding from her eyebrows.

"Excuse me?"

She looked up.

The mom with the twins was back. "I think maybe Oskie dropped his binkie when we were here earlier."

54

"Binkie?"

"His pacifier," the woman said. "He won't go to sleep without it . . ."

Kerry put down her sketch and walked twice around the booth. Finally, she saw a glint of silver protruding from beneath the base of one of the trees, reached down, and retrieved it.

Both twins had clambered out of the stroller while she searched, and they were both squatted down, lavishing head pats and neck scratches on Queenie, who seemed to be enjoying all the attention.

"Is this it?" Kerry asked, holding the pacifier by the silver ring attached to the rubber nipple.

"Oh, thank God," the woman said.

"Mine!" Oscar reached for the binkie.

"Wait!" his mom said sharply. "We have to wash it first. It's been in the dirt."

Kerry grabbed a water bottle from beneath the card-table-turned-cash-stand, and handed it to the mom.

The mother quickly uncapped the bottle and poured water over the pacifier. "It'll have to do," she said under her breath, before handing the pacifier over to her son.

Oscar thrust the binkie into his mouth and sucked vigorously.

"I owe you one," the woman said. "So, are

you Murph's girlfriend?"

"His sister," Kerry said quickly. "You know my brother?"

"Oh, sure. We always buy our trees from Tolliver's." She stuck out her hand and Kerry shook it. "I'm Taryn Kaplan. We just live right down the block at number 110."

"Nice to meet you," Kerry said. "I currently live in that trailer with my brother, who snores like a grizzly bear." She pointed at Spammy.

Taryn shot her a sympathetic smile. "And I'm betting Murphy didn't tell you that we always leave a key for you guys so you can shower at our place while you're in the city."

Kerry's eyes widened. "No. I'd kill for a hot shower right now."

Taryn reached into the pocket of her jacket and held out a brass key ring. "We're on the second floor, unit four. Ring the doorbell and I'll buzz you up. Come over anytime."

"That's so nice of you," Kerry said. She glanced over at the twins. Oscar was curled up next to Queenie on her blanket, eyes half closed, blissfully sucking away on his pacifier, while Elmo had climbed back into the stroller.

"Uh-oh, time to get these monkeys home for their naps," Taryn said.

"Wait!" Kerry pulled her phone from her pocket and snapped off a series of photos of both the boys.

"Hope you don't mind," she told their mother. "They're so cute, I was thinking I'd love to sketch them."

"You're an artist?" Taryn didn't bother to hide her surprise.

"Oh no. Not really," Kerry said quickly. "I mean, I went to art school, but my career has been in graphics. I haven't drawn in ages, but since I've currently got time on my hands . . ."

Taryn sighed. "Time on your hands. What's that like?"

Kerry studied the photo she'd taken of Oscar, curled up beside Queenie. She drew the curve of the little boy's cheek, the long lashes, the cupid's bow lips clamped tight around the pacifier. She leaned backward, sighed, and applied the pencil's eraser to the pacifier. It was a jarring note. She worked for another hour, drawing, erasing, shading, finally giving up and returning to the sketch of Queenie.

She'd gotten really rusty at something that had once come so easily. Growing up, Kerry always had a sketchpad, pencils, watercolors, and brushes at hand.

She had few friends, preferring to spend time drawing, or reading the art books her mother checked out for her from Tarburton's small public library. Her classmates weren't mean to her, they just didn't understand a kid like Kerry. Her family didn't really understand her either.

"You need to get outside in the sunshine," Jock would say, on her infrequent visits to the farm. "It ain't right to spend all your time with your nose stuck in a book."

Kerry knew better than to argue, so she'd retreat to the barn, where she'd climb up into the hayloft and retrieve the sketch pad she kept hidden there, along with her treasured copy of E. B. White's *Charlotte's Web.* Although she loved the story, she was actually more fascinated with Garth Williams's entrancing ink-and-graphite illustrations of Wilbur, Charlotte, Fern, and even Templeton the rat. She'd spend hours stretched out in the hay, studying the way the artist managed to convey emotion on the face of a pig.

Now she looked over again at Queenie, and back at her sketch, attacking it again with her eraser.

A man's voice interrupted her concentration. "You're not bad at drawing dogs, but you really don't know anything about drawing people, do you?"

She glanced up. She'd been so absorbed in her drawing she hadn't noticed the old man who stood looking down at her steno pad. Kerry instinctively covered it with her free hand.

"What? You ashamed?"

The man was enveloped in a dusty-looking heavy wool overcoat that buttoned up to his chin. A red wool scarf wrapped around his throat, and he wore a battered tweed fedora. His face was a mass of wrinkles and he had a scruffy white mustache and goatee. He was thin, almost to the point of emaciation, and his shoulders were rounded into a permanent stoop.

"It's just a doodle," Kerry said, closing the cardboard cover of the notebook.

"Eh," he said, his tone dismissive. "Doodle is too nice a word for this."

"Were you interested in finding a Christmas tree?" she asked.

"Just passing by." His voice was gravelly, with a hint of an accent. He touched his hand to the brim of his hat. "Keep trying." He walked away, his steps halting, a brass-tipped cane tapping at the pavement.

CHAPTER 7

Kerry studied her sketch again. She sighed. The annoying geezer's criticism was annoyingly valid. She'd succeeded in capturing the essence of Queenie, but her depiction of little Oscar was awkward, even clunky. He looked stiff and inhuman, more like a toy than a child.

She'd always struggled with drawing people, barely making passing grades when she studied figure drawing back in her art school days. She flipped the steno pad to a blank page and started over, blocking in the figure of the child first this time.

"Whatcha doing?"

It was Austin, Patrick's son. He was dressed in a private school uniform; blue blazer with an embroidered patch on the breast pocket, a somewhat wrinkled white shirt, and khaki pants. He had a red backpack slung over his shoulder and was sipping from a juice box.

"I'm trying to draw a picture," Kerry said. She was instantly fascinated with the child's face. His dark blue eyes were fringed by long, dark lashes and a tiny constellation of freckles was scattered across his snub nose and pale cheeks. He had dark-blond hair cut short to the scalp, with bangs that had been carefully gelled back from his forehead.

Kerry gazed around the stand. They were alone. "Are you supposed to be down here by yourself?"

Austin pointed to the building just to the left of Lombardi's. "I'm not alone. My dad is upstairs. He watches me through the window. I'm not allowed to cross the street or talk to strangers."

"Aren't I a stranger?" she asked, raising an eyebrow.

"No. My dad says you're nice."

Kerry felt herself blushing.

"Because you're Murphy's sister," the boy added. He pointed at the trailer, where Kerry's brother was just emerging. His serious face brightened. "Hi, Murphy!"

Murphy stretched, rolled one shoulder, then the other. "Oh hey, Austin. What's up? Did you get kicked out of school?"

"No!" The boy giggled. "School's over. My dad said it was okay if I helped you out."

"Cool." Murphy shook his head. "I was

just thinking we could use some cheap labor around here. Right, Kerry?"

"Definitely." She closed the steno pad.

"Good job on the Christmas lights," Murphy said, gazing around. "But it doesn't look like you sold too many trees. Maybe we need to make Austin here our sales manager."

"Okay by me," Kerry told him. "I did sell one tree. To Taryn Kaplan. She said her husband will come by after work to pick it up. And, she said we can shower at her place? Something you somehow forgot to mention to me?"

"Oh yeah," Murphy said carelessly. "Did she leave the key?"

"She did," Kerry said. "And tonight, I intend to take the longest, hottest shower in the world."

"Good for you." He glanced at his watch. "Almost four. Business should start picking up pretty soon." He pointed to a pile of fir branches he'd trimmed from the trees, then a wooden crate beneath the cash stand. "The clippers and wire are in there. Rolls of ribbon too. Maybe you could make some more wreaths. You remember how, right?"

Kerry rolled her eyes. As a teenager, she and Birdie had crafted the Christmas wreaths Jock and Murphy sold during their holiday stay in the city, wiring the prickly fir branches together into long garlands, forming some of them into a circle, then attaching sprigs of blue juniper, red-berried holly, and white tallow berries foraged from the woods surrounding the tree farm. In a good year, Jock would pay her five bucks apiece for her handiwork, money she eagerly saved to buy the clothes and makeup Birdie couldn't (or wouldn't) buy her.

"I think I can figure it out again," she drawled. Kerry pulled out the supplies.

"What can I do?" Austin piped up.

Murphy dragged a large black plastic trash bag from the bed of his pickup truck. "This here is full of mistletoe. You can break off some of these pieces, like maybe three pieces to a bunch, and wrap some red ribbon around 'em. And tie a bow. You can tie a bow, right?"

"Sure thing," Austin said. "That's easy."

"Don't eat any of those berries. Okay? Cuz they're poison. And your dad's likely to get real annoyed with me if we have to take you to the hospital in an ambulance and pump out your stomach."

"I never been in an ambulance," Austin said, perking up.

"You ain't going on my watch," Murphy told him. "No sirreebob."

Kerry wrinkled her nose when she saw the roll of cheap ribbon Murphy handed Austin to tie around the sprigs of mistletoe.

"Don't you have anything else?"

"What's wrong with it?"

"Where'd you get this crap? A truck stop?"

He shrugged. "We been using it for years. No complaints."

"How much do you get for wreaths these days?"

"Twenty-five bucks, same as always."

"I'm gonna find some decent ribbon. Nice, wide, wired grosgrain. Did you bring any other greenery, like Mom and I always used to use?"

"Look, just make the wreaths and tie on the damn ribbon. It don't need to be fancy."

Austin looked uneasily from Murphy to Kerry, his cheeks reddening.

She gave the little boy's shoulder a reassuring pat. "It's okay, Austin. Murphy isn't mad at you. He just doesn't like taking advice from a girl."

CHAPTER 8

The next day, while it was still dark and Murphy was snoring away in his bunk, Kerry set out walking to the wholesale flower market that was less than a mile away. She'd done her research online, knew what she wanted, and where to get it.

Happily wandering the flower stalls with a steaming latte in hand, she picked out bundles of seeded eucalyptus, glossy holly branches with fat red berries, and blue juniper. She bought green floral wire and spools of ribbon in luscious colors.

Back at the tree stand, she set out her materials on the card table and started wiring the greenery to one of the plain wreaths she'd created the day before. By the time Murphy emerged from the camper she'd created half a dozen wreaths loaded with the variegated greenery and luxe ribbon she'd bought at the flower market.

"Where'd you get all that?" he commented, glancing at her creations. "And what'd you spend?"

"I went to the wholesale market. I spent what I needed." She finished plumping the gold satin ribbon on a wreath and held it out for his inspection. "What do you think?"

"How much?" he asked.

"I looked in the window of a fancy florist on Greenwich Avenue. They sell wreaths like this for a hundred and fifty dollars, and their greens aren't anywhere near as fresh as ours," Kerry said. "I've got about twenty dollars of materials in these, so I'll price these first half dozen at ninety-nine apiece. And if they don't sell, I can always reduce the price, right?"

Murphy shrugged and walked away, toward the bakery, muttering to himself.

"Oh my!" A woman in workout clothes had stopped to inspect the wreath Kerry had just finished. "These are gorgeous. Are you selling them?"

"Yes, ma'am," Kerry said, deliberately laying on a thick Southern accent.

The woman stroked the gold satin ribbon. "I've got double doors in my entryway, so I'd need a pair of these. Do you have another just like this one?"

"I can make you a second one, if you give me about an hour," Kerry said.

"Perfect," the woman said, beaming. "I'm on my way to Pilates, but I can stop here on the way back. How much are they, by the way?"

"Two hundred for the pair," Kerry said, holding her breath, hoping the woman wouldn't change her mind.

"Okay. Sold." The customer reached into the pocket of her Patagonia jacket and pulled out some folded-up bills. She plucked four fifties and handed them to Kerry. "I'm Lorna. And I'll see you in a bit."

Kerry was winding tartan ribbon around a twenty-six-inch wreath when a tall, slender man approached with a small fluffy dog on a leash. He wore a brown leather bomber jacket with a Burberry scarf wrapped around his neck, and a tweed newsboy's cap.

Queenie, who'd been lounging on her moving blanket, walked over and gave the dog an inquisitive sniff, and the smaller dog responded by rolling onto his back and wriggling on the sidewalk.

"Oooh," the dog's owner said, pausing to watch what Kerry was doing. "That's super cute. I can totally see that tied to one of the glass doors on my husband's grandmother's mahogany secretary. If I buy it, could you add a loop of ribbon to hang it with?"

"Of course," Kerry said.

He cocked his head and gave it some thought. "But I'm wondering if that red plaid will clash with all the oranges and browns in the rug. It's an Oushak, very old."

"I can use whatever ribbon you like," Kerry said quickly. She held up the roll of gold satin ribbon. "What about this?"

"Yaaaasss," he drawled, looking around the Christmas tree stand. "You're new this year, right? I don't remember Murphy and Jock selling wreaths this nice before."

Kerry laughed. "I'm Murphy's sister, Kerry. My dad couldn't make the trip up from North Carolina this year, so I'm his substitute."

He took her hand in his. "Well, welcome to the neighborhood, Kerry. I'm John." He gestured toward the dog. "And this is Ruby."

The dog gave a short, enthusiastic bark and wagged its tail so vigorously, Kerry couldn't help but laugh.

"What kind of dog is Ruby?"

"She's a very entitled, spoiled mini gold-endoodle," John said. He reached in his pocket and brought out a small business card. "She's got her own Instagram account, in case you do that sort of thing. By the way, you're coming Saturday night, right?"

"Saturday night?"

"We, that is, everyone in our building, always have a holiday open house, the second Saturday night in December. Just a little potluck affair, you know?"

He pointed to the same building Kerry had seen Patrick and Austin emerge from the previous day. "You must come! And remind Murphy too. We're hoping he'll bring his dobro."

"His dobro?" Kerry glanced at the bakery window, where her brother was apparently waiting for his breakfast muffin to get heated up.

"Of course. We have to practically beg him to play, but once he gets started, he's really an amazing musician." John gave her a quizzical look. "Is this somehow news to you?"

"Sort of," Kerry said, not wanting to explain her family's complicated history.

"Anyway, come around six. Dress is holiday festive."

"Holiday festive," she repeated. "And what can I bring?"

"Oh, don't worry about that. We always have an embarrassing amount of food."

"I'll figure out something to bring," Kerry said firmly. "Southerners never show up anywhere empty-handed."

"I'll tell you what," he said slowly. "Maybe you could bring some kind of centerpiece?

69

Old Mrs. Gaskins on the second floor usually brings one of her tragic fake poinsettia creations, but she's gone to stay with her daughter in Florida this year."

"I'd be happy to," Kerry said. She hesitated for a moment. "It sounds like you know most of the people who live in the neighborhood."

"I should. We've lived here for twenty years. Why? Has someone been bothering you?"

"Nothing like that," she said. "I was sketching earlier, and an older man dressed in a big heavy black coat sort of wandered over and gave me some unsolicited criticism."

"Does he walk with a cane? Bundled up in a scarf?"

"That's him." She nodded her head.

"That's just Heinz. Sort of a crank, but he's harmless. Say, when do you think you can have my wreath ready?"

"This evening," Kerry said.

He looked over at Ruby, who was now rolling around on the ground gnawing on a stiff, furry brown article. "Ruby, no!"

"Just a dead chipmunk," Kerry said helpfully. "I think Queenie found it in the park."

"Ruby, drop it!" He tugged at the leash, but the dog ignored him.

His voice took on the stern tone of a disapproving parent. "Right now, young lady."

Ruby crouched down and gave a short, gleeful bark.

"Here." Kerry picked up a plastic bag, leaned down, and deftly extricated the chipmunk from Ruby's grasp, then dropped it in the trash barrel.

"Oh God," John moaned. "Do chipmunks carry rabies?"

"Doubtful," Kerry said, laughing. "You don't want to know the gross dead stuff our dogs find back home. Possums, squirrels, rats . . ."

"Rats!" He clutched his chest in horror. "I can't."

Ruby was sniffing the base of the trash barrel, whining and straining at her leash.

"Let's go," John said. "I'm taking you straight to Pups and Pearls to get disinfected. See you Saturday, Kerry. And don't forget to tell Murphy to bring that dobro."

CHAPTER 9

Wednesday morning, Kerry was drinking coffee, sitting at her folding chair on the sidewalk, when a huge tractor trailer pulled up across the intersection. A worker in brown coveralls jumped out and plopped a set of traffic cones in front and back of the truck.

A pickup pulled up and parked behind the trailer, and two more men emerged, one tall and thin in quilted navy coveralls, the other shorter and stouter, in jeans and a faded gray sweatshirt. The men began unloading stacks of plywood and power tools and swiftly began erecting scaffolding on the sidewalk outside Happy Days, the neighborhood bodega.

The whine of the power saws and nail guns soon roused Murphy.

He stepped out of the camper, dressed only in his long johns, and blinked in the bright sunlight. "What the hell's going on?"

Kerry pointed at the construction project across the intersection. "That. I can't quite figure out what they're doing over there."

"I can." Murphy's expression was grim. He climbed back into the camper, and when he reappeared five minutes later, he was dressed and ready for action.

He bolted across the street, dodging cars and buses as he ran.

"Hey!" he shouted. "What do you think you're doing?"

The tall thin man turned, grinned, and nudged the chunky one.

"You can't set up here," Murphy shouted, his voice cutting through the noise of traffic. "This is our block. Our corner. Always has been."

The thin man's voice was surprisingly high and shrill. "Not no more, buddy. You don't own this block. So beat it." He took a step forward, brandishing a two-by-four.

Murphy stood in the street, with his hands on his hips, glaring at the crew, until a cab blared its horn and he beat a reluctant retreat back across the street.

"Who are those guys, and what are they doing?" Kerry asked.

"They're the Brody brothers," Murphy said, slumping down onto his lawn chair. "They own a bunch of tree stands in Brooklyn and the Upper West Side. They're wholesalers, don't know a Scotch pine from Scotch tape. Setting up over there is no accident. They've been scheming to take over our block for years now."

Kerry sighed, picked up a broom, and began tidying the booth. Murphy yawned. "I'm gonna try and grab some more z's."

"Okay."

The Brody brothers had been busy. By mid-afternoon, neon orange poster boards with crude hand-lettering were tacked on each corner of their makeshift stand.

FRESHEST TREES IN THE CITY —
$75
FREE DELIVERY!
NO TREE OVER $100!
OUR PRICES ARE CRAZY
AND SO ARE WE!

By late afternoon, people were streaming into the Christmas tree stand across the street. Every time Kerry looked up, someone was loading a tree into their car, or one of the brothers was setting off from the stand, carting a tree tied to a red wagon.

Business was notably slower at the Tolliver tree stand. Kerry crafted four more wreaths, using up all the floral supplies she'd purchased that morning, setting aside the ones she'd already promised to earlier customers. She sold a total of two trees, which were to be delivered by Murphy, later in the evening.

At three, she pulled the bungee cords across the trees at the entrance to the stand and posted a GONE TO LUNCH sign. She walked across the street to get a close-up view of the Brodys' enterprise. She strolled around the bodega, filling up a shopping basket with random groceries, stopping at the front of the store to peer out the window at the competition.

The tall, skinny brother darted around the stand, chatting up potential buyers, gesturing wildly as he haggled over prices. The brother in the Santa hat lounged on a folding chair, idly scrolling on his cell phone while puffing on a cigarette.

When she returned to her post, Murphy was prowling around the booth, picking up stray branches and glowering at the competition across the street.

"I thought you were sleeping," Kerry said, tossing Queenie a dog biscuit from the bag she'd picked up on her shopping/spying excursion.

"I did, for a while, but then I got too riled

up. Where'd you go?"

"Over there," she said, nodding in the direction of the Brodys. "I wanted to check them out up close and personal. They're wheeling and dealing, that's for sure. I bet they've sold a dozen trees, in the same time I only managed to sell two."

"Those assholes!" he growled. "They know this is our corner. Our street. Has been for thirty years. I can't believe the Sorensens let them set up in front of Happy Days."

Kerry followed his gaze. "What can we do about them?"

"Nothing. Claudia says old man Sorensen has basically retired, so their kids are running the show. Eric Sorensen told her the Brodys are paying them two K a week."

"Why would they move right across the street from another Christmas tree stand?" Kerry asked.

"They're assholes, but they're not stupid. This corner is prime real estate. It gets amazing foot traffic. That's why Dad chose Abingdon Square way back when. Couple years ago, the Brodys even went to the neighborhood association that runs the park, to offer them more money than we pay to set up here. Fortunately, we've got friends on the association board."

"I was wondering how that worked," Kerry said.

"We make a generous donation to the park foundation," Murphy said. "We keep the place picked up and neat while we're here, and they like what they call the ambience. You know? No trashy neon signs, that kind of thing."

She nodded her understanding. "Got it."

"And that's why the Brodys showed up this year. To underprice us and try to drive us out of business."

"So what do we do now?"

"We do what we do," Murphy said. "We've got the freshest, prettiest trees in the city. Our customers can afford to pay more for the best. And they like that we have a history here."

CHAPTER 10

"That's it," Kerry told Queenie, the next morning. "Today's the day I get an honest to Gawd shower."

Queenie turned her head and gave Kerry a quizzical look, before returning to her own grooming project, which consisted of delicately licking her paws.

Taryn Kaplan picked up her phone on the first ring. "Kerry! I was wondering when you were gonna give in and take me up on my offer."

"Is now a convenient time?" Kerry felt unexpectedly shy, asking for such a personal favor.

"Now's perfect. The boys are at preschool, so they won't be underfoot, and I'm just catching up on some phone calls."

"Great," Kerry said. "I'll be right over."

"Bring your laundry if you want," Taryn said.

"Oh my God, you're an angel," Kerry said

fervently.

She found Murphy, wrapped burrito style in a sleeping bag, dozing in his lawn chair outside the camper. She touched his shoulder lightly and he stirred awake. "What's up?"

"I'm going to go take a shower at the Kaplans', and do some laundry while I'm there," she said. "Want to give me your stuff to wash?"

"Nah. But don't be gone long, okay? I need to get some real shuteye."

Taryn was waiting when the elevator doors opened on the fourth floor, holding the door to her apartment open. She looked impossibly glamorous in a black velour tracksuit, with her long hair done up in a topknot, her face dewy and impeccably made up, which made Kerry feel even more self-conscious about her own unkempt appearance.

"Right this way," her hostess said, gesturing her down a wide hallway. The wood floor was painted in a black-and-white diamond pattern, and the walls were lined, floor to ceiling, with art of every description: portraits, landscapes, still lifes, oil paintings, charcoal drawings, sketches, watercolors, and prints.

They paused at a set of curtained French

79

doors. "The laundry room," Taryn said, opening the door to a long, narrow room. One wall held a washer and dryer and a table stacked high with folded clothing. The room was warm and smelled like bleach and lavender. "Go ahead and throw your clothes in," Taryn said. She opened another door and pointed. "Guest bath. You should have everything you need."

When Kerry emerged from the bathroom, pink-faced and relaxed after her shower, she could hear Taryn's voice echoing from the back of the apartment. She padded, barefoot, down the hallway, drawn to the carefully arranged art.

She was so intent on studying a small vividly colored abstract collage she didn't notice Taryn until she was standing right beside her.

"I was wondering where you'd gotten to," Taryn said. She pointed at the artwork Kerry was gazing at. "You like this piece?"

"I love everything you've got," Kerry said. "The colors in this one, all these intense blues and greens, really appeal to me."

"Me too," Taryn said. "I bought it at a little street market in Greece in my college days, for five bucks. I'm transported back to Mykonos every time I look at it."

Kerry's gaze fell on a piece hanging nearby, a pen-and-ink study of a young man. He had a high, wide forehead, wavy hair, a delicate, aquiline nose, dark, moody eyes, and full lips that were curved into a tentative smile. The portrait was unsigned, except for an abstract silhouette of a tree in the lower right-hand corner.

"I really like this one. A lot," Kerry said. "It's so . . . . evocative. I want to know this man."

"It's one of my favorites," Taryn agreed. "Would you believe — I found it in a pile of trash on the street the first week we moved into this building. It was rolled up, with a rubber band around it. I couldn't believe my eyes when I saw it. I snatched it up so fast, and ran with it to the framer's."

"Who would throw away something like this?" Kerry asked.

"Don't know. But I have to admit, every time I see a pile of trash on the street out front, I stop to check — hoping maybe I'll strike gold twice. It drives my husband insane."

A loud buzzer sounded from the hallway. "There's my laundry," Kerry said.

CHAPTER 11

Kerry was bent over her pad with a fine-tipped black marker, so immersed in her drawing she didn't notice she had company until a small voice piped up.

"What's that supposed to be?"

She glanced up. Austin stood beside the table, staring down at her sketch. He was dressed in his school uniform. Red mittens dangled from the sleeves of his jacket, and his cheeks were pink from the cold.

She pointed at the Brodys' stand across the street. "It's them."

Kerry watched as the old gentleman in the black coat approached. He'd added a faded silk scarf to his ensemble today, and an equally faded black wool beret.

Queenie scrambled to her feet as the old man drew closer, her tail wagging. The man's craggy face brightened, and he reached into his coat pocket and drew out a dog biscuit, offering it on the palm of his flattened hand.

"Good girl," he said, scratching Queenie's ears.

"What are we drawing today, then, hmm?" he asked, peering over the top of Austin's head.

"Hi, Mr. Heinz," Austin said. "She's drawing those guys!" He pointed indignantly across the street. "They're bad."

"Oh?"

The old man glanced at the Brodys and then down at Kerry's sketch pad. "This is a little better," he said, tapping his index finger on the drawing. "You're a moderately adequate draftsman, but your work lacks heart. Finally, here, I see something approaching emotion. What is this about?"

Kerry chewed the cap of her pen. "We don't actually know yet."

Heinz gestured to the sketch pad. "May I?"

"Please." Kerry stood up and indicated that her guest should take her chair.

He sank down onto the chair and turned to a new page in the sketchbook. He picked up one of Kerry's pencils and gazed around at the Christmas tree lot for a minute or so. Finally, he began drawing, the pencil moving so quickly over the paper, it was almost a blur.

As Kerry and Austin watched, they saw the Tolliver Christmas tree stand take shape: the wooden structure, the rows of shaggy firs, the strings of lights crisscrossing above and outlining the perimeter. Heinz's pencil paused for a moment, and then picking up speed again, sketched a flattened oval, adding in a door, and tiny windows, and a set of steps.

"That's Spammy," Austin said gleefully.

The old man nodded but kept drawing. Now the outline of Jock's pickup truck appeared, the bed filled with a pile of Christmas trees. A familiar furry head emerged, peeking over the edge of the truck bed, with a heart-shaped brown patch on its nose, and a feathery tail.

"There's Queenie," Austin said.

The old man drew the figure of a burly man, cross-hatching a jacket, sketching a bearded man's head of wild, dark hair topped with a knitted cap. The man rode a bicycle, with a medium-sized tree strapped across the handlebars.

"There's Murph, but where's Kerry?" Austin asked.

The artist grabbed Kerry's trucker cap and tossed it onto the table.

"Ughhh, no. I'm a mess."

He ignored her protest and touched Kerry's chin. "Turn, please, so I can see you in profile."

She tilted her head to the left, and his pencil flew across the paper.

Austin watched raptly, his eyes following the artist's progress.

"Hmm. No." The old man grabbed an eraser and attacked the drawing, then went back to work.

"Hahahahaha," Austin chortled.

Kerry looked down. Heinz had sketched her, standing defiantly by the truck, wielding a push broom as though it were a saber.

"She's guarding the trees," Austin said. "But what about me?"

"Austin!" Patrick called from the doorway of the brownstone. "Time to come inside and get ready for dinner."

"I'm not hungry," the child called, turning back to his friends. "Are you gonna draw me now?"

"Austin?" Patrick's voice sounded a warning note.

Heinz picked up a pen and went to work. In a matter of seconds the figure of a boy appeared on the paper. He was slender, with tousled dark hair and a sprinkling of freckles across his cheeks, and he seemed to tower over a forest of abstract-shaped evergreens. He had an ax slung over one shoulder, and an outsized squirrel perched on the other. A bird nested in his hair, and a mischievous raccoon peered down at him from the lower branch of one of the trees.

"That's me!" Austin said, his face glowing with excitement. "It's me, isn't it, Mr. Heinz?"

"I think so," Heinz said, studying the boy's face. "But wait. Something is missing." He picked up the pen and placed a baseball cap between the raccoon's paws.

"He stole my hat," Austin said.

"Only borrowed it," the old man corrected, his pale lips curving into a smile. "I'm sure his intentions are pure."

"James Austin?"

Kerry looked up. Patrick was standing on the sidewalk, hands on his hips, a dish towel tucked into his waistband, his dark dress pants dusted with flour. "I just burned the first batch of pancakes," he announced. "And it's your fault."

"Sorry, Dad," Austin said. "But we were doing something important." He pointed at the drawing. "See? Me and Kerry and Mr. Heinz are drawing a story."

Patrick walked over and examined the sketches laid out on the tabletop. "What kind of a story?"

"Kerry drew those guys across the street,"

Austin said, breathless with excitement. "And then Mr. Heinz drew Kerry, guarding the tree stand. And he drew Murphy. So then I asked him to draw me . . ."

"Mr. Heinz?" Patrick asked.

"Yeah." Austin stabbed the drawing with his index finger. "See? That's me."

For the first time, Kerry realized that the old man had quietly drifted away, into the darkening streets.

"Hey," the boy said, looking around. "Where did Mr. Heinz go?"

"Maybe he went home," Kerry suggested.

"He probably realized it was time for dinner," Patrick said, placing a hand on his son's shoulder.

"Pancakes again?" Austin scrunched his face in disgust.

"You love my pancakes," his father said.

"Do they have blueberries in them?"

"Well, no. The ones in the fridge grew some Grinchy-looking green fur, so I had to throw them out. But we have bacon."

"And maple syrup?"

"Not exactly. I found a jar of strawberry jam, though, which is even better."

"Eeeeewwww," Austin howled. "Nobody puts jelly on pancakes. Gross!"

Patrick threw Kerry a pleading look.

"Are you kidding?" Kerry said. "Strawberry jam on pancakes is awesome sauce. It's way better than boring old maple syrup. Murphy and I love to make pancake and strawberry jam sandwiches for dinner. And then you put bacon in the middle, and it's salty and crunchy and sweet all at the same time."

"Bacon in the middle, huh?" Patrick said. "Never thought of that."

"Oh yeah. It's an old Tolliver Tree Farm tradition in my family. Goes back generations."

"Well, now we have to try it out, right, buddy?"

"I guess," Austin said. "Hey, Kerry, maybe you could come over and show my dad how to make it."

"Good idea," Patrick agreed.

"I couldn't," Kerry said.

The boy's face fell and his shoulders drooped.

"I mean, I'd love to," she added. "But Murphy is out delivering trees, and I can't just close down the stand. People will be getting off work, and heading home, and that's when lots of people decide to buy a Christmas tree. On impulse."

"Another time then," Patrick said. He tapped his son's arm. "Come on, then.

We've got a whole new culinary tradition to explore."

CHAPTER 12

Early Saturday morning, Kerry surveyed her wardrobe options for the holiday party with mounting despair. Per Birdie's suggestion, she'd packed light for the trip to the big city: three pairs of well-worn jeans, a couple of sweatshirts, a flannel shirt she'd swiped from her college boyfriend. There was a tattered blue sweater that the same boyfriend had given her for her twenty-first birthday. It was undeniably cozy and warm, but the cuffs had begun to unravel. Was that a metaphor for her life, she wondered?

The nicest items she'd brought were a black cashmere turtleneck and her worn black leather riding boots. Hardly the makings for a holiday-festive ensemble.

Murphy flung the trailer door open. "Kere? Got a customer wants one of your wreaths." He looked down at the clothes scattered across Kerry's made-up bunk. "What's all this?"

"My fashion options for tonight's party,"
Kerry said, sighing.

"What party?"

"The neighborhood holiday open house.
At John and Thomas's place? It's tonight.
Remember?"

"That's tonight? Already?"

"Yes, Murphy. I promised John we'd both
be there. And they want you to bring your
dobro."

He collapsed onto his bunk. "We'll see.
But in the meantime, you need to get out
there and start hustling Christmas trees."

Kerry bit her lip. "I will, but can you take
over for me for an hour or so after that?"

Murphy yawned widely. "I just worked a
fourteen-hour shift. Delivered seven trees
last night — including dragging an eight-
footer up six flights of stairs. I'm toast."

He closed his eyes.

"Please, Murph?" Kerry leaned over and
pried his eyes open with her fingers. "I'll
work this morning, but I really need to find
something decent to wear to this party
tonight. You can sleep till noon, okay? And
then spell me for an hour or so?"

Murphy batted her hand away and rolled
onto his side, with his back to his little
sister. "Just go sell some trees, will ya?"

91

The customer was a thirty-something woman with flaming red hair that spilled over the fur-trimmed collar of her white wool car coat. She was pacing around the stand, her stiletto-heeled boots clicking on the pavement, holding up trees, frowning, then letting them drop back onto the pile she'd picked them from.

The woman loudly cleared her throat. "Ahh-hemm."

"Hi," Kerry said. "I hear you're looking for a wreath?"

"Among other things," the woman said. "My neighbor bought one from you earlier in the week. I'd like something very similar, only with white berries instead of red, some of those dried flowers like hers had, but with purple ribbon."

"Oh-kay . . ." Kerry glanced down at the card table she'd come to regard as her workshop. She'd sold at least two dozen wreaths this week and her supplies were dwindling. She had some dried rose hips, a couple sprigs of mistletoe, but she was totally out of ribbon. She needed to make a trip to the flower market again, but there wouldn't be time today.

"I don't really have the materials to make a wreath like you want," she said. "But if you come back Monday afternoon, after I've had a chance to restock . . ."

The woman shook her head vigorously. "Monday's too late. I'm hosting my book club Christmas brunch Sunday. And I need trees and wreaths and garlands . . ."

"But that's tomorrow," Kerry pointed out.

"That's the point," the redhead said. She marched over to the stack of ten-foot trees and held one out. "I need a pair of these. But they need to be identical, because they go on either side of the fireplace in the living room." She picked up a roll of fir garland that Kerry had spent the previous day crafting. Her fingertips were still sore and full of minute pricks from the sticky needles.

"How long is this?" the woman asked.

"Um. Maybe thirty feet?"

"I need twice that much, but I'll take what you have," the woman said, turning to look around the tree stand. She pointed at a three-foot tree. "One of those, for the buffet table."

Kerry grabbed a receipt book and began jotting down the woman's purchases. The trees alone came to nearly seven hundred dollars. She hadn't calculated the price for the garland, but quickly decided the labor-intense project was easily worth one hundred and fifty.

"Anything else?"

"That should do it." The woman rummaged in her oversized Louis Vuitton handbag, drew out a credit card, and handed it to Kerry. "You take cards, right?"

"We do," Kerry said. "Just a moment, please."

She plugged the square into her cell phone and swiped the woman's card.

"That's one thousand, one hundred and sixty dollars," she told the woman.

"Including the wreath?"

"Well, no, since I don't have the materials to make one today."

"But you could get the materials, right? And make the wreath before tomorrow morning?"

Kerry paused. It was nearly nine A.M. now. She didn't dare wake Murphy to ask him to watch the stand while she made a trek to the wholesale flower market. And he'd pitch a fit if she closed up the stand on a Saturday morning, which should be their best day of business.

"I really wish I could," she told the customer. "But I'm working alone this morning."

The woman frowned and fidgeted with a lock of her hair. "I really, really need that wreath. The brunch starts at eleven."

"I don't know. The wholesale flower market closes at noon today . . ."

"Then forget it," the redhead snapped. "Just cancel out the transaction. I'll find someone else —"

"Wait," Kerry said. She couldn't just let a sale this big walk away. "I'll figure it out. White berries, dried flowers. Purple ribbon, right? What size wreath?"

"The biggest one you have," the woman said.

"That's a twenty-eight-inch wreath," Kerry said. She took a deep breath. "It'll probably cost around one twenty-five."

The woman waved her hand carelessly. "Whatever. In the meantime, you deliver, right? I'm in the neighborhood. Just a few blocks over."

"Uh, my brother does the deliveries, but he's not here right now . . ."

"He'll be back soon, right? My assistant is coming at noon to start decorating."

Kerry glanced nervously at the trailer, where she could hear Murphy's muffled snores.

"I'll take care of it," Kerry said, handing her the receipt book. "Just write your name and address on the top here, and your phone number."

"I'm Susannah," the redhead said. "Don't forget. Noon."

The morning passed in a blur. The weather cleared, the sun came out, but she estimated that the temperature hovered in the twenties. People streamed in and out of Anna's, coffees in hand, ready to pick out their tree. Customers arrived by cab and by bus. Most took their trees with them, but at least half a dozen were added to the pile for Murphy to deliver. She chatted with neighbors asking about Jock and her brother, and she assured them that her father was on the mend, and Murphy was only napping.

At ten, Patrick and Austin joined the crowd.

"Here," Austin said, handing her a foil-wrapped package. "We made this for you."

Patrick's lips twitched with a barely suppressed smile.

Kerry peeled back the foil and peered at the contents. A fat, roundish brown blob inside oozed a thick red fluid.

"It's a pancake and strawberry jelly sandwich!" Austin announced, unable to contain his excitement.

"With low-sodium turkey bacon," his

father added. "Super healthy, right?"

"Oh. Wow. That's so . . . thoughtful."

"Try it!" Austin urged.

Patrick handed her a foam cup of steaming coffee. She took a sip, then lifted the sandwich to her mouth and took a small bite.

The pancake was tough on the outside and undercooked on the inside. But the contrast of the sweet, fruity jam and the salty, crunchy bacon was, she decided, a pleasant surprise. She chewed and swallowed, then beamed at her young friend.

"This is the best pancake sandwich I've ever tasted. Even better than my mom makes."

Father and son were dressed for the outdoors. Austin wore his blue puffer jacket, corduroy pants, red snow boots, and a red knit ski cap. Patrick had on jeans and a quilted flannel jacket. He was bareheaded. Both wore waterproof gloves.

"Where are you two headed?" she asked. "Hiking?"

"Nooo," Austin said. "We came to help you sell trees."

"I tried to talk him into going ice skating in Central Park, or to the puppet show at the children's museum, or something outdoorsy, but he insisted on coming down here."

"That's so sweet," Kerry said. "But I couldn't let you give up a Saturday working here with me."

"I want to!" Austin exclaimed. "Murphy lets me help, doesn't he, Dad?"

Patrick shrugged. "But Murphy's not here right now, bud."

"He worked pretty late last night. But if you're really serious, I actually could use some help," Kerry said.

"Name it," Patrick said.

"I've got a customer who needs a custom wreath by tomorrow morning, but I'm out of supplies and the wholesale flower mart closes at noon. If you guys wouldn't mind manning the stand, I'll cab over there, get what I need, then come right back."

"Cool!" Austin said.

Kerry scribbled her cell phone number on the top of the receipt book. "Call me if you have any problems or questions. Okay?"

Kerry hustled through the market, turning a blind eye to buckets of gorgeous blooming blossoms, instead concentrating on what she needed for wreaths. She chose dried white and purple statice, milky-colored wax berries, more sprigs of mistletoe, tiny

98

pinecones, and sprays of seeded eucalyptus. In the ribbon aisle she found a roll of wide amethyst-colored ribbon.

After paying for her purchases she walked out to the sidewalk and for the first time, noticed a small pop-up vintage market in a vacant parking lot across the street. She still hadn't solved her wardrobe dilemma for tonight's party.

She hesitated, then darted across the street. Patrick would call if there were any problems, right? What difference would another fifteen minutes make?

An older woman with a short silvery bob, dressed in a moth-eaten leopard-print fur jacket, black leather miniskirt, fishnet hose, and platform ankle boots sat at a high-top table at the entrance to a booth called Frock of Ages.

"Looking for anything in particular?" she asked.

"Something to wear to a party tonight. Holiday festive," Kerry said.

The woman pointed a long crimson-polished finger at a rack of dresses. "Start there."

The dresses were crammed in tightly and formed a rainbow of eclectic styles and decades; chiffon and taffeta '50s prom

99

dresses, eye-popping psychedelic prints from the '60s, and poofy '80s bridesmaids' dresses. Kerry checked the tag on a cranberry satin jumpsuit and gasped. It was one hundred and fifty dollars.

She was on her way out of the booth when she spied a dark green velvet sleeve poking out of a box of clothing. It was a men's Ralph Lauren jacket, but in a small size. She removed her barn jacket and slipped the blazer on. It was big in the shoulders, and smelled like it had been in someone's basement, and there was no price tag, but this, she decided, was as good as it was going to get.

Her phone rang as she was starting to dig through the rest of the box's contents.

The call was from what she recognized as a New York City area code.

"Kerry?" It was Patrick.

"Everything okay?"

"Uh, well, there's a cop here, and he says your trailer's parked illegally."

"What? Where's Murphy?"

"He woke up a little while ago and went to deliver a tree. It's just Austin and me, and uh, I'm kind of concerned cuz the cop just called for a tow truck."

"Did you call Murphy?"

"I don't have his number."

"Oh God." Kerry tucked the velvet jacket under her arm and race-walked toward the shopkeeper. "I'm headed back now. Just don't let them tow Spammy away. Please!"

"I'll do what I can," Patrick said.

The shopkeeper was chatting on the phone in a language Kerry didn't recognize when she approached.

"Price?"

The woman held up her hand and kept talking.

"Price, please?" Kerry held out a twenty-dollar bill. Without stopping her chat, the shopkeeper plucked the money from her fingertips.

CHAPTER 13

By the time Kerry emerged from the flea market it had started to sleet. Buses and cars and cabs whizzed by as she frantically waved from the curb, trying to hail a cab. Finally, she stepped into the street, the way she'd seen it done in the movies, jumping in front of a cab as it slowed for the traffic light, then ran around and got in the back seat.

"Hey!" The driver turned an outraged face to her. "I'm off duty."

"Oh. Sorry."

"Friggin' tourists."

Kerry backed out of the cab and it sped away.

She tried calling her brother, but the calls went directly to voice mail. She walked two more miserable blocks, sleet pelting her face and bare head, before finally managing to flag down a cab. She called again, her fingers stiff from the cold.

"Murphy! You've got to get back to the stand. A cop showed up and says we're parked there illegally. He called a tow truck. I'm on my way there now, but I don't know what I'll do when I get there."

Traffic was slow and Kerry peered anxiously over the cabdriver's shoulder. "Isn't there a shortcut you can take?"

The cabbie didn't turn his head.

Ten agonizing minutes passed before they arrived at Abingdon Square. She shoved some bills in the cash slot in the partition and jumped out of the cab.

A small crowd had gathered around the tree stand, where a tow truck was parked in front of the trailer. A heavyset man in a bright yellow rain slicker stood on the sidewalk, engaged in what looked like a heated conversation with her brother.

Utilizing her new big-city skills, Kerry managed to elbow her way through the onlookers.

"Murph?"

Her brother turned and glared. "Where you been?"

Kerry felt her face redden. "I went to the flower market. A customer — she bought nearly fifteen hundred dollars' worth of trees — wants a wreath for her party tomorrow, and I was out of materials."

"Never mind," he said curtly. He put his hand on the tow truck driver's sleeve. "Do we have an understanding?"

The driver stomped back to the tow truck, revved the engine, and slowly pulled away from the square.

People began to drift away. But Patrick and Austin stood their ground.

"Sorry," Patrick said. "That cop must be new on the beat. I've never known the police to mess with your family before."

Kerry watched as Murphy loaded two trees onto the wagon he'd rigged to trail behind his bike. "My brother told me we've always had an understanding with the cops in this neighborhood. I wonder what changed?"

Murphy walked back to where she stood. His face was tight with barely controlled anger. She'd never seen her even-tempered brother like this.

"Kerry? You think you can maybe manage to stay here and do your job while I go deliver these trees? Maybe I should hire Austin, here, to take your place?"

Austin was wide-eyed, sensing the tension between the siblings.

"It's okay, bud," she told the little boy, patting his shoulder.

"We're, uh, gonna go grab some lunch,"

Patrick said. "You're coming to the party tonight, right?"

"We'll see," Kerry said.

Kerry hurried into Lombardi's at three to use their restroom. Claudia offered her a cup of espresso.

"Only if you can make it to go," Kerry said. "I'm already on my brother's shit list."

Claudia rolled her eyes, but fetched a cardboard cup and drew her a cup of the inky black espresso.

"I'll see you at the party tonight, right?" Claudia asked.

"Not sure. I found a jacket at a flea market this morning, but it's kind of wrinkly and stinky. And I don't have anything to wear with it. Plus, Murphy's in a real mood."

Claudia followed her outside the restaurant. "You leave your brother to me. And in the meantime, why don't you give me that jacket? I've got a little hand steamer upstairs in my apartment that works miracles."

CHAPTER 14

The sleet had finally slacked off, but now the sky was darkening and the temperature had dropped another ten degrees while Kerry finished up her wreaths.

She was searching for the gloves she'd removed while crafting when she heard the trailer door open and saw Murphy step out, stretching and yawning like a grizzly bear after a long winter nap. She felt herself involuntarily flinch as he approached her work station.

"How'd we do today?" he asked, slumping down into his lawn chair. "How many trees?"

She consulted her steno pad, where she'd made hash marks for every tree sold.

"Eighteen trees. Not bad, right?"

"Not good," he said, shaking his head. He lifted one hip and extracted a small notebook from his pocket. He leafed through well-thumbed pages of what looked like handwritten hieroglyphics and muttered under his breath.

"What?"

He ran an index finger down the page he'd opened the notebook to. "We're way behind. Last year, by now, we'd sold thirty-two trees."

Kerry craned her neck to get a look at the page, but the scratchings were illegible.

"Kerry, I don't think you appreciate what all is on the line here. These next three weeks, right here on this corner, this is what keeps Tolliver Tree Farm in business next year. We're operating on a razor-thin profit margin, as it is. We're getting killed with expenses. Had to buy a new baling machine last month, and the cost of fuel is sky high. We lost all those trees last spring. And now, missing the first week of sales, plus all these hospital expenses from Dad's heart attack . . ."

A chill ran down her spine. "What are you trying to say? We might lose the farm?"

"Not saying that," Murphy said, running his hands through his already wild mane. For the first time she noticed that his dark reddish hair was shot through with silver, as was his beard.

"I'm saying we gotta pay attention. Gotta maximize sales. Especially with those two goons over across the street calling the cops on us to try and make trouble."

"You think it was the Brodys?"

"Hundred percent it was them. We know every cop in this precinct. They know us. I deliver a Tolliver tree to the station house every year, and give all the cops half-price trees."

"Hey." Claudia stood a few feet away, holding up the green velvet blazer.

"This jacket doesn't even look like the one I bought," Kerry marveled, taking it from her. "It looks brand new."

"It is brand new. Or it was a few years ago. I found the price tag in the inside breast pocket. I don't think it was ever worn."

Kerry sniffed the collar and smelled something like lavender. "Smells new too."

"Gave it a toss with a scented dryer sheet then ran my steamer over it," Claudia said.

"Well, you're awesome." She poked her brother in the ribs. "Isn't she?"

"Yeah, totally," he said dutifully.

Claudia looked Murphy up and down. "So what are you wearing tonight, big fella?"

"I forgot about that party. And, uh . . ."

Claudia raised an eyebrow. "Let's have a chat."

CHAPTER 15

Spammy's bathroom mirror was only slightly larger than a pie pan, and the forty-watt bulb in the tiny space cast a dim yellow light on the faded pink walls.

Kerry twisted her dark-blond hair into a knot at the nape of her neck, then rolled and tucked the ends into a French knot. She finished her makeup with a coat of Chanel red lipstick, the same shade she'd been using since Birdie gave her a tube for her eighteenth birthday.

She studied her reflection in the mirror. Gray eyes, the one on the left slightly smaller than the one on the right, stubby nose — just like Jock's — and full lips, like her mother's, and all the women on her side of the family.

The trailer door opened and Murphy stuck his head inside.

"Gimme a minute."

She looked down at her ensemble. The

rich bottle-green velvet of the jacket suited her coloring. The white blouse was nothing special, just something she'd tossed in her suitcase at the last minute. She'd tucked it into her best pair of jeans, which were at least clean, improvised a belt from red satin ribbon, and polished her old black riding boots to a high sheen.

When she stepped out of the bathroom, Murphy was perched on the edge of his bunk, plucking at a small stringed instrument.

His conference with Claudia had apparently worked a miracle. His hair was damp, with comb marks. He wore black jeans, a black collared shirt, black loafers, and a silly green felt bow tie made to resemble a sprig of holly, complete with a blinking red light in the middle.

"I didn't know you played the dobro," Kerry said.

"Been playing for years," he said, playing a bar of a mournful song she vaguely recognized.

"Don't you know something less depressing and more seasonal?"

He closed his eyes and picked out a few bars of "Frosty the Snowman."

"Perfect. You look nice, by the way. Especially love the bow tie."

"Claudia's contribution."

"You two seem pretty friendly," Kerry observed.

"We are. Especially since she finally filed papers on her loser ex last year. Actually, the shirt and shoes are his. Were his."

He stood up and slung the dobro over his shoulder. "Okay. You ready to roll?"

"I guess. But compared to you, I look pretty sad."

"You look fine." It was as close to a compliment as she could expect from her taciturn brother.

Kerry grabbed her pocketbook, then, out of the corner of her eye, noticed the fringe of a red plaid blanket in the rumpled bedding on Murphy's bunk.

It was a wool stadium blanket, in a vivid Stewart tartan. "Where did this come from?"

"Dad's house, I guess."

Kerry wrapped the blanket around her waist.

She slid off her riding boots and unzipped her jeans.

"What's going on?" he asked, politely averting his gaze.

"Just a quick costume change. Give me five minutes, will ya?"

"I'll go walk Queenie, but then you better

111

be ready."

Kerry had noticed her grandmother's dusty mending basket under the bathroom vanity. Inside, she found tiny spools of thread, and a small pincushion bristling with straight pins and needles and safety pins. There was also an old jar of buttons, and a tiny pair of scissors.

She fastened the stadium blanket around her waist, and awkwardly pinned it together so that the fringed edges overlapped. She stepped out of the makeshift skirt, threaded the largest needle she could find, and basted a fast but messy seam, ending three-quarters of the way down the edge of the blanket.

She donned a pair of black tights and pulled the skirt on, fastening the opening with the largest safety pin she'd found. She cinched the waist of the skirt with her black leather belt, then pulled her boots on again.

"You decent?" Murphy yelled, banging on the door of the trailer.

She opened the door and stepped down to the pavement.

Murphy gave her a puzzled look. "You're wearing my blanket to a Christmas party?"

"Uh-huh. Just like you're wearing your girlfriend's ex-husband's shirt and shoes. It is what it is."

CHAPTER 16

"Wait up," Kerry called. She reached under the work table and pulled out the centerpiece she'd completed the day before.

"What's that?" he asked, as she hefted it onto the table.

"My contribution to John's party."

Kerry had filled the bottom of a fruit crate she'd found on the curb with crumpled paper, then piled in Granny Smith apples, green pears, limes, baby artichokes, and bunches of green grapes. She'd filled in gaps in the fruit with greenery and white roses, all bought at the bodega.

"Looks like dessert," Murphy said, snagging a grape, before Kerry slapped his hand away.

"It's a centerpiece and it's heavy," Kerry said, staggering under the weight. "How about you carry it and I'll carry the dobro?"

John's apartment was on the third floor of a

redbrick building with a spacious arched entryway, half a block from the Christmas tree stand. They rang the buzzer and a moment later heard the front door unlock. As soon as they emerged from the elevator, they heard strains of music, laughter, and the clink of glasses coming from the partially open door at the end of the hall.

Other doors on the hallway were open too, and people drifted out of their apartments, carrying bottles of wine or covered dishes and trays of food. The women were dressed in chic, short cocktail dresses, the men in crisply pressed slacks and tweed blazers.

Kerry felt frumpy and ill at ease in her thrown-together flea market/bedspread attire. She had a sudden urge to run back home to Spammy, but before she could act, John was there, pulling her into an impulsive hug. He held Ruby, resplendent in a green-and-white knitted Christmas sweater, with a matching cap that sported felt reindeer antlers.

"Kerry! Murphy! We're so glad you could come," John exclaimed. He took the arrangement from Murphy. "Oh my God, this centerpiece! Kerry, it's divine. It's fabulous. I can't believe you made this yourself. Wait till Thomas sees it! The whole thing is gorgeous. Rustic and elegant, and Kerry, you wizard, how did you know our dining room is done in greens and gold?" He linked his arm through Kerry's. "Now you two get in here and let's get you something to eat and drink."

The apartment was high-ceilinged and spacious and thronged with people, most of whom seemed to know her brother.

"Murphy! Good to see you!"

"Hey, Murph! What's shakin'? How are things down south in the mountains?"

There was much back-slapping and cheek-kissing, and Kerry was amazed how well her brother seemed to fit in with these urbane residents of the West Village, while she, by contrast, felt like a miserable country-come-to-town mouse.

She followed John into the dining room, where he put the arrangement in the middle of a gleaming oval mahogany table loaded with trays of food.

It was the most elegant room Kerry had ever seen, with wallpaper in a rich green-and-gold damask. Silk curtains puddled on the hardwood floor. A chandelier dripping with crystals illuminated the room, and a mahogany Hepplewhite sideboard held dozens of glowing candles set in silver candlesticks. The wall opposite the sideboard held a huge gilt-framed oil portrait of an elegant woman in a gauzy aqua '50s-era evening gown.

John noticed her staring at the painting. "My great-grandmother," he said. "GeeGee. She was quite a dame. Made her debut with Jackie Kennedy, slept with two cabinet members in the Johnson administration. This apartment and a lot of the furniture in here was hers."

He looked over Kerry's head and waved. "I just realized you haven't met Thomas yet. He's been on the road with a touring production of *Annie* and just got home yesterday."

John's partner Thomas had the bluest eyes Kerry had ever seen, and a neatly trimmed graying beard.

"Babe? This is my friend Kerry that I've been telling you about. She's Murphy's sister, but more importantly, she created the wreath hanging on your grandmother's secretary and that divine centerpiece."

Thomas's eyes widened in appreciation. He took her hand in both of his. "Kerry, it's so nice to meet you. We both love your work."

"Thanks," she said. "So you've been on the road with a show? Are you an actor?"

"God no," the two men drawled in unison.

"I'm a theatrical producer," Thomas explained.

"And John's a writer. He'll never tell you this himself, but he's a *New York Times* bestseller," Thomas said proudly. "His books terrify me. How does a gay man write such seriously spooky stuff?"

"You're *gay*?" John lowered his voice to a whisper. "I've been sleeping with you for twenty-five years, and now you tell me?"

"Funny, honey," Thomas said. "Okay, enough about us. This lady has been here for at least ten minutes and she doesn't even have a drink in her hand."

"What'll you have?" John asked. "Wine? Martini? Champagne? Or some of Thomas's infamous Christmas punch?"

"The punch sounds delicious but dangerous, so maybe just a glass of champagne."

She sipped from a delicate crystal flute and wandered into the living room, where Taryn Kaplan spotted her and began introducing her to some of the other partygoers. Kerry felt a tug at the sleeve of her jacket.

Austin beamed up at her. He looked especially natty, wearing a red-and-white-striped dress shirt, red plaid vest, and a necklace of winking plastic Christmas tree lights.

"Hey, Kerry!" the boy said, his voice pitched with excitement.

"Austin, hi," Kerry said. "Where's your dad tonight?"

"He's at his place. It's my mom's turn to stay with me. You look real pretty," Austin said. He reached into his pants pocket and pulled out an iced sugar cookie and took a bite. "Did you get any of the cookies? I helped make 'em."

"I didn't, but I'll certainly get one, now that I know you baked them."

"Get the ones with the silver sprinkles," he advised.

"Austin?" A woman, slender with hair worn in a sleek dark bob, approached and pointed to the cookie the boy was munching on. Kerry recognized her from their brief encounter at the tree stand. "How many of those have you eaten tonight?"

"Not that many. Only five."

"Austin?" She brushed away the cookie crumbs cascading down his vest.

"Maybe it was six? I forget."

"Okay, no more cookies for you," the woman said sternly. She favored Kerry with a lukewarm smile.

"Hi there. I'm Gretchen McCaleb. Austin's mom."

"And I'm Kerry. My brother and I run

118

the Christmas tree stand. Austin's been a big help this week."

"Really? How so?"

"My brother was sleeping and I had to run an errand, so Patrick and Austin very generously offered to mind the stand. It was barely an hour," Kerry explained.

"But then the police came, and somebody called a tow truck and they were gonna hook Spammy up to the truck and take her away. But Murphy yelled at the guy and made him go away," the boy continued.

"The police?"

"It was a misunderstanding," Kerry assured her.

Gretchen nodded. "You're the artist, right? Austin has been telling me all about the story you two have been writing and illustrating together."

"Mr. Heinz has been helping too. He draws really good. You should see the picture he drew of me and Kerry."

"Are you talking about that batty old homeless guy in the dusty coat, Austin? I'm not sure you should be hanging around with him. There's something off about that man. Always wandering the street, day and night, muttering to himself."

"He seems harmless to me," Kerry said.

Gretchen gave her an impassive stare.

119

"You've been here, what? A week? I've been seeing him around the neighborhood for years. He scowls every time he sees me." She put a protective hand on Austin's shoulder. "I saw him take his cane and beat the hood of a cab last year when it honked at him for jaywalking. He could be a dangerous kook. I'd really rather that man not spend any time with my child."

"What's all this about?"

Patrick had eased, unannounced, into their little circle.

Austin's face brightened. "Dad! You came."

Patrick high-fived his son. "Of course I came. Can't miss the best Christmas party of the year."

"I thought you had dinner with a client tonight," Gretchen said.

"More like drinks and appetizers. And the restaurant was only a few blocks away."

"How nice," Gretchen murmured. Kerry almost laughed. She could tell the woman was totally pissed to see her ex.

Gretchen took a sip of her martini. "I was just telling Kerry that I don't like our son spending time around that homeless man. He seems deranged."

"Oh, I don't think Heinz is deranged. And look, it's not like Austin has ever been alone with him."

Austin tugged at the hem of Patrick's Harris tweed sport coat. "Dad, there's Murphy. And he brought his banjo."

Claudia had Murphy by the arm, dragging him toward the living room fireplace, where a chair had been set up in front of a roaring fire.

"Everyone!" she announced. "We've got a treat tonight. Murphy Tolliver has volunteered to get us in the Christmas spirit by playing his dobro."

Guests drifted in from the dining room, glasses and plates in hand, and formed a semicircle around him. The room grew silent as all eyes were trained on the musician.

Finally, Murphy looked up and cleared his throat. "Uh, what d'ya'll want to hear?"

"Play 'Frosty the Snowman,' " Austin piped up.

Laughter rippled through the crowd and the awkward silence was broken.

CHAPTER 17

Murphy closed his eyes and positioned his large, chapped hands on the flat bridge of the dobro. He was still for a moment and looked almost prayerful. His fingers were like Jock's, thick and calloused, with dirt under the nails that no amount of scrubbing would ever entirely erase.

But then, his fingers flew over the strings. Kerry looked down at Austin, whose eyes were alive with excitement. Patrick was watching him too, and for a moment, he glanced over at Kerry and grinned.

From "Frosty the Snowman," Murphy plowed without stopping into "Jingle Bells," and then, with a nod in Austin's direction, "Rudolph the Red-Nosed Reindeer." Finally, he paused and looked up, his cheeks pink with excitement or embarrassment, Kerry couldn't tell which.

The room erupted in applause, and he ducked his head. Their hosts had drifted into the room and stood in front of the huge Christmas tree that dominated the rest of the room. It was strung with what appeared to be thousands of tiny, twinkling white lights.

"Murphy, can you play something, I don't know, like maybe the kind of music you might play back at home?" John asked.

"You mean like bluegrass, country, something like that?"

"Whatever you like," John said.

Murphy's hand began patting out a beat on the dobro's neck and a minute later he started playing the first notes of "I'll Fly Away." Soon, everyone in the crowd was clapping and tapping their feet.

"More!" someone called out.

For the next fifteen minutes, Murphy performed a virtuoso one-man concert, following up with bluegrass standards Kerry had grown up listening to back home in the southern Appalachian Mountains: "Man of Constant Sorrows," "Foggy Mountain Breakdown," and "Orange Blossom Special."

More applause, cheers, and hoots of approval from the guests.

Following that, he rested his hands on the dobro and took a deep breath. Claudia, who'd been standing close by, beaming her approval, handed him a bottle of beer. He took a long pull from the bottle, then wiped his perspiring brow with the back of his hand.

"Just one more song, Murphy. Please?" John coaxed.

Murphy took another long drink of beer, then started playing.

At first, Kerry couldn't place the song. It was familiar, but the tune was slow, melancholy almost. But then Thomas stepped forward and in a clear, strong tenor, began singing.

" 'Have yourself a merry little Christmas. . . .' "

John chimed in on the next verse, amid scattered laughter from the party guests.

" 'Make the yuletide gay. . . .' "

And then the others started singing, hesitantly at first, some humming when they didn't know the words. Kerry only remembered a few of the verses, so she sang in a near whisper.

" 'Have yourself a merry little Christmas, let your heart be light. . . .' "

A loud, somewhat wobbly baritone voice was very near. It was Patrick. He'd scooped Austin into his arms and the little boy's head rested on his shoulder, his eyelids fluttering in a desperate attempt to stay awake.

"Here. Let me take him up to bed. It's way past his bedtime." Gretchen reached out for the child, but Austin shook his head.

"I wanna stay."

"Austin? You heard your mom." Patrick handed the boy off. Gretchen gave Kerry a curt nod of recognition, then melted into the crowd. Austin gave a brief, weary good-bye wave.

Kerry wanted to congratulate her brother, to tell him how proud she was of his performance, but he was surrounded by well-wishers.

Claudia drifted over to her side. Like Murphy, tonight she looked strikingly glamorous, wearing a winter-white silk blouse tucked into voluminous white wool palazzo pants. Her hair fell to her shoulders, clipped back behind one ear with a rhinestone-studded comb.

"You look amazing," Kerry said. "And I can't believe the transformation in my brother. I don't think he's been that dressed up since my dad's last wedding."

"He cleans up pretty nice, doesn't he?" Claudia said fondly. "Despite all his bitching and moaning, I think he kind of enjoyed all the attention tonight."

"I can't get over it. He's a completely dif-

125

ferent person once he starts to play," Kerry said.

"I better go rescue him," Claudia said.

Kerry's stomach rumbled and she realized she'd barely eaten all day. She made her way to the dining room, where the table resembled a glossy magazine spread, thanks in part to her hand-crafted centerpiece, but also to the silver platters holding thinly sliced smoked salmon, rare roast beef, an enormous cut-glass punchbowl with marinated shrimp, plates of cheeses and crackers, and a vegetable tray that looked like a still life by a Dutch master.

Grabbing a plate, she worked her way around the table, making a sandwich with a small, pillowy yeast roll and some roast beef, heaping shrimp and cubes of cheese and a mound of crackers and artichoke dip onto her plate. The crowd was starting to thin out, so she isolated herself in a corner of the room, nibbling on her dinner.

Kerry popped a tiny Napoleon in her mouth and nearly moaned in ecstasy. She looked around to make sure she couldn't be seen, then loaded half a dozen of the pastries into a paper napkin, which she was in the process of stashing in her shoulder bag when a husky voice whispered in her ear.

"I saw that."

Startled, she jumped and dropped a strawberry tartlet onto the Oriental carpet. She whirled around to see Patrick, standing directly behind her.

"Hmm. Grand theft cannoli?"

Her face went crimson. "Guilty as charged. Okay? I haven't had time to eat today, and tomorrow morning's not looking good, either."

Wordlessly, he turned to the buffet table, then made a show of scooping a handful of cookies into a damask dinner napkin, which he carefully folded and stowed in his jacket pocket.

"Guess that makes me an accessory to the crime," he said, folding his hands innocently at his waist.

"I won't tell if you won't," Kerry said, picking up the errant tartlet and depositing it on a stack of used dishes.

"Well then, since that makes us co-conspirators, can I fetch you a drink?" He pointed to her empty champagne flute.

Kerry considered. "Maybe just a small glass of white wine? I don't dare drink two glasses of champagne. Gotta open the stand bright and early in the morning."

Patrick went through a swinging door into what she assumed was the kitchen and returned a minute later with a half-full wine-glass.

"Thanks," she said, taking a sip. The wine was nicely chilled and very good. She could get used to this kind of life.

Patrick had a cut glass tumbler filled with what looked and smelled like bourbon. He clinked his glass against hers. He nodded in the direction of the living room, where Murphy and Claudia were huddled in a corner, standing very close together.

Kerry followed his gaze and laughed. "I think he's smitten." She raised her glass to her lips and emptied it. "I better go."

"Already?" Patrick's face fell. "It's barely nine o'clock." He gestured toward the living room. "I was thinking we could kind of hang out for a while, since it's Gretchen's night to have Austin."

"Wish I could," she said, meaning it.

"Then I'll walk you home," Patrick said, putting his glass down.

She almost protested but changed her mind. "That'd be nice."

CHAPTER 18

Patrick and Kerry were crossing the street when they saw a young couple standing hand in hand, peering into the roped-off Christmas tree stand.

"Hey," the man called as they approached. "Are you guys open?"

"We are now," Kerry said. Even one more tree sold today would help the bottom line.

She unfastened the bungee cord and gestured for the two to enter. Patrick sat down in Murphy's vacant lawn chair.

The girl gestured toward Spammy. "I love the little trailer. So adorable! Does somebody actually live in it?"

"Two somebodies," Kerry said. "And a dog. Right up until Christmas Eve."

"Oooh! Like something out of a fairy tale," the girl squealed.

"More like a horror story," Kerry said, as she was sizing the couple up for their tree-buying potential.

She estimated that they were in their early twenties. The girl could have been a model for skiwear, with a pink knitted beanie pulled over her long blond hair, a white quilted jacket, and skinny jeans tucked into fur-trimmed suede boots. Her partner was also dressed for the slopes. He wore wire-rimmed glasses and had a glorious mop of strawberry-blond curls.

"This might sound kinda creepy, but is there any way I could look inside your camper?"

"Ashley, no. That's definitely super creepy," the boyfriend said.

The girl flashed a winsome smile. "Please?"

"It's a big mess inside," Kerry protested. "I'm living with a slob, and his dog sheds. And I was getting ready for a party . . ."

"No judgment," Ashley promised. "Just a peek?"

Kerry sighed, then climbed up and opened the trailer door. Queenie, who'd been dozing on Murphy's bunk, gave a short, quizzical bark, then stood and squeezed past the visitor.

Ashley poked her head inside. "It's pink! And turquoise! And that teensy kitchen! Does it actually work?"

"Not in a long time," Kerry told her.

"Does it have a name?"

"My mom named her Spammy; you know, because it looks like a canned ham," Kerry said.

"Ash? I thought we were buying a tree." The boyfriend's voice sounded a warning.

"Oh, right."

She did a quick circle around the lot. "Ooh, Shaun, look at this one." She pointed at a ten-foot tree.

Her partner shook his head and laughed. "Babe, that thing is as big as the tree at Rockefeller Plaza. How are we gonna drag that up three flights of stairs?"

"But it's so pretty," she protested.

He kissed the tip of her nose. "Think smaller."

She circled the lot, pulling out and sizing up trees, for the next ten minutes.

Kerry didn't bother to suppress a yawn.

"Ashley, these folks are ready to close up shop," the boyfriend said.

"It's okay," Kerry said, smiling brightly.

The girl stopped in front of the stack of smaller trees and picked up a four-foot model.

She set it on the pavement and twirled it around. "This is it. This is the one."

"You sure?" Shaun asked.

"Positive. It's super sweet. We can put it

on the table in front of the window."

"And what's gonna happen when Billy decides to climb your super-sweet Christmas tree?" Shaun asked. "Billy's her cat. Her obnoxious, spoiled rotten cat."

"He's not spoiled," Ashley said. "He's . . . entitled, but I promise I will speak to Billy about staying away from this Christmas tree."

Shaun turned to Kerry and Patrick. "See what I'm dealing with here?" He put a finger to his forehead. "She's loco in the cabeza. Nuts."

Ashley wrapped her arms around him. "Yeah, I'm nuts. Nuts about you, Shaun Hettinger."

"Okay," he relented. "We'll get the tree. Are you gonna make me spend hours and hours stringing and then rearranging and then re-rearranging all the lights?"

"Definitely."

He pulled out his billfold, and she gave a happy, high-pitched squeal of delight.

"This is our first Christmas together," she told Patrick and Kerry.

"What?" Shaun said. "We've been together for two years."

"I mean, it's our first Christmas living together in our own place," Ashley said. She held out her left hand, wriggling her fingers to show off the tiny diamond chip on her ring finger. "We just got engaged Thanksgiving Day."

Patrick beamed at the happy couple. "Congratulations! It's great that you'll be celebrating your first Christmas together with a Tolliver Christmas tree. In fact, we'd love to offer you our first-Christmas-together discount. Right?"

He glanced at Kerry for approval, giving her a subtle nod.

"Really?" Ashley asked. "So how much is the tree?"

Kerry got the hint. She glanced across the street at the Brodys' tree stand. Their light-up sign advertised *Fresh Trees — Cheap! Starting at $40.*

"It's thirty-eight dollars," Kerry said.

"Cool." Shaun opened his billfold and handed Kerry cash for the tree.

Ashley whipped her cell phone from her jacket pocket. "Would it be okay if I took some pictures of your tree stand for my social media?"

"Guess so," Kerry said.

"Put the tree over your shoulder, babe," she instructed her fiancé. "Like you just cut it and hauled it down the mountain."

He obediently balanced the tree over one shoulder, and she handed the phone to

Kerry, before posing herself beside him, hand rested on one hip.

Kerry clicked off a few frames.

"Now get one of us standing by Spammy," Ashley instructed. "And then another by your sign, so my fans will know where to find you."

Kerry did as requested. Ashley took the phone and studied the photos. "Mmm. Not bad." She looked up. "Now let me take one of you and your boyfriend in front of the sign. Good publicity, right?"

Kerry felt the heat rise in her neck and cheeks. "He's not my —"

"No problem," Patrick said cheerfully. He whistled and Queenie trotted over, then he took Kerry's arm and steered her over to the sign.

"What are you doing?" she hissed.

"Just smile and act like you adore me," he said under his breath, flinging an arm around her shoulder, as Ashley clicked the camera's shutter. "I'll fill you in later."

When the impromptu photo shoot was done and the happy couple were walking away with their bargain Christmas tree, Kerry turned to Patrick. "Okay. What was that all about?"

"The girl, Ashley. I knew I recognized her from somewhere. Then it struck me. That's

Ashley, from AshleyActually. She's a huge social media influencer."

Now it was Patrick's turn to consult his phone. He opened the Instagram app, typed something in the search bar, and showed Kerry the results.

AshleyActually had 1.2 million followers, and her feed featured an endless stream of artfully styled shots of her shopping, strolling, sipping, nibbling, and sightseeing.

"How do you happen to know about someone like her?" Kerry asked.

"One of our clients paid a lot of money recently to have her do a paid promotion for their new coffee brand."

With his fingertip he scrolled through Ashley's feed, pausing at a backlit photo of the girl sipping from a mug of coffee, with a Siamese cat resting in her lap. She was dreamily looking out a window through a gauzy curtain.

Morning Musings with my #KoolBeans-Roasters coffee and my bff #SillyBillyCat. Two things I can't do without — my #Kool-BeansRoasters coffee and my Billy. Link in bio to get a 20% discount and enter to win a KoolBeans giveaway.

"She got paid for that?" Kerry asked.

135

"Major bucks. And our client was deliriously happy. Look at the number of likes and comments. The account netted like two thousand new followers and the discount got them a nice sales bump."

"Huh."

"If she actually mentions Tolliver Tree Farms on Instagram it could be huge," Patrick said. "Ashley and Shaun won't promote just any product. They're pretty picky."

Kerry was pondering the possibilities when Patrick's cell phone rang. His easy smile tensed. "Gretchen. Wonder what she's mad at me about now?"

He tapped Connect on the phone.

"Hi. What's up?"

His face softened as he listened. "Okay. Yeah. Glad you caught me. I'll come right up."

"Everything okay?" she asked.

"Austin wants me to come up and read him a bedtime story. Gotta go."

"See ya," Kerry said. "And thanks, by the way, for the intel about Ashley."

"Happy to help," Patrick murmured. He leaned in and kissed her, very lightly, on the lips. "Hope something comes of it."

CHAPTER 19

When her phone started ringing the next morning, Kerry groped around on her bunk, then finally found it on the floor, on top of the mound of clothes she'd dumped the night before.

She blinked a few times when she saw the caller ID, and then the time. It was barely seven.

"Mom? What's wrong?"

"Nothing's wrong. Is your brother around?"

She glanced over at Murphy's bunk, where Queenie was sleeping. She walked to the door in her stocking feet, opened it, and peeked out. The CLOSED sign was still hanging where she'd left it the night before.

Shivering, she returned to her bunk and pulled the blankets up to her chin. "I don't see him. Why don't you call his phone instead of mine?"

"I did, but you know how he is. Half the

time he doesn't even know where his phone is, the other half, he only picks up if he feels like it."

Kerry recalled Claudia's parting words the previous evening. Clearly, Murphy had spent the night out.

"Guess he must have gone out for coffee. Or to deliver a tree."

"At this time of the morning?"

"Mom, it's New York. The city that never sleeps. Anything I can help you with?"

She sensed a note of hesitation in her mother's voice. "No. Nothing important. Your dad had a question for him. Something about a piece of equipment."

"I'll tell Murphy to call you as soon as he gets back," Kerry promised.

"Fine. How's it going with you two? Are you getting along okay?"

"Sometimes yes, sometimes no. You know Murphy. He can be really prickly . . . And so closed off. I can never tell what he's thinking."

"Takes after his daddy," Birdie said. "But give him time. He's a good man, Kerry. Other than that, how's business?"

"I thought it was going pretty well, but Murphy says we're way behind on his usual sales numbers."

"You'll catch up."

"How's Dad?" Kerry asked.

There was a long pause.

"Mom? Are you there?"

Birdie sighed. "Fine. Cranky as ever."

As if on cue, Kerry heard her father's voice, querulous, demanding . . .

"Bird? Are you fixing my breakfast? You know I can't take my pills until I eat . . ."

"You heard the man," Birdie said. "Gotta go. Tell Murphy to call me when he gets back."

Kerry stayed in bed for another fifteen minutes, her thoughts drifting to the night before, and Patrick's parting kiss. What did it mean? In the South, people, even strangers, routinely hugged and kissed when they met, and when they parted ways. But this was New York City.

Finally, she dragged herself out of bed. Despite the space heater, it was still chilly enough that she could see her breath in the air. She longed for a hot shower, but there was no way she could impose on the Kaplans this early on a Sunday morning.

Kerry pulled on her jacket and snapped a leash to Queenie's collar before walking her outside to the park to do her business. Finally, she filled the dog's bowl with water and food and directed her to her moving blanket beneath the worktable outside. She heard church bells ringing from St. Egbert's on the next corner. The sun shone down. The sidewalk was alive with people walking dogs or pushing babies in strollers. A man dressed in tights and a sleeveless T-shirt jogged past, and Kerry shivered on his behalf. Delivery trucks rolled down the street, and two teenagers whizzed past on electric scooters. The door of a diner opened and she caught the aroma of frying bacon and what? Dill pickles? It struck Kerry that this corner of the West Village really was a little village, full of life and the sounds and smells of a big city, and after only a week it felt a lot like home.

She pulled out the custom purple-and-white wreath and finished attaching the last few bits of mistletoe. Just as she was finishing tying the bow, a sleek black sedan pulled up to the curb and Susannah, the redheaded customer, jumped out of the back seat.

Kerry held the wreath up so she could inspect it. "It's perfect," the woman gushed. "Better than I could have hoped. The trees are wonderful too. Your brother even put them in the stands for me. My apartment smells like an alpine forest. Heavenly." She handed a wad of bills to Kerry.

"But . . . but . . . you already paid me,"

Kerry babbled.

"That was before I saw the finished product. And, take a piece of advice from someone who's been in business for herself for a very long time. Never argue with a customer who wants to pay you what you're worth. Too many women undervalue themselves."

Susannah jumped back into the sedan and it rolled away. Kerry unfolded the bills. There were five twenty-dollar bills. Not a bad start for the morning.

In the next hour, she sold three more trees, all to customers who either promised to return to pick up their purchase after returning from brunch, or who wanted their trees delivered.

Still no sign of Murphy. She should have been annoyed, but then, she decided, why shouldn't he have a night off? Especially when it involved a sleepover with the glamorous Claudia.

She got out her drawing pad and pencils and began to sketch, placing Queenie in the middle of the page, with the pigeons, looking like fussy old ladies, bobbing and pecking around her. On a whim, she pulled out colored pencils and began sketching in the Christmas tree lot, adding a border enclosing Spammy, the dog, and the pigeons with a semicircle of trees. She drew in the Tolliver Family Christmas tree sign festooned with a big red bow.

When she looked up from her work she saw a stooped figure in a long black coat slowly making his way down the sidewalk. Queenie got up and walked over to him, sniffling at the old man's coat.

"She's a smart girl, this one," Heinz chuckled, pointing at her worktable. "So, what are you working on today?"

"Nothing, really," she said.

"Will you let me see?"

Kerry shrugged and opened the sketchbook to this morning's drawing. He put on a pair of spectacles and studied her work.

"It's just a doodle," Kerry said. "Not even a doodle."

"No, no. I quite like it," Heinz said. He turned to the page with the drawing of Queenie. "I like the expression on Queenie's face while she watches the pigeons. You're quite good with animals, you know. But tell me, how does all this fit into our story?"

"Our story?" Kerry raised an eyebrow.

"Certainly." He stuffed his hand into his coat pocket and brought out a single dog biscuit. He extended his hand, palm out. Queenie crept closer, crouched, and after a moment, delicately swept the biscuit into her mouth with her tongue.

"Good girl," Heinz said. He looked around the stand.

"Where is our young friend today?"

"It's his mom's week to stay with him, so I sort of doubt he'll be hanging out here."

She leaned in and lowered her voice. "I don't think Gretchen approves of me."

"Gretchen? The brunette?" He snorted. "She crosses the street when she sees me. Like I have something contagious. I don't think she approves of me, either. So, you are in good company. And that reminds me. I don't believe I know your name, young lady."

"I'm Kerry," she said, smiling. "Kerry Tolliver."

Kerry had just sold a tree to the Moodys, a middle-aged couple whom she'd met the night before at the Christmas party, when Murphy came limping into the stand with his dobro tucked under his arm.

He wore only one shoe. His hair was wild, he was bleary-eyed, and his shirt was untucked and half unbuttoned.

"Hey, Debra, hey, Dale," he said, giving a half-hearted nod to the customers.

"Morning, Murphy," Debra Moody said. "We sure enjoyed your music last night." Murphy gave a wan smile in return, then he slumped down onto his chair and sighed.

"Jesus, Murphy," Kerry said after the Moodys walked away, "what happened? You look like you got hit by a truck. Or mugged. Or both."

"I feel like I got hit by a truck full of muggers," he moaned, massaging his forehead.

"I mean, it's none of my business, but

144

what did you and Claudia get up to last night?"

"Me and Claudia?" He opened one bloodshot eye. "Nothing. I wasn't with her."

"But I thought . . . the way you two were cuddling in the corner . . ."

"Nah. Get your mind out of the gutter, Kerry. I walked her back to her place, then I headed over to Augie's Pub to play darts. Some guys I know turned up, and they begged me to play my dobro . . . and pretty soon it was after three, and I didn't want to wake you up, so I just spent the night there."

"In a bar?" She leaned over and sniffed her brother. He did indeed smell like beer. And barf.

"Well, on a couch down in the basement." He shivered. "Kinda cold, ain't it?"

"I guess so. What happened to your jacket? And your other shoe?"

"Damned if I know."

Kerry tried to tamp down her mounting annoyance. She pointed at the stack of Christmas trees with sold tags attached. "You've got a bunch of deliveries to make. And I promised everyone they'd get their trees today."

Murphy wiped his nose on the sleeve of his borrowed shirt. "I got it covered." He looked up and nodded. "Here comes my helper now."

A kid coasted toward them in the bike lane on a bright yellow twelve-speed bike. He had a wagon rigged to the back of the bike, and an eager smile.

"Hey, Murph!" the kid said as he braked. "Reporting for duty!"

"Vic, this is my sister Kerry. She's helping me out this year."

"Hello, ma'am," the kid said, doing a stiff bow at the waist.

"Vic just got home from boarding school yesterday," Murphy explained. "He's gonna be delivering trees and doing whatever else we need for the next couple weeks."

"Like an internship," Vic said eagerly. He was maybe fourteen, at that loose-limbed gangly phase boys went through. He had white-blond hair cut short to the scalp, and just the slightest shadow of what might someday be a beard.

Kerry turned to her brother. "We need to talk."

"Okay."

"Alone."

Murphy scratched his beard and groaned. "Hey, Vic, why don't you start loading one of those trees there on your wagon. Okay, sport?"

While they were alone, Kerry unloaded

146

on her brother.

"I can't believe you have the nerve to show up here half dead and hungover. You said it's our busiest day — and I've been working here all by myself. Also, I was worried about you. You couldn't have called?"

Her brother blinked and dug in his pocket, bringing out his cell phone. "Sorry. It's dead."

"Figures," she said. "Mom called me and woke me up at seven this morning. I had to lie to cover up for you."

"What'd Mom want?"

"She wants to talk to you. I think she's being deliberately evasive."

"About what?"

"What else? Dad's health."

"Did you ask her how he's feeling?"

"She says he's okay, but I think she just doesn't want me to worry about him."

"Then don't," Murphy said. "They're adults, Kerry. They can take care of themselves. Now, if there's nothing else, I gotta get some sleep."

"What about the kid?" she demanded. "We can't afford to pay a helper, especially since our sales are off." She pointed at the Brodys' bustling stand. "They're killing us."

"Relax. We're not paying Vic. He works for tips." He massaged his temples again.

147

"You get tips?" Kerry had wondered why Murphy never complained about all the deliveries he had to make, and now she knew.

"Of course. This is New York City. Nobody works for free."

"Like, how much?"

"Ground-floor apartment, around ten bucks. Unless it's a rich old lady. They're usually the cheapest. They open their wallets and moths fly out. If I gotta carry the tree up a couple flights of stairs, maybe twenty. The higher the floor, the higher the tip."

"Susannah said you set up both her trees when you got to her apartment. She was very grateful."

"Very, very grateful. She gave me fifty bucks, even though there's an elevator in her building."

Kerry decided not to mention the hundred-dollar tip she'd received for her custom-made wreath.

CHAPTER 21

Vic arrived at the Tolliver Tree Farm stand on Monday, promptly at eight o'clock — or "oh eight hundred" as he called it. He was neat and clean and cheerful, and Kerry was none of these things. The day was cold and gray, like her mood.

Kerry had already fed Queenie. "I'm going to the flower market to pick up some supplies. I should be back in an hour or so, but if I'm not back by nine, go ahead and open up the stand. I don't expect we'll have much business on a Monday morning, but hopefully I'm wrong. The trees are all priced." She pulled the cashbox from beneath the work table and unlocked it.

"There's enough cash in here to make change. No checks, and no credit cards though."

"Understood, ma'am. Cash only."

Kerry had to smile at his enthusiasm. "Anybody has any questions, call me. Do not, unless your hair is on fire, wake up Murphy. He's kind of a bear in the mornings."

"Yes, ma'am. What else can I do?"

"You could walk Queenie a little bit, but don't venture too far, just to the end of the block and back."

She cast a wary eye at the now-deserted Brody brothers' tree stand.

"Watch out for those two dudes across the street," she advised.

Vic's easygoing expression darkened in an instant, his spine straightening, his eyes narrowing. "Do you think they're armed?"

"What? No! I mean, just watch they don't try any funny business — like trying to steal our customers."

Kerry scribbled her cell phone number on a slip of paper and handed it to him. "Call me if you have any questions."

"Yes, ma'am." He did everything but snap a salute.

The hundred-dollar tip from Susannah emboldened Kerry to spend a little more freely at the flower market. She added rolls of wide red wired ribbon, and on impulse, a case of battery-operated twinkle lights. Then she popped into a nearby deli for breakfast: a bagel for her and a bacon, egg, and cheese

150

roll for Vic.

He was bustling around the tree stand when she got back. "I sold two trees," he said excitedly. "But I told them I couldn't deliver until you returned."

"That's great," she said, handing him a white paper bag. "I brought you a bacon, egg, and cheese roll."

"Oh man, I mean, ma'am. Thanks. I didn't have time to grab breakfast at home."

He demolished the sandwich and washed it down with an energy drink. "What now?"

"You can deliver those trees if you want. I'm gonna get busy making wreaths, but when you get back I've got a little project you could help with."

Vic loaded the trees onto his wagon and happily pedaled off in search of tips.

As she'd predicted, business was slow, so she concentrated on wreath making. By the time Vic returned from his deliveries she was putting the finishing touches on two enormous wreaths, fastening both with bright red bows.

"Okay," Vic said, warming his hands over the fire. "Ready for my next assignment."

"There's a stepladder in the truck," she said, handing him the keys. "You can help me hang these wreaths, and then we'll be stringing lights. Lots and lots of lights."

While Vic was hammering nails to the uprights supporting the Tolliver Family Tree Farm sign, Kerry opened the boxes of twinkle lights, loaded them with batteries, and tested the tiny plastic remote controls.

"All done," Vic reported.

She pointed at the pile of lights on the worktable. "Okay. We're gonna string these lights on the big trees at the corners of the stand."

He took the first string and awkwardly looped it around the middle of the tree, like tightening a belt around a chubby toddler.

"Not like that," she said, sighing. Kerry picked up a string of lights and knelt at the base of the first tree. "Start at the bottom. Shove the strand toward the trunk, and then wind it around the branch two or three times. Like so. Then, move around the tree, and start another row, maybe six inches up."

After lunch Kerry wrapped the remaining strands of lights around the Tolliver sign. She was standing back admiring her handiwork when two women paused at the entry to the stand.

The older woman was expensively dressed and carrying a designer shopping tote, and the younger one was pushing a stroller with a drowsy toddler.

"Look at this big tree, Holly. I love how many lights are on it. And the shape is beautiful."

"You should get this one, Mom."

"Remember how your dad used to do the lights on our tree every year? He was so particular about it, fussed over it for hours. And I was strictly forbidden from going anywhere near it until he was done." She looked wistful at the memory.

"My mom has always been the same way," Kerry confided. "She's the one who taught me to string the lights this way."

The younger woman tugged at her mother's sleeve. "Mom, you should see if she" — nodding at Kerry — "would hang the lights on your tree."

"Do you do that sort of thing?" the mother asked.

"As a matter of fact, I do." As of now, Kerry thought.

"Can I ask what you charge?"

Kerry thought quickly. "Seventy-five dollars an hour, with a two-hour minimum."

"Oh, I don't know," the mother murmured. "It seems like such an extravagance."

"Mom, you didn't even have a tree last year, because you said thinking about it stressed you out too much. And I know it

153

made you sad," Holly said.

"Well . . . I really didn't think I'd miss having a tree, but it's true. It just didn't seem like the holidays last year. It didn't seem right."

"Okay," Holly said. "We'll hire . . . What's your name?"

"Kerry Tolliver."

"Right. We'll hire Kerry to deliver your tree, set it up, and decorate it."

Kerry gestured toward the wreaths she'd been making. "Would you want a wreath too? They're seventy-five for the small ones, a hundred dollars for the large."

"Yes, she would. A large one for her, and one for me. Come to think of it, could you do the same for me? Deliver, set up, and decorate?"

"If you're in the neighborhood, I could come tomorrow, after five."

"That's perfect," the mother said. She reached into her pocketbook and brought out a slim leather card case. She extracted a card and handed it to Kerry.

"I'm Adele, and this is my address."

"I live one floor above Mom," Holly said. "Oh, and why don't you just plan to bring us all new sets of lights, like the ones you have here. No telling what kind of shape ours are in. I get anxiety just thinking about untangling that mess."

CHAPTER 22

"Kerry?"

It was Tuesday. Kerry looked up to see a harried-looking Gretchen McCaleb, standing at the entrance to the tree stand. She wore a black cashmere coat, fur-trimmed boots, and demure pearl earrings, and her hand rested lightly on her son's shoulder.

"Oh, hi, Gretchen. Hi, Austin. Did you change your mind about getting a Christmas tree?"

"Heavens, no. Look, I'm in a terrible bind. I have an important meeting outside the city this morning, but the school has one of those stupid in-service days today, and my babysitter canceled. I can't reach Pat. I realize it's a terrible imposition, but Austin is so fond of you . . ."

"I'd love for Austin to hang around with me and Queenie today," Kerry said quickly. "I could use the extra help."

"See, Mom?" Austin said, beaming. "I told

156

you they needed me here."

"All right then," Gretchen said, consulting a slim gold watch on her wrist. "I've got a car picking me up in ten minutes." She reached into her tote and thrust a quilted red Spider-Man lunch box at Kerry. "Here's his lunch, and some fruit for a snack. No telling how long my meeting will be. Hopefully, his father can come this afternoon and . . ."

A black town car glided to the curb and the driver blinked the headlights. "Oh no. He's early. I really do have to go."

She leaned down and kissed the top of her son's head. "Bye, love."

Kerry and Austin looked at each other. She liked kids and was certainly fond of this particular kid, but she'd never actually been in charge of a small human before. Unlike most teenagers, she'd never done any babysitting, and most of her friends back in North Carolina were either single or still childless.

They turned to see Murphy standing in Spammy's doorway. His hair stood on end and he was dressed in thermal long johns, his preferred sleeping attire.

"You're up early," Kerry drawled.

"Mom just called," he said, keeping his

voice low. "Dad had to go back in the hospital."

Kerry stared. "How bad is it?"

"Not that bad," he said. "He was refusing to eat right, got dehydrated, and because nobody can tell the great and mighty Jock Tolliver there's anything he can't do, he decided last night would be an excellent time to go out and chop some firewood."

Kerry closed her eyes and groaned.

"He passed out, hit his head on a tree stump. Mom called the ambulance, and they took him to the hospital. He's got a gash on his forehead, they gave him some stitches, and they're keeping him for observation, giving him IV fluids and running some tests."

"Thank God it's not worse," Kerry said. Her heart was racing. "Maybe we should close up shop and go home —"

"No way," he said, cutting her off. "Mom won't hear of it. She knows we need to sell these trees to get back in the black. And she swears she's got it under control."

"Really? She's gonna stop Jock from being Jock? She couldn't do it while they were married, so how's she gonna manage it now?"

Murphy's expression was grim. "I'm gonna stop him. I called him up just now, cussed him out and called him every name in the book."

"So? The two of you fuss at each other like that all the time."

"This time is different. I told him if he don't do exactly what Mom and the doctors say, I'm out. I'll get a job with the Forestry Service, get my own place."

She studied her brother's face. "You'd do that?"

"In a heartbeat. That old man is so stuck in his ways. I go to all these agribusiness seminars the state puts on, take classes at the university, but every time I try to do something different on the farm than the way him and Granddad have always done it, he shuts me down. I'm nearly forty years old. He's gotta start treating me like a man, listen to some of my ideas."

Murphy ran a hand through his unruly hair. "I need to get dressed."

She reached out and touched his elbow. "You still haven't told me what Dad said to that."

He laughed sheepishly. "I guess I finally got through to him. He bawled like a baby, begged me not to move on. He promised to listen to Mom, really quit smoking, and do exactly what the docs said."

"I'm glad," Kerry said. "You don't really

159

want to leave the farm, do you?"

"Nah," he admitted. "Last thing I want. But I will if I have to."

Vic rode up on his bike while Murphy was getting dressed.

"Who's the little kid?" he asked, jerking his thumb in Austin's direction.

"That's Austin. He lives in the neighborhood and he's gonna hang out here today and give us a hand. He can be your helper. Right after he walks Queenie for me."

Murphy emerged from the trailer and headed off, without a word, in the direction of Anna's. He came back with two large cups of coffee, handed one to Kerry, and sat down.

A moment later, he went back to the trailer and came out with his notebook. He thumbed through the pages, sipped his coffee, and shook his head. "This ain't good."

"The coffee? Mine was great."

"No, dummy. The tree sales."

"It's picking up," Kerry said. "I sold ten trees yesterday, and you sold how many overnight?"

"Eight. But it ain't enough. We're way behind our usual numbers. And we have those idiots across the street to thank for it."

"I'll think of something," Kerry said. "But I need to run back to the flower market to buy more lights for my decorating job tonight."

"Huh?"

"I sold a couple trees to this mother and daughter yesterday, and they asked if I could put lights on their trees the way I did ours. So I said yes. Vic delivered their trees, and this evening, I'm going to go over and hang the lights."

"You getting paid for that?"

"As you pointed out, this is the city. Nobody does anything for free. I'm charging them seventy-five an hour with a two-hour minimum, and they didn't bat an eye."

"That's crazy," he declared.

CHAPTER 23

Kerry opened her laptop to check her email. She'd posted her contact information in an online forum for freelance designers, hoping to snag a new account, but her in-box was depressingly empty.

She'd invoiced another client before leaving town, but there was no reply. Since she was living rent-free with Birdie, things weren't dire yet, but they would be soon if she didn't line up more work.

"Okay, Austin," Kerry said, setting her laptop aside and opening the sketchbook. "Where were we?"

"In the forest of Christmas trees," Austin prompted. "And the birds and squirrels were my friends."

On impulse, she added a large, elaborate wrought-iron gate to the drawing she'd made previously, with a leafy vine curling around it. Trees and bushes crowded up against the other side of the gate.

"What's that?" Austin asked.

"I was thinking, it's the gate to a magical, mysterious forest kingdom, right in the middle of the city."

"But it should be a secret forest. That nobody else knows about but me. And I have the key."

"I like it," Kerry said.

"You like what?"

Patrick smiled down at them. He was carrying two foam carry-out cups. "Who wants hot chocolate?"

"Me!" Austin said, eagerly grabbing one of the cups. "Dad, what are you doing here?"

"Your mom called and asked me to come pick you up."

"I can't leave yet. Me and Kerry are working on our story."

"Kerry and I," he corrected. "Can I take a peek?"

"We were just goofing off," Kerry said, feeling awkward and self-conscious around Patrick. He beamed as he looked down at the drawings, and she noticed the crinkles at the corners of his eyes, and that he needed a shave, and that he had a mole in precisely the same place as Robert Redford, whom she'd crushed on years ago the first of dozens of times she'd watched Birdie's

163

DVD of *Butch Cassidy and the Sundance Kid.*

"These are great," Patrick said. "Let's go back to the apartment. It's getting cold, and it's going to be dinnertime pretty soon."

Austin's face fell for a moment, but then he perked back up. "I know. Kerry can come to dinner with us, and then we can keep drawing our story."

"Good idea," Patrick said, turning to Kerry. "How about it?"

"I'd love to, but I'm afraid I've got to work tonight." She glanced at her phone and was startled to see it was nearly five. "In fact, I need to leave as soon as Murphy gets back."

Patrick looked as disappointed as his son. "Another time then, okay? So I can properly thank you for babysitting Austin."

"No need to thank me. We had fun today. To tell you the truth, I've missed seeing him for the past couple days."

He raised one eyebrow. "What about me?"

"Okay, yes. I've missed both of you." She was annoyed to realize she was blushing.

Patrick looked pleased and then turned serious, lowering his voice to avoid being overheard. "I have to apologize for Gretchen. I can't believe she just . . . dumped our son off with you and then fled. She had no right . . ."

Kerry touched his arm. "She was obviously in a bind. And I'm happy we got to spend time with Austin. He's such a funny, entertaining little guy. He can hang out with us anytime."

"He clearly adores you and Murphy. And what about that dinner? Can we set a date?"

"Uh . . ." She knew she was blushing again. "Anytime you like. It's not like I've got a crowded social calendar."

"Friday night, then? Around seven? Guess I know where to pick you up, right?"

"Right." She hesitated. "Can we make it someplace casual?"

"Casual it is," he said. He gave her a quick peck on the cheek.

The kiss didn't escape Austin's sharp eyes. "Dad! Let's go. I'm hungry."

CHAPTER 24

"Murphy." Kerry shook her brother's shoulder. He'd fallen asleep in his lawn chair, swaddled in his sleeping bag, and was softly snoring. The fire in the barrel had gone out sometime during the night, and the worktable was littered with empty Red Bull cans, foam coffee cups, and the remains of a bucket of takeout fried chicken.

"Ugh." She threw all of it into the trash. It was early, just past seven, so she decided to let him sleep while she ran to the Kaplans' apartment for a quick shower.

Murphy was awake when she returned. "What happened to my fried chicken?"

"I threw it out, along with all your other trash."

"That was gonna be my breakfast," he groused. "How did last night go? You never said."

"You never asked," she pointed out. By the time she'd gotten back to the stand the

166

night before, Murphy and a couple pals were sitting around the fire, passing around a Mason jar of Jock Tolliver's moonshine, while Murphy played his dobro.

"I'm asking now."

"It went really well. The mother's apartment was very contemporary and minimalist. By the time I got the lights on the tree, she decided she liked the bare look, so I didn't even put any ornaments on it. Only took an hour but I got paid my two-hour minimum, and she was overjoyed with the results. The daughter's place took longer. We ended up moving the tree to a different corner of the room, but it worked out, and I made three hundred bucks, plus a forty-dollar tip. Not bad for one night's work. How did it go here?"

"Business sucked. I only sold four trees."

She reached into her pocket and handed him three fifty-dollar bills.

"What's this supposed to be?"

"Your share of the profits," she said. "And last night's customers promised to tell all their friends and neighbors to buy their trees from us."

Kerry sold two more Christmas trees in the early afternoon. When business slowed again, she went back to working on her drawings of the forest that Austin had conjured. She'd finished drawing oval borders around the sketches, each a little different, with twining vines, pinecones, and butterflies, and had begun lettering the text on the pages when Heinz seemingly materialized from thin air.

He stood over the worktable, examining her work. "This is coming along quite nicely."

"Austin spent the day with me yesterday, and of course he wanted to work on his story," she said.

Heinz pointed at the drawing of the gateway to the forest. "Ahh. This looks very magical."

"I'm so glad you see that. He wanted his own private forest, inhabited with all kinds of creatures."

He stabbed the border she'd just drawn. "The oval motif is a nice touch. Fanciful. And your calligraphy is excellent. Did you learn this in art school?"

"No. I taught myself by watching YouTube videos. It was how I earned spending money when I was in school, addressing wedding invitations and place cards."

He nodded. "What happens next in this story of yours?"

"I'm not quite sure. Austin will think of

something."

Heinz shook his head. "What an imagination that child has."

"He's very smart. And sweet. He was asking about you yesterday."

Heinz looked away. "I've been attending to business."

Kerry tilted her head. "Do you live in the neighborhood? I mean, I see you walking here most days."

"In the vicinity," he said. He picked up the sketchbook, abruptly changing the subject, and began leafing through the pages.

"Ahhhh. These dogs. What personality you've given them!"

"I do enjoy drawing dogs," she admitted. "There's something about the openness, their vibrant personalities." She turned to see Gretchen approaching.

"I must be going," he said, nodding in her direction. "That one thinks that I am the bogeyman."

If Gretchen saw the older man chatting with Kerry, she didn't mention it. She walked quickly, with purpose.

"Kerry, Austin told me how much he enjoyed yesterday, and I can't thank you enough." She paused. "Pat seems to think it was wildly inappropriate of me to even ask you."

Gretchen shook her head to indicate that she disagreed with her ex. "Be that as it may, I got you this." She thrust an envelope into Kerry's hand, then turned and hurried away.

"Wait," Kerry called. "That's not . . ."

Kerry looked down at the envelope, shrugged, and slit it open with her thumbnail. When a two-hundred-dollar American Express gift card slid out, she was speechless.

"This is too much," she murmured.

CHAPTER 25

Two days later, Kerry stood outside the window of a nearby boutique, gazing at the racks of designer clothes inside.

"Nothing in here for me," she told herself. But it was in the neighborhood, and she promised Vic that she'd be back to the tree stand within half an hour.

Her mission this morning was simple: to buy something suitable for tonight's "casual" dinner date with Patrick — and Austin.

But this shop? The scalloped dark-green-and-white-striped awning over the storefront, the creamy brick façade and dark-green-painted trim, not to mention the subtle lighting and understated elegance of the display window — all of it screamed money.

Of which Kerry currently had only two hundred dollars, in the form of the AmEx gift card that Gretchen had insisted she accept.

Two women passed her on the sidewalk, their arms laden with shopping bags. They gave her a quick, curious glance, then ducked into the shop.

She was about to enter too, when she caught sight of her reflection in the shop window. Just standing in the shadow of that mannequin made her feel inadequate. And tacky, and shabby, despite the fact that she'd showered and blown her hair dry earlier at the Kaplans' apartment and was wearing her best (and only) pair of designer jeans, and the velvet blazer, which she'd felt elegant in — until just this minute.

It was cold on that sidewalk, and a clerk inside the shop was openly staring at her.

The air in the shop was perfumed, the carpet thick, and the ceiling high, with one huge chandelier dripping with crystal baubles. She flipped the tag on a perfectly simple navy sweater and winced. Fifteen hundred dollars, which was more than her first car had cost.

"Hi." The salesgirl was young, barely twenty, Kerry guessed, with very blond hair pulled back from her face in a severe ponytail. She was dressed in all black. The girl touched the cuff of Kerry's jacket. "I love

172

this! Is it vintage?"

"Um, yeah," Kerry said, surprised at the girl's friendly manner. "At least I think so. I got it at a flea market."

"I love shopping vintage." She lowered her voice. "But don't tell my manager. Now, what can I help you with?"

Kerry felt her anxiety level drop a notch. "I need something . . . special. But I'm not sure I can afford anything in here."

The girl studied Kerry, and she felt even smaller and shabbier than when she was outside the shop. This was a mistake. She turned to go.

"Hey," the girl said. "Don't leave. I wasn't judging you. I was just trying to figure out your sign."

"My sign?"

"You know. Your astrological sign. I'll bet you're a Virgo. Am I right?"

Kerry's jaw dropped. "How did you know?"

"Oh, astrology is my superpower, along with hailing cabs and my flawless ability to shape eyebrows. And I'm a Virgo too, so I can spot one a mile away. I'm Astrid, by the way. We're logical, practical, perfectionists with an eye for detail. That's you too, I bet."

"Guilty," Kerry admitted. "I'm Kerry and I need something to wear for a dinner date tonight, and I'm panicky because I need to get back to work."

"Where are you from? I swear I detect a Southern accent."

"North Carolina."

"The mountains, not the coast, right?"

"How did you . . ."

"I'm from Raleigh," Astrid said. "You don't meet a lot of Tarheels up here in the city."

"You don't have an accent at all," Kerry said.

"Oh, honey," Astrid drawled. "I'm an actress. I put it on and take it off as needed, like a pair of Spanx. Now, let's find you a killer outfit. What were you thinking of spending?"

Kerry felt herself flush. "I'm kind of on a tight budget."

"How tight a budget?"

"Two hundred," Kerry whispered. "Impossible, I know . . ."

Astrid touched the cuff of Kerry's jacket. "I gotchu, girl."

She steered Kerry toward the back of the shop. "You're an eight, right?"

"More like a ten."

"Wait right here. I've been hoarding this one sweater for just the right customer."

When Astrid reappeared, she was holding

a cashmere sweater in a luscious deep teal. It had a keyhole neckline tied with a bow, and elbow-length sleeves.

"Isn't this yummy? It'll be spectacular with your coloring."

Kerry ran her hand down the fabric. "How much?"

"It's not that expensive," the salesgirl said. "It's marked way down because we're already starting to get in our spring resort wear."

"How bad is not bad?"

"One eighty-nine," Astrid said, handing her the sweater. "Go put it on. I swear, it's like this thing was waiting for you to walk in here and take it home."

In the dressing room, Kerry removed her shirt and blazer and pulled the sweater over her head.

She held her breath when she turned to look in the mirror. The fit was perfect. The color was lovely, and the cashmere was softer than a baby's sigh. She was changing back to her own clothes when she heard her phone ding to signal an incoming text. It was from Murphy, and in true Murphy form, it was short and to the point.

WHERE THE HELL R U?

"How'd you like it?" Astrid asked, pushing aside the curtain.

"I'll take it, but I have to get back to work, like now," Kerry said.

She followed the girl to the cash register and handed her the gift card.

"Do you work around here?" Astrid asked, as she rang up the sale.

"I'm working at our family's Christmas tree stand on Abingdon Square. My brother just texted me that I need to get back there."

"Wait. Is your brother Murphy?"

Kerry answered the question with another question. "You know my brother?"

Astrid laughed and flashed a dimple. "Honey, everybody in the neighborhood knows Murphy Tolliver. My boyfriend and I always get our trees from y'all."

She wrapped the sweater in tissue and slipped it into a glossy shopping bag.

Kerry reached for the bag.

"Wait," Astrid said. She darted over to a jewelry display. When she came back, she dropped something into the bag.

"That's a little sercy from one Tarheel to another," she said. "We can't have you going out tonight without some pretty new earrings."

"Now I know you're a Southerner," Kerry said. "I've never met anybody from outside

North Carolina who knows that a sercy is a gift."

"Like a lagniappe, if you're from New Orleans," Astrid agreed.

"But I can't let you do this," Kerry protested.

"Already done," the girl said. "At my price, they're practically free anyway."

"Thanks," Kerry said. "And when you come get your tree, I'll throw in a free wreath."

"It's a deal," Astrid said.

CHAPTER 26

Kerry was half a block away from Abingdon Square when she spotted the crowd. People were swarming around the Christmas tree stand, waiting in line on the sidewalk, taking selfies in front of the TOLLIVER FAMILY CHRISTMAS TREE FARM sign and standing beside Spammy.

"What on earth?" she murmured, breaking into a trot, and then a full-out dash.

Murphy was standing in the middle of a knot of mostly women, all of them chattering, although there was a sprinkling of men in the crowd too. She saw Vic, struggling as he tried to strap three trees onto his bike-hitched wagon.

Her brother looked trapped. And panicky. As she arrived at the stand his eyes met hers over the crowd and he mouthed one word: *Help.*

"Hi," she said, wading into the fray. "Sorry. Let me just put my bag in the trailer . . ."

"Miss!" a woman called. She had her arms wrapped around a small tabletop tree. "How much is this? And do you have any more this size?"

"Miss." A middle-aged woman butted her way around the one with the tabletop tree. "I was here before, and I need . . ."

She heard a twenty-something exclaim to her friend, "Oh my God. That trailer is just the cutest ever. I just want to move in and live here."

Kerry opened the door to the trailer, tossed in her bag, and turned around to find a middle-aged man shoving his credit card at her. "I have an appointment and need to pay for my tree right now."

"In a minute, please. We only have one credit card reader, and my brother is using it." When he started to protest, she turned away and made her way to Murphy's side.

"What's going on here? Where did all these people come from?"

"That's what I want to know. These women are about to start a rumble over Christmas trees. They say they read it on Ashley somebody. Who the hell is that?"

"They must be talking about AshleyActually. She and her fiancé bought a tree here last week. Turns out this woman is a big-deal lifestyle influencer. She's got a social media following of over a million people."

Kerry pulled out her cell phone, tapped the Instagram icon, and typed "ASHLEY ACTUALLY" into the search bar. She immediately recognized the stylish blonde and her fiancé, standing beside the Tolliver sign, and then another of herself and the duo, with the caption:

Last week Shaun and I discovered the coolest spot in New York City to buy a Christmas tree and soak up some holiday cheer. Run, don't walk to the West Village and Tolliver Family Farms Christmas tree stand to support a great family business. Their trees are fresh-cut from their farm in the North Carolina mountains and smell amazing. And don't forget to check out the cute little camper they call Spammy. They actually live there during the Christmas season!

She passed her phone to Murphy. "There are over eight thousand likes and more than seventeen hundred comments. And she only just posted this a couple hours ago."

"Some girl you never met before is responsible for all this . . . . chaos?"

"Apparently. Isn't it great?"

180

"Did they all have to descend on us at the same time?"

"Sir? Sir?" A young woman dressed in head-to-toe purple waved a credit card. "I want a six-foot tree, and where do you keep those cute wreaths like the one Ashley showed on her IG post?"

"The wreaths are on back order," Kerry said. She handed the woman her notebook. "Write down your name and phone number and I'll text you when they come in again in the next day or so."

"Hey!" A man with a tree slung over his shoulder pushed his way toward the siblings, narrowly avoiding poking someone in the eye with the tip of the tree. "Bro, can you cash me out? My Uber is only a block away." He had a handful of bills in his hand. Kerry plucked the money and gave him his change.

The next two hours were a blur, as fresh waves of customers arrived at the stand, clamoring for trees and wreaths and for Kerry and Murphy to pose for selfies or for permission to tour Spammy.

The pile of trees awaiting delivery grew precariously tall, and Vic pedaled away from the stand countless times, with a sweaty face and an ear-to-ear grin.

Shortly before four, the crowds subsided

and brother and sister collapsed, in tandem, onto their folding chairs.

"This is nuts," Murphy said, surveying the picked-over assortment of trees, some of which had been knocked down during the crush of business. "Look at this place. If business keeps up at this pace, we'll be out of trees by Sunday. Maybe before."

"What happens if we actually do run out of trees?" Kerry asked.

"Not sure. We've never had it happen before Christmas Eve. We sure as shooting haven't ever sold out this far ahead of Christmas. I mean, usually we hold back a few trees so we can still help out the last-minute crowd. I guess, if we run out, we just pack up and go home."

Kerry's mouth went dry and her stomach did a little dip. A few days ago, she would have jumped at the thought of heading home, to a real bed, plumbing, and an actual silent night not punctuated with Murphy's snores. But now?

She looked around, at the square, with the pigeons pecking at the bread crumbs left by the elderly woman who tottered out to the park on her walker every morning with a sleeve of stale crackers, at the now-familiar businesses and their owners, who'd quickly become like family, and the neighbors walking their dogs along the sidewalk — she knew all their names and their dogs' names too. She thought about her visits with Heinz, and his tactless, but spot-on critiques of her art. Mostly though, she thought about Austin, and their unfinished story, and about Austin's father, Patrick.

"Can we get more trees?"

"You want me to cab over to Central Park and chop some down?" he asked.

"I mean, do we have any more trees back on the farm?"

Murphy tugged at his beard. "I'm not sure. Dad always holds back a certain number to sell at the roadside stand, and to a couple guys over in Asheville for their stands."

"Maybe you should call him and ask," Kerry suggested. "Or how about the Joyners, or the Fletchers? Maybe they've got some extra Christmas trees they'd be willing to sell us?"

"Even if they still had some to sell, how would we get them up here? Those guys aren't gonna drop everything and truck a couple hundred trees up here at the drop of a hat."

"Could you drive down and pick them up?" she asked.

"And who'd run the stand while I was gone?"

"Me," she said. "Vic can help. We'll pay him a regular hourly salary. And maybe he can enlist a buddy. It would just be until you get back."

"Ten hours' drive down to the mountains and then back? Not to mention the time it'll take to load the trees? And who knows if I could even get trees at this late date."

"But what if you can? If business keeps up like this, think of what it could mean for Dad and the farm. It would put you in the black and then some. And maybe, just maybe, it would show Dad you actually do have some expertise in the business. Will you at least think about it?"

"Maybe." He disappeared into the trailer.

CHAPTER 27

The next wave of customers materialized fifteen minutes later. Another dozen chattering, hyper women with an apparently endless number of questions, and requests.

"Do you deliver to Queens?"

"Can you get me this exact shape tree, but flocked?"

When Vic returned from his deliveries, she put him in charge of writing receipts and taking down orders for deliveries — half a dozen — and three tree-lighting gigs.

"Wait till I tell Murphy," she said under her breath as she made change and processed credit cards.

At one point, when she had four people in line waiting to make their purchases, she happened to glance across the street. She noted that the Brody brothers were standing on the sidewalk, scowling at her. She gave them a triumphant finger wave.

"Um, Miss Kerry, ma'am?" It was Vic. He

185

looked as tired as she felt. "Sorry, but I really gotta get home now. My mom's been calling to ask where I am."

"Oh, gosh, Vic. I'm sorry. I don't know what we would have done without you today."

He smiled a toothy grin, and began pulling fives, tens, and twenties from his jacket pockets. "Today was awesome! I bet I made over two hundred dollars, easy."

"You earned it. Let me ask you something. There's a chance Murphy might need to drive home and pick up another load of trees. If so, would you be able to help out full time?"

"Maybe," he said. "Can I let you know in the morning?"

"Of course." She patted him on the back.

For the first time that day, Kerry was alone. She slipped inside the trailer, which was rattling with her brother's snoring. It was nearly six, but she didn't have the heart to awaken him. Instead, she donned her warmest down jacket and returned to her post just as Patrick and Austin appeared. Patrick wore a sport coat under his jacket and she saw that Austin was wearing a snappy red bow tie.

"Kerry," Austin called. "Are you ready for our date?"

She gasped. "Oh my gosh. We've been so busy, I totally lost track of time."

"I've been texting you," Patrick said gently. "I thought maybe we should come over and make sure you were still available. But if you're too busy . . ."

She pulled her phone from her pocket and spotted three texts from him.

"I've been looking forward to tonight all week, but we've been absolutely crushed with business all day. I never even saw any of your texts." She gestured around at the stand, which was looking notably emptier than it had been eight hours earlier.

"Wow," Patrick said. "You must have sold a bunch of trees today. What happened?"

"AshleyActually posted a story on her Instagram feed and the masses descended. I actually had women fighting over trees."

"That's a good thing, right?"

"Depends on how you look at it. Murphy says we might totally sell out of trees this weekend. And if that happens, he says we pack up and go home."

"Home?" Austin yelped. "What about our story?"

"Hang on, pal," Patrick said, putting a hand on his son's shoulder. "Is it possible to buy more trees somewhere?"

"That's what I suggested, but Murphy

isn't keen to sell just any old trees. He's pretty picky about quality. I guess I agree. It's the family brand, and we don't want to harm that."

"He's got a valid point."

"What about our date?" Austin clamored. "When do we eat? I'm hungry. Aren't you hungry, Kerry?"

"You know what? I'm starved," she said. "I didn't even get lunch."

"Then let's go," Austin said.

"Can you?" Patrick asked.

Kerry glanced at the trailer. She could hear her brother's muffled snores.

"I'd have to wake up Murphy. He worked all day too." She looked down at herself. Her jeans were smudged with dirt and her hands were sticky from pine sap.

She longed for a hot shower and the chance to show off her new sweater.

"Can you just close up the stand?" Patrick asked. "There aren't a whole lot of trees left to sell tonight."

"Look at me," she protested. "I'm a hot mess."

"We won't go far," Patrick promised.

She looked down at Austin, whose face was scrunched up with hope.

She untied her green Tolliver Tree Farm apron and tossed it on the back of the chair.

"I'm officially off the clock. If Murphy wakes up, he can take the next shift."

CHAPTER 28

"Bernie's Burgerz," Austin said, as they entered the restaurant. "My favorite."

Patrick offered Kerry an apologetic smile. "We usually go out to dinner whenever he's with me, and it was his turn to choose, so here we are."

A middle-aged Black woman with close-cropped silver hair came out from behind the hostess stand and greeted Austin like a beloved celebrity.

"Austin, where you been lately? I been missing you," the woman exclaimed, kneeling on the floor and enveloping the boy in a hug.

"Hi, Bernie. I go to school now, you know."

She ruffled his hair. "I knew there was something different about you since the last time you were in here. You're all grown up." She tapped his bow tie. "And all dressed up too. Like your daddy. Is it somebody's birthday tonight?"

"No. Me and Dad are having a date with her." He jerked his thumb in Kerry's direction. "Her name is Kerry. She sells Christmas trees and draws pictures. And she's my friend."

Bernie took Kerry's hand in both of hers and pressed them together. "Well, isn't she a lucky lady? Y'all go on back over. I've got your favorite booth, right over there by the window."

After they were settled with wine for the adults and lemonade for Austin, Patrick ordered an appetizer of chili-cheese-smothered tater tots.

"Oh my gosh," Kerry moaned, at the first bite. "This is heaven."

"The hamburgers are the best. In the whole world," Austin advised.

"Of course, there are lots of other choices on the menu," Patrick said. "Chicken, fish, steaks. They have great salads . . ."

"Who orders salad in a place called Bernie's Burgerz? That would be an outrage. I'll have a burger, medium rare, with all the fixings."

"Don't forget the French fries," Austin said.

Once their orders arrived, it was all she

could do not to fall on her burger and devour it like a half-starved hyena.

The flow of conversation over dinner was so relaxed and easy, she forgot about her usual first-date jitters. No sweaty palms, butterflies, or angsting over what she was wearing or how she looked. She was sure her father would have described her as looking "like you been rode hard and put up wet," but Patrick didn't seem to mind.

He was an easy conversationalist. "What was it like, growing up on a Christmas tree farm?" he asked.

"You'd have to ask Murphy," Kerry said. "I haven't lived on the farm full time since my parents split up when I was about Austin's age."

The boy looked up. "Kerry, did your mom and dad get a divorce too?"

She glanced at Patrick, who shrugged.

"They did."

"Were you sad?"

"It was a very long time ago, but yes, I was sad at first."

"Me too," he said, in a matter-of-fact way.

Kerry chose her next words carefully. "My mom promised that she and my dad still loved me, but they just didn't need to be married anymore. After a while, I realized my mom was happier, so that made me happier too."

Austin gave that some thought. "Huh. I wonder when my mom will be happier again. She still yells at my dad and acts mad at him."

Patrick winced. "She's not mad at you, buddy. Neither of us is."

"I know." He picked up another French fry and dipped it in ketchup.

She tried to steer the conversation back into neutral territory. "I did spend weekends and parts of the summer on the farm. And it seemed pretty magical when I was there. Dad had chickens, because he just likes chickens, and he kept goats, to help keep the weeds in check, and I even had a pet baby goat of my own."

Austin's eyes widened. "A baby goat? Cool. What was his name?"

"Cookie. Because she would come whenever I fed her cookies. But Cookie would eat anything at all. She even ate my favorite doll and one of my sneakers."

"Sneakers!" The boy giggled. "Were there a lot of Christmas trees too?"

"Acres and acres of them. The whole side of a mountain. It was a great place to go sledding when we got snow. Dad would put hay bales at the bottom of the hill, and we'd crash into them on purpose."

"Sounds like a fun place to grow up," Patrick said. "How far away did your mom live?"

"Not even five miles. But in town. She was a teacher, and since the school was only a few blocks away, I could walk there."

"Tell me some more," Austin urged. "About the farm."

"Dad kept a big garden, and there was a spooky old barn full of broken-down tractors and farm equipment where we played hide-and-seek. One time, I was hiding, and a mouse ran across my foot, and I screamed bloody murder, and everybody thought I'd been bitten by a snake. I still hate mice."

"Did you have a dog?"

"Always," Kerry said. "Mostly just strays that would wander up to the house. I think word got out that Jock was an easy mark. And my mom always had dogs too. She has an English setter right now, named Alfie. He was supposed to be Murphy's bird dog, but turns out, he's gun-shy. So he came to live with Mom. And now, he's a big, spoiled baby."

"What else?" Austin yawned widely.

"Apple trees. I had my own special apple tree. I used to climb up there and hide out from Murphy. I'd read my library books and daydream and draw."

"I wish I could have my own special apple tree to climb," Austin said. "And a baby goat." His eyelids fluttered. "And a dog and my own forest of Christmas trees."

Patrick caught the waiter's eye and signaled for the check. "We'd better get you home to bed, bud. Your aunt Suzie is taking you to see Santa Claus in the morning."

"I'm not tired! Besides, I want an ice-cream sundae for dessert," the boy protested.

"You know, a long time ago Santa Claus lived in my hometown," Kerry said.

He looked up at her with the eyes of a skeptic. "I thought Santa lived at the North Pole."

"Well, maybe he wasn't real, but the Santa suit was, and it was full of magic. I'll tell you about it while we walk home, okay?"

They walked the two blocks back to Abingdon Square slowly, with Austin in the middle, holding both their hands. It had grown colder, and she was glad for the warmth of the little boy's mittened hand.

"Tell me about the Santa Claus suit, Kerry," Austin said.

"A lady moved into an old house just down the road from our farm, and she found a beautiful Santa Claus suit in a closet," Kerry began. "And it turns out, the man who lived in that house for many, many years played Santa Claus every year for all the children in the area. And every year, he and his wife would have thousands and thousands of Christmas lights on his house. He did a lot of other wonderful things for our community too. His name was Santa Bob, and I went to see him too, when I was a little girl.

"But after Santa Bob was a very old man, he died, and the house was empty. Until this lady moved in. She asked a man who sold her the house if he wanted to wear the suit for this big holiday celebration we have every year in our town — called the Christmas Stroll. So he did, and then, he and the lady fell in love. And a lot of other magical stuff happened, and now, every year since then, he's the Santa Claus for the Christmas Stroll. And now, they have a little boy, and his name is Nick."

The CLOSED sign was still stretched across the entrance to the stand. "I guess Murphy is in for the night," Kerry said.

"It's not that late. Why don't you come up to the apartment?" Patrick suggested. "I'll get this guy in bed, and then we can have a drink."

The apartment was on the fourth floor of a handsome yellow-brick building. She could understand why neither Patrick nor Gretchen wanted to give the place up.

It was smaller and much less grand than Taryn's place. But it had high ceilings and dark-stained wooden floors. There was a large, somewhat ratty leather sofa facing a fireplace, mismatched armchairs and end tables, and a coffee table that had seen better days. It looked like the aftermath of a breakup, where the parties had divvied up the best pieces and left behind the rest. A large, fake Christmas tree decorated with ornaments made of popsicle sticks, glitter, and construction paper stood in the corner near the fireplace, its lights twinkling.

But the star of the room was the wall of almost floor-to-ceiling windows that looked out on the street and the square. A child-sized table and chair had been placed there, and the space around it was littered with art supplies and toys. Lego bricks and picture books spilled out of plastic bins lined up beneath the windows.

Patrick pointed at a bar cart in front of some bookshelves. "Help yourself to whatever you want. I think there's a bottle of white wine in the fridge. I'll get this guy settled and be right back." He disappeared down a narrow hallway lined with framed family photos.

Kerry found a bottle of bourbon in a brand she'd never seen before and poured a couple fingers of the amber liquid into a crystal rocks glass. She went to the kitchen in search of ice, and returned to the living room, drawn immediately to the wall of windows.

She sat on the window seat and gazed out at the scene below. The old-fashioned streetlights shone down on the square, where people strolled past, stopping to look at Spammy and the lit-up Christmas trees in the stand. Diners were coming and going from Lombardi's, and a couple sat on the bench outside Anna's, cuddled close together against the cold. Looking past the tops of the trees in the park, she spotted the Empire State Building, lit up in red and green. Buses and cars rumbled past on Hudson Street, and even the sound of a far-off siren made the bustle and rush of the city seem enchanting and exciting.

A door closed softly behind her and a minute later, Patrick joined her on the window seat, sitting so close their shoulders touched. "What are you looking at?"

"All this." She gestured to the scene below. "The city, the neighborhood. You've got quite a view here. I can see why you didn't want to give up this apartment."

"Yeah. Austin loves it here too. Most mornings, he sits right here, eating his Pop-Tarts for breakfast. He loves watching you and Murphy setting up the stand in the mornings."

"Pop-Tarts?" Kerry gave a look of mock horror. "Does his mom know you're feeding that junk to her son?"

"Pfft. They're fruit, right?"

"I got addicted to Pop-Tarts my freshman year of college," Kerry confided. "My mom is kind of a health-food nut. She was appalled the first time I came home for the holidays with a box of Pop-Tarts in my backpack."

"Sounds like you and your mom are pretty close," he observed.

"We're total opposites, but she loves and accepts who I am, and I'm so lucky that she does."

"What will you do, when all the Christmas trees are sold?" he asked, sliding an arm around her shoulder. "Will you go back to . . . what's the name of the town?"

"Tarburton. For the short run, until I can figure out my next move. The only thing I know for sure is that I don't want to live there permanently."

"Really? You make it sound so idyllic, the farm, the mountains, the apple trees . . ."

"What's that people say about New York City — a nice place to visit, but I wouldn't want to live there? That's how I feel about Tarburton. I don't fit in there. I never did."

She felt the prick of tears. The thought of going back to the stifling confines of the tiny town in the mountains filled her with dread.

Patrick placed his hand under her chin and gently turned her face toward his. "I hope you don't go," he murmured, as his lips met hers. "Not anytime soon."

Kerry kissed him back. "Let's not talk about it," she whispered. "Carpe diem, right?"

"Dad?" Austin's voice echoed through the apartment. "We didn't read our story."

"Not tonight, buddy," Patrick said, but Kerry touched his arm. "It's okay. I need to get up early anyway. I'll let myself out." She kissed him lightly. "To be continued?"

CHAPTER 29

Murphy's truck was double-parked in front of Spammy with the motor running. He was emerging from the trailer as she walked up. "What's going on?" she asked.

"I was just getting ready to call you. I'm heading back to the farm."

"Right now?" She was incredulous. "For real? You don't want to wait till morning?"

"If I leave now, I can be there by sunrise, load the truck, and deadhead it back here by Sunday. Dad swears he can get a helper to cut and bale the trees. He's got sixty or seventy-five trees down near the creek bottom, although he says we don't have many of the big ones left."

"That's actually better," Kerry said. "Seems like people prefer the tabletop trees. And some more six- or eight-foot ones would be good too."

Murphy gave her a sour look. "So you're the expert now? You can predict what my customers, who Dad and I have been selling trees to for thirty years — you know what they do and don't want?"

Kerry's jaw dropped at the intensity of his anger.

"Hey. Don't go if you're gonna be all pissy and belligerent, Murphy. I don't get why you're so furious that we're finally selling trees and making some money. Isn't that what this trip is about? Seeing to it that we get the farm back in the black so Dad doesn't worry about it and give himself another heart attack?"

He leaned against the trailer, his body stiff with barely suppressed fury. "Yeah, it's about that. But I resent you telling me what to do, parachuting in here and changing everything around. Dad and I have a system . . ."

"Which wasn't working so hot, was it? You were the one bellyaching about how the numbers this year were off and waving that notebook of Dad's around. So instead of sitting here and watching the Brody brothers steal our customers —"

"*My* customers," Murphy said, from between gritted teeth.

"See? That's the real problem. I get it. You don't want a woman telling you what to do. Especially if the woman happens to be your little sister."

"Screw you." Murphy reached for the backpack he'd left on the trailer steps and headed for the truck. "I gotta get to the storage yard and get the trailer hitched up. I don't have time for your crap."

"When will you be back?" Kerry asked, suddenly panicked.

"Tomorrow night or early Sunday morning." He climbed into the cab of the truck. "I'm leaving Queenie here with you. She'll raise hell if anybody tries to mess with you."

"And how am I supposed to run the tree stand by myself?"

"You're an expert. Figure it out."

"C'mon, Queenie," Kerry called. "Let's call it a night." The dog wagged her tail in approval and followed her into the trailer.

She sat on her bunk and looked around the cramped space, which looked like a cyclone had blown through. Her brother's dirty clothes were strewn around the floor, which bore his muddy boot prints, and his bed was a lumpy jumble of blankets, sleeping bag, pillow, and a pile of clothes of indeterminate cleanliness.

Without giving it much thought, she dumped the clothes in a laundry bag, folded the blankets, and remade his bed. She went outside to grab the broom, and while she was there, went to Jock's truck and retrieved the baseball bat he kept stowed under the front seat.

"Security," she told herself. She had to admit she was already feeling uneasy about her first night alone in the city.

After she finished rage cleaning, she got ready for bed. Queenie jumped up and settled herself on Murphy's bunk. Kerry locked the door and retrieved Murphy's notebook, and thumbed through to the page for the previous year's sales. He'd circled the number of trees in red. Forty-two.

When her cell phone rang, she grabbed it, hoping it might be Patrick.

It was her mother.

"So it's true?" Birdie asked. "Murphy's really driving back down here for another load of trees? Your dad is all worked up about it. He hasn't said so yet, but I know what he's thinking — that he'll ride back up there with your brother. It's killing him having to stay home this year."

"Mom, no!" Kerry yelped. "You absolutely can't let him come up here."

"I told that old fool if he leaves this house, I'm done. He can go back on Silver Singles and find him a new girlfriend to cook and clean and remind him to take his meds."

"Hah! He'd never date anybody old enough to be on Silver Singles," Kerry said. "But you better tell Murphy the same thing. I'm sure he'd love to have Dad replace me."

Mother and daughter both sighed at the same time.

"Tolliver men," Birdie said. "My mama tried to warn me, but . . ." Her voice trailed off. "Are you gonna be able to run the stand by yourself? That's a lot."

"We do have a pretty conscientious high school kid who's been helping out. I'm hoping he can recruit a friend so I'll have somebody in the stand while Vic's out making deliveries."

"I hope so too," Birdie said.

"Tomorrow's Saturday. According to Murphy's notebook, it should be the busiest day of the season."

"I wish there was something I could do to help," her mother said. "Honey, I'm so proud of you and the way you stepped up. I know you're going through a rough patch in your own life. Have you heard from Blake at all?"

"Blake is old news. But Mom, I've been thinking. As soon as the holidays are over, I'm going to seriously start looking for a place of my own."

"Here in town?"

"No. You were right. I've got to quit hiding out and playing safe with my life. It's time to reinvent myself. I don't know exactly what that will look like yet. But I've started drawing and painting. And it feels like I can breathe again. Like my creative soul has been set free."

"That's what I've been praying for," Birdie said. "That's all I want for both my children. For you to be happy and fulfilled. And safe. Good night, honey."

"G'night," Kerry said, not bothering to stifle a yawn.

"Don't forget to lock the door," Birdie said, right before she disconnected.

Ten minutes later, her phone rang again. It was Murphy.

"Hey," he said. There was a long silence. She could dimly hear his radio, playing country music, of course.

"Hey," Kerry said, just to break the silence. "What's up?"

"Uh, I been thinking. I guess I was sort of a prick earlier tonight."

"Sort of?"

"Not gonna let me off the hook, are you?"

"Not even a little bit," she said.

He took a deep breath. "Anyway, I think I was out of line yelling at you. It's actually a good thing that we almost sold out of trees today. And that was all you."

Kerry laughed. "Mom called and read you the riot act, didn't she?"

"Yeah." He sounded sheepish. "Okay, that's about it. Let me know how it goes tomorrow."

"I will. And Murph?"

"Yeah?"

"Thanks for calling. Drive safe."

CHAPTER 30

It was Saturday morning and the trailer, even with the space heater turned up as high as it would go, was cold as . . . what was Jock's favorite metaphor? A well-digger's ass? Kerry shivered as she splashed icy bottled water onto her face — the closest she'd get to a shower today.

Someone was knocking at the trailer door. Already? It was barely seven.

Queenie jumped down from her bunk and gave a menacing bark.

"Yeah?" she hollered.

"Ma'am? It's me. Vic. Just wanted to let you know I'm here."

"Hang on a sec." She donned a thick sweater over her flannel shirt and pulled a knit beanie over her messy hair before opening the door.

"Hi," she said. "I'll be out in a minute. Can you take Queenie for a quick walk?" She handed him the dog's leash with a poop bag tied onto it, and Queenie eagerly bounded outside.

Kerry picked her jacket from the hook by the door and stepped into the morning.

The darkness was punctuated by the twinkle lights strung around the tree stand's perimeter. Murphy had them on a timer, set to turn off at daylight — which hadn't arrived.

The street was relatively quiet. A delivery truck was unloading goods at the bodega. Commuters walked past at a brisk pace, headed for the Fourteenth Street subway stop.

She filled Queenie's bowls with food and water, then walked around the stand, picking up stray tree branches and tossing them into the fire barrel.

"I'm back," Vic reported a minute later. She patted Queenie's head and unclipped her leash.

Kerry gazed up at the low-hanging clouds overhead. "Do you think it might snow today?"

"Maybe. It's sure cold enough. Uh, Miss Kerry . . ." Vic stared down at his feet.

"You can just call me Kerry, Vic," she said gently. "I'm not one of your teachers."

"Okay, uh, well, the thing is, I can only work until noon today."

Her gray mood darkened. "Oh no. Today of all days?"

"I'm real sorry, but my mom says I gotta go upstate today to see my dad and step-mom before the holiday. She says it's kind of a command performance. You know?"

She nodded. "I get it. Not your fault." She looked over at Anna's, where the lights had just blinked on. "I'm gonna need some coffee. And carbs. Mind the store, okay?"

When she returned, she handed Vic a steaming cup of cocoa and a cruller. He had a wide smile as he bit off a huge hunk of pastry and chewed enthusiastically. She envied his energy and his metabolism.

He pointed at the last remaining big tree on the lot. "A guy came by while you were gone. He wants to buy that tree. As long as he can have the lights on it."

"Awesome. He can have all the lights. Did you tell him the price?"

Vic gulped some cocoa. "I wasn't sure what it was. There's no tag."

"It's twelve hundred. And if he goes ahead and buys it, you've just earned yourself a fatty commission."

"Cool! He wants it delivered today. But no way that tree will fit on my bike."

"Wonder if it would fit on Murphy's bike

trailer?"

She looked around the stand, but the bike and trailer, which her brother usually kept chained to the utility pole, were missing.

Kerry pulled out her phone and called Murphy. "Hey. Are you home yet?"

"Just crossing the line into North Carolina. What's up?"

"Did you move the bike and trailer?"

"No. When I left last night it was chained to the pole, like always."

"It's gone this morning," Kerry said. "No sign of it."

"Damn. Somebody must have stolen it. But where was Queenie? She didn't bark?"

"Not a peep."

Murphy let off a string of expletives. "It's those friggin' Brody brothers."

"Probably so. They were royally pissed yesterday when they saw how much business we were doing. What now?"

"I've got another bike at the farm. I can bring it back with me, but I had to build that trailer rig myself. No time to make another one. Guess you'll just have to make do with Vic and his bike for now."

"More bad news. Vic can only work till noon today."

"See if he has a buddy?"

Kerry looked up at Vic. "Do you have a

friend who might want to help out today?"

"Sorry. I called a couple guys, but everybody already had plans." He polished off the cruller and wiped his hands on his jeans.

"No dice," Kerry reported. "Never mind. I'll figure something out. In the meantime, should I call the cops and make a report?"

"Forget it," Murphy advised. "New York ain't Tarburton. The bike and trailer are history. Just do what you can until I get back. Then I'll deal with those punks myself."

Kerry hooked her phone up to a Bluetooth speaker she'd bought at a nearby electronics store and downloaded a playlist of up-tempo holiday music.

By nine, the Tolliver Family Tree Farm stand was packed with customers, all of them clamoring for trees and selfies with Spammy and quaint stories about life on a Christmas tree farm. She resisted the temptation to start fabricating stories about magical elves, watch owls, and dastardly bike-stealing trolls, and concentrated on pasting on a (mostly) cheery smile.

Vic scurried around the stand, helping buyers choose trees, wielding the chain saw to cut down trunks, and carrying their purchases to cars or nearby addresses.

The pile of larger trees needing delivery

kept growing, as Kerry promised Murphy and his bike should be back on the premises by Sunday.

By noon, the tree stand had been nearly stripped of the remaining unsold trees.

"Go ahead and leave," Kerry told Vic, as she counted out his earnings into his outstretched palm. "If Murphy gets back with another load of trees, we could probably use your help again tomorrow, if you're available."

"Have to check with my mom," he said. "Can I text you in the morning?"

"Of course. Great job today, Vic. Don't know what I would have done without you."

He grinned and pointed to his jacket's pockets, bulging with tip money. "Are you kidding? I made bank today!"

"Maybe just one more favor?" she asked. "Can you run down to the hardware store and bring me back a load of firewood? This Southern girl is about to freeze to death out here."

The afternoon was as slow as the morning was harried. Kerry took Queenie for a quick walk to Anna's for a sandwich and some coffee.

She fetched her sketchbook from the trailer and resumed doodling with a sketch of a saucy Westie she'd spotted down the block. She drew him wearing a handsome plaid jacket that matched his owner's, a woman she recognized from the Kaplans' building.

"Hi, Kerry." Austin raced to her side. He was bundled up in a thick puffer jacket, snow boots, mittens, and a green-and-red-striped ski cap.

"Can we work on our story now? My dad said it doesn't look like you're too busy right now."

She handed him the sketchbook. "Where were we?"

He flipped through the pages. "Here," he said, stabbing his finger on the page with the elaborate gate and the secret forest. "I think what happens next is, the bad guys figure out how to get into the forest, to steal the trees."

Kerry glanced across the street, where one of the Brody brothers was standing in the street, flipping his cheap trees sign around like a majorette's baton.

"What if," she said, musing out loud, "we made the bad guys brothers?"

"Yeah!" Austin said.

Suddenly, Patrick was on the sidewalk, directly behind her. He placed his hands on her shoulders and gave them a slight

214

squeeze in greeting.

"What did those two do now?" he asked, gesturing at the Brodys.

"Pretty sure they stole Murphy's bike and trailer last night," she said.

"Here comes Mr. Heinz," Austin announced, pointing at the elderly man, who was walking slowly toward them.

He made his way into the stand and nodded a hello to Patrick and Kerry.

"Well, look who's here today," Heinz said. "I've missed seeing you this week, young man. Any new ideas for our story?"

"Yeah. The bad guys are brothers, cuz they stole Murphy's bike," Austin said indignantly.

"Really?" Heinz held out his hand for a pencil.

He turned to a blank page in the sketchbook. His gnarled fingers clutched the pencil, and it flew over the paper. In the blink of an eye, he'd drawn two menacing figures, black clad, crouched in front of the merest suggestion of the gate Kerry had drawn, and peeking furtively in at the forest beyond.

"That's them," Austin said, nodding vigorously. "But what are their names?"

"Malvolio and Iago," Heinz suggested.

"Those are funny names," Austin said,

wrinkling his nose.

"Two of Shakespeare's most despicable villains," the old man informed him. "Unfortunately, you're correct. Those names are hardly familiar to young people these days."

"Sad but true," Patrick agreed.

"I know. Gordy and Payton," Austin said. "Those are the two worst kids in first grade."

"What makes these children so bad?" Heinz asked.

"Well. Gordy is a biter, and Payton sits behind me and kicks my desk when the teacher isn't looking," the boy reported.

"Looks like we have our villains," Kerry agreed. "Nobody likes a biter. Now. How do they manage to sneak into the forest?"

"I think they should parachute in out of a helicopter," Patrick said. "And then maybe throw in some smoke grenades."

"Daaad." Austin rolled his eyes. "Isn't that what happens in those movies Mom won't let me watch?"

Kerry got up and walked to the front of the trailer, where she'd just noticed something she'd overlooked earlier in the day. It was the chain Murphy used to secure his bike and trailer.

"I think they used bolt cutters," she said, showing the men the chain.

CHAPTER 31

Patrick extended his hand. "May I?"

She handed him the bike chain. He turned it over and over, then handed it back, his expression troubled. "When did this happen?"

"Last night. Sometime after I fell asleep. I think those two creeps across the street probably saw Murphy loading his stuff into the truck and saw their chance to mess with us."

"Where did Murphy go?" he asked.

"He's making a run back to the farm to pick up another load of trees."

Patrick cursed under his breath. "That's pretty bold, coming over here, with you asleep only a few inches away. Queenie didn't raise the alarm?"

"No. We were both dead tired."

"This is terrible," Heinz said, tsk-tsking. "Does your brother know?"

"I called him a little while ago. He's furi-

217

ous, of course, but he said it's a waste of time to call the cops. He should be back late tonight or in the morning."

Kerry shivered, stood, and went over to the fire barrel to throw on another log. Sparks rose into the chilly air. The reality of having thieves standing right outside the trailer the previous night while she was sleeping was just starting to sink in.

"I don't like the idea of you staying here alone tonight," Patrick said. "Maybe you should stay at our place until Murphy gets back. I can bunk in with Austin and you can have my room."

"Yeah," Austin said, hopping up and down with excitement. "A sleepover."

The idea of sleeping in an actual bed, with working heat, in close proximity to a hot shower, with a bonus of being close to a hot man, namely Patrick, was oh so tempting.

"I can't just abandon my post. What if they come back, to take something else, or do something worse? Besides, I'm not gonna let those two goons scare me away. I'm not just some sweet, shrinking magnolia. I'm from the mountains."

She ran to the trailer and came back, brandishing the baseball bat, then stalked over to the edge of the sidewalk and, addressing the Brody brothers, shouted loud

218

enough to be heard over the sound of the passing traffic. "I've got my daddy's baseball bat, and I'm not afraid to use it." She sliced the air two or three times in what she felt was a distinctly menacing fashion.

The skinnier brother's response was lewd and direct, followed by a loud braying laugh.

"Y'all really don't know who you're messing with," she yelled, then turned her back and walked away.

"I would not mess with you," Heinz said, and he and Patrick laughed together, breaking the tension of the moment.

"I bet they're mad because you sold more trees than they did," Austin said.

"Probably so," Kerry said.

"Mr. Heinz," Austin said, looking up at the old man. "Did you buy your Christmas tree yet?"

"Oh no," Heinz said. "I have a very small apartment, and live alone, so there's really no need to indulge in such foolishness."

Before the child could reason with him, he rose slowly and tipped his hat; a black wool Borsalino, with a tiny feather tucked into the band. He glanced down at his watch. It was thick and gold and looked like a fine antique to Kerry's unschooled eye.

"I must be going now."

Queenie had crept out from beneath the

table, and now she gently nudged his hand with her nose and wagged her tail.

"Oh my goodness," Heinz said. "I almost forgot." He reached into his pocket and held out a small dog biscuit, which the dog gobbled down. He patted her head. "You take good care of your mistress tonight, will you? If anyone comes close, attack!"

Kerry had to laugh. "If anyone comes close, she'd probably lick them to death."

Tree shoppers came and went from the stand, with Patrick acting as her assistant, loading trees onto cars and wagons while Austin kept the stand swept.

"What happened to your helper?" Patrick asked, after he added another tree to the stack to be delivered.

"His mom had other plans for him today, so I'm working solo," Kerry said.

Patrick glanced at his watch. "My sister's in town for the day and I promised to take her for a late lunch. After that, we'll come back and help out."

Austin flexed his muscles. "Me and my dad are really strong."

Patrick struck his best strong-man pose too.

"Wow, check out the gun show," Kerry said. "I'll see you guys later."

The temperature continued to drop for the next two hours. The sky darkened, and Kerry looked up in time to see the first flurry of snowflakes. She threw another log on the fire and stood over it, warming her hands.

She propped her phone on her worktable and tapped her Spotify playlist. Soon she had Bing Crosby and Nat King Cole crooning about sleigh rides and chestnuts roasting on an open fire as she was warmed by the sights and sounds of Christmas in the city.

Customers drifted in, most of them prompted by seeing AshleyActually's Instagram post about the Tolliver Family Tree Farm. She sold six more trees, leaving her with only a total of seven left, and was grateful that all the customers didn't mind toting their trees home themselves.

Austin and Patrick came back to the tree stand at dusk. Austin was wearing an obviously new yellow-and-blue-striped knit Steelers ski cap and scarf, and Patrick carried a large flat cardboard box.

"Looks like you sold a bunch more trees," Patrick said, setting the box on the worktable beside her, as Austin crawled under the table to snuggle with Queenie.

Kerry pointed to the box. "Is that what I

think it is?"

He lifted the lid. "From Arturo's. Only the best authentic pizza in the Village. Sorry to be so late. I love my sister, but she can draw out a goodbye like nobody else."

Kerry inhaled the spicy tomato aroma and lifted a slice from the box. She took a bite, chewed, and let out a sigh of contentment. "Oh my Gawd. This is so good."

She polished off the slice in an embarrassingly short amount of time.

"I know you can't get pizza like this down in North Carolina," Patrick said.

She wiped her hands on a paper napkin and dabbed her lips with it. "On the other hand, you also can't get real barbecue in Greenwich Village, or anywhere in New York City."

"Hah! There's a place over on Greenwich Avenue, called Mighty Quinn's. It's got incredible authentic barbecue."

"I bet they serve brisket," Kerry said with a dismissive sniff. "Not the same thing at all. And also, what's the sauce? Is it eastern Carolina sauce, or western Carolina?"

"There's a difference?"

"Don't get me started. Blood feuds have erupted over this very issue. Eastern Carolina barbecue can be any cut of meat and the sauce is thin and vinegar and pepper based. To me, it tastes like bitterness and regret. On the other hand, western Carolina barbecue is divine. It's smoked pork butt with a thick rich sauce that uses ketchup and some brown sugar."

Patrick raised one eyebrow. "Do I detect some bias on your part?"

"Just reliable reporting," Kerry said. "Now, my dad's sauce is a little bit of a mash-up of the two. Although, it's actually my grandmother's original secret recipe. Muv would fill up recycled wine bottles with her sauce and give them out as Christmas gifts. And if she really liked you, she'd urge you to bring it back later in the year for a refill."

"I'd like to try that sauce," Patrick said.

"Murphy usually carries some around in his truck — for barbecue emergencies. When he gets back, I'll ask him to give you a taste. Or maybe, when I go home, I'll send you a bottle."

"Why do you gotta go home?" Austin asked plaintively.

"Because . . . I just do," Kerry said. "I can't live in this little camper forever."

"Why not? I love Spammy. I would live there forever if my dad would let me."

"Spammy doesn't have a working bathroom, or a kitchen. And we can't park here much longer, because this space doesn't belong to us. Right after Christmas, I have to find a new job and a new place to live," she explained.

"But . . ."

Patrick ruffled his son's hair. "I want her to stay too, Austin, but the lady says she's only here til Christmas, so we have to respect that. Okay?"

Austin ducked his chin and she could see that he was fighting back tears. Kerry was getting a little teary-eyed herself at the prospect of all the changes looming post-holiday.

She gathered the boy into her arms. "Hey. Let's not think about goodbyes right now.

"He's shivering," she told Patrick. "Maybe y'all should call it a night."

Austin struggled out of her embrace. "Dad, can we have a campout tonight? Please? I've never been camping before. And this will be like camping in a forest." His blue eyes shone as he pleaded his case.

Patrick checked with Kerry.

"Believe me, camping is highly overrated. And I should know."

"He has a point though. We can't just leave you defenseless against those bad guys."

Kerry picked up her bat again. "They're

the ones who need to be worried about me."

Patrick took a half step backward. "Maybe we'll just hang out for a while and sing campfire songs and do camping things. Just till Murphy gets back?"

"It's awful cold out here," Kerry said. "More snow flurries are possible."

"My grammy gave me a sleeping bag for my birthday," Austin said pointedly.

Patrick considered, and then easily caved to his son's entreaties.

"All right. We'll run upstairs and get our 'camping' gear, such as it is. In the meantime, Kerry, please try not to start World War Three with the new kids on the block."

She twirled the bat. "I can make no such promises."

CHAPTER 32

"We're baaaack." Austin was loaded down with a backpack that nearly dwarfed him in size, with a rolled-up sleeping bag under his arm. His father was pushing a small shopping cart with a lantern, blankets, a thermos, and a couple of folding soccer chairs.

"You call this camping?" Kerry plucked a bottle of champagne from the cart.

"This is how we do it in our neck of the Village," Patrick said.

Austin struggled out of his backpack and settled into the smaller of the two chairs.

Patrick unfolded his own chair and sneezed.

"Bless you," she said.

He sneezed twice more in rapid succession, and she noticed that his eyes were red and watery. "You really are allergic to pine trees," she said.

"I really am." He sniffled into a handkerchief he'd produced from his jacket pocket.

"Will you be okay?"

"I took a couple allergy capsules before we came down just now," he said. "Just warning you, I may get a little drowsy."

"Me too," Kerry said, stretching her legs toward the fire in the oil drum.

Patrick unscrewed the cap of the thermos. "Hot cocoa, anyone?"

"I'm good. But I wouldn't say no to some champagne."

"Ahhh. A woman after my own heart."

He made a show of uncorking the bottle, and she held out one of the flutes.

"Very nice," Kerry said, sipping.

"Will you sing a campfire song?" Austin barely succeeded in stifling a yawn.

"Do you know this one?" Kerry hummed a little, then began to remember the verses.

"Puff, the magic dragon . . ."

"Lived by the sea," Patrick chimed in softly.

"I love dragons," Austin said, his eyelids fluttering.

Haltingly, Kerry and Patrick sang the rest of the song as Austin's chin began to sag slowly to his chest.

Kerry stood and gathered the drowsy boy into her arms. "Hey, buddy," she whispered. "You wanna go check out Murphy's bunk?"

His eyes fluttered open. "In Spammy?"

"Yeah."

"But I gotta watch out for the bad guys."

"There's a window right beside Murphy's bunk. You'll have a perfect view in case anybody tries to make trouble," she said.

"Okay, but I need my light saber and my binoculars," he said.

Patrick picked up the backpack. "Got it right here," he assured his son, as Kerry transferred Austin to his arms.

She opened the trailer door and pointed at her brother's bunk. Patrick deposited him on the bunk and she unzipped the sleeping bag and pulled it over him.

In a moment, the boy's breathing slowed and softened.

"He's out," Patrick whispered, looking up at Kerry. "Hot cocoa for the win."

CHAPTER 33

"Did your whole family really live here for an entire month?" Patrick asked, stretching out on the opposite bunk, looking around the cramped trailer.

Kerry sat down on the edge of her bunk. "We did. As a little kid, it seemed fun. Back then the bathroom and stove worked. Mom fixed a lot of soups and stews in a crockpot. She made even the mundane seem magical. Once we went to the Macy's at Herald Square to see Santa. We took the subway and I thought that was just the most awesome thing ever. Even better than our Santa back home in Tarburton."

Patrick smiled and leaned back against a stack of pillows. "I'd like to have seen New York through the eyes of seven-year-old Kerry."

He leaned in and kissed her cheek and stroked her hair. Slowly, she turned her face and her lips met his. The first kiss was tentative, but slowly, things grew more fevered.

Kerry wrapped her arms around Patrick's neck. Being with him like this felt so warm, so right. She sighed.

"What?" he whispered. "Are you sad?" He kissed her forehead and then pressed his lips to hers. "Don't be sad."

"I'm not. I'm thinking how nice this is. I'm . . . content."

He pulled his face a few inches away from hers and frowned. "Is that supposed to be a compliment? My kisses make you feel . . . content?"

She touched a fingertip to his chin, tracing the stubble with her nail. "It's definitely a compliment. This . . . snuggled up in here with you, it feels right."

Patrick reached for the folded blanket at the foot of the bed, and stretched it until it covered them both. He managed to unzip her quilted jacket and started to slide his hands under her sweater, but paused.

Austin stirred slightly and mumbled something incoherent.

"It would feel a lot nicer if my kid weren't sleeping two feet away from us," Patrick grumbled, glancing over at his sleeping child. "When can we be alone?"

"Shh. He's asleep, right?" Kerry kissed his frown away, and he tugged at the hem of the sweater, only to encounter the flannel shirt she wore underneath.

"Just how many layers of clothes are you currently wearing?" His whisper was urgent.

"I work outdoors, remember?" She sat up and swung her legs over the edge of the bunk. She leaned down and unlaced her work boots, then stood up.

"Where are you going?"

"Just gonna step into the bathroom to remove some of these pesky clothes," she said, giggling. "Maybe you could do the same while I'm gone?"

"Ahhhh."

Kerry tiptoed into the bathroom in her stocking feet, shedding the heavy jacket along the way. Somehow, in the space that was smaller than a phone booth, she managed to extricate herself from her jeans. Next came the sweater, then the flannel shirt, then the thermal underwear top. Hopping on first one foot and then the other, she pulled off the thermal bottoms. Finally, shivering and dressed only in panties and her wool socks, she leaned into the mirror to check her appearance, and wished she hadn't. Her hair was lank and she had dark circles under both eyes, and she hadn't actually had a real shower that day. In desperation, she squeezed some toothpaste into her mouth and swished it around, then spritzed herself with the only thing at hand, which happened to be a can of Murphy's Axe spray deodorant. She fluffed her hair, then dashed, in the cold, back to the bunk.

Patrick was still propped up on the pillows, with the blanket pulled up over his bare chest. And he was dead asleep.

She sat down on the bunk and tentatively touched his face. He didn't move. She put her hand on his chest. It was a nice chest, muscled, not overly hairy. She lifted the blanket and peeked. He'd stripped down to his boxers. They were red, with a festive pattern of prancing reindeers.

"Patrick?" She put her lips to his ear and whispered, "Patrick?"

His eyelids fluttered.

Kerry went back to the bathroom to fetch the clothes she'd just struggled out of.

He was snoring softly when she joined him on the bunk. She shook his shoulder. "Patrick. Hey, wake up."

"Huh?" His voice was hoarse with sleep, and he seemed confused to find her half dressed.

"You fell asleep," she said.

He sat halfway up, and groaned as he sank back down onto the bed.

"It's the damned antihistamines." He

grabbed her hand. "But I'm awake now."

"It's okay," she said. "Don't worry about it. It's late and I'm beat too. And there's no telling how soon Murphy will come rolling in here."

The mention of her brother brought Patrick fully awake. He raked his fingers through his hair, sighed, and reached for the clothes he'd discarded on the floor.

"Probably not a great idea all around, huh?"

She leaned in and kissed him hard, on the mouth. "Sometimes even the best ideas don't work out. Ya know?"

He kissed her back and touched her check. "Can I get a rain check? Can we have a real date — just the two of us?"

"I'd like that."

She helped him bundle Austin in the sleeping bag, and tucked the flashlight and binoculars into the child's backpack before walking Patrick back outside with his son slung over his shoulder.

"One more thing," she called, as he started back across the street.

"What's that?"

"Promise me, when we have our date, you'll wear those cute red reindeer undies?"

He blushed, then winked. "It's a deal."

■ ■ ■ ■

After Patrick and Austin were gone, Kerry walked all the way around the Christmas tree lot one last time. It was nearly midnight. She saw the lights blinking off at Lombardi's, saw the last of the help straggling out the door and locking it behind them. Traffic was light, and the snow was still softly falling on the damp pavement of Hudson Street.

She took out her phone and called her brother.

"Yo," Murphy said. He sounded as tired as she felt.

"Everything going okay?" she asked.

"Just super. Mom had to practically hogtie Dad to keep him from riding back with me. How's it going there?"

"Pretty good. We're down to less than half a dozen trees now. How far away are you?"

"Another couple hours at least. I'm gonna pull over in a truck stop pretty soon and get a couple hours' sleep. I should be there by no later than five."

"I'll be here," Kerry said. "Hey, Murph?"

"Yeah?"

"Drive safe, okay?"

"Always, little sister."

234

Kerry disconnected the call. She pulled the bungee cord across the entrance and posted the CLOSED sign. Then she whistled for Queenie, who followed her back inside the trailer.

CHAPTER 34

Kerry was floating somewhere beneath the sea, or maybe it was the clouds. She was dimly aware of muted sounds: low voices, thuds, footsteps. But she was beyond touch of the earth, floating free, relaxed. Time and space did not exist.

Until she was rudely yanked back to earth. The trailer door slammed, hard. She battled her way back to the surface. She sat up and blinked, shocked at the blinding sunlight streaming through the open door.

"You up?" Murphy held two cups of steaming coffee and now he handed her one.

"I am now."

"About damn time."

Kerry breathed in the coffee fumes. "When did you get here? And what time is it?"

Outside, rows of freshly cut Christmas trees were stacked up three deep.

"How did you unload all those trees by

236

yourself? You should have woken me up."

"I got one of the busboys over at Lombardi's to help. We got the trees unloaded, then I took the trailer back to the yard in Brooklyn, dumped it, and headed back here. Didn't want to wake you up, so I slept in the truck. And by the way, it's nearly nine, and I'm dead on my feet."

"Sorry," Kerry said, grabbing for her clothes. "I've gotta get a shower at the Kaplans'. I'll be back in ten minutes. Okay?"

He collapsed onto his bunk. "Do not wake me when you get back."

A fire was blazing away in the oil barrel when she returned to the tree stand, and her brother's snores could be heard from the sidewalk.

Kerry worked her phone, calling all the customers who'd left orders for trees over the weekend, to let them know the new shipment had arrived. In between calls she managed to craft a few more wreaths, and even sold three trees to people from the neighborhood.

Shortly after noon, she stretched the bungee cord across the entrance to the tree stand and dashed over to Lombardi's to place a to-go order.

Claudia bustled around the busy main

room, chatting with regulars. She wore a tight-fitting green sweater adorned with silver-tinsel-draped Christmas trees.

She met Kerry at the bar. "Well, hey there. Haven't seen you in a while. How's business?"

"Like a roller coaster. Down, then up, up, up — so much so that we sold out of trees and Murphy had to make a run back to the farm to pick up another load. He just got back."

"Yeah, he called to let me know when he was on his way down there," Claudia said, tucking a wisp of blond hair into her updo.

Kerry did a double take. "He did?"

Claudia laughed at her shocked expression. "Don't be so surprised. He knew I'd be pissed. We were supposed to go out Friday night."

"My fault," Kerry confessed. "I kinda guilt-tripped him into going back to the farm."

"He did blame it on you. But we both know you can't make Murphy Tolliver do something he doesn't want to."

The bartender arrived with Kerry's order.

"What'd you get?" Claudia asked.

Kerry opened the bag and inhaled the scent of garlic, oregano, and tomatoes. "Your minestrone, and an order of garlic bread. Gotta have something warm in my belly today."

"Good choice," Claudia said.

"Anyway, I'm sorry I ruined your weekend plans," Kerry said.

"He's got one more chance to make things right," Claudia confided. "No more grabbing a late dinner here at the bar after we close the place down. I told your brother he's gotta make real plans. I want to dress up and go out on the town on an honest-to-God date."

"Good for you." Kerry glanced out the restaurant's plate-glass window and saw a young couple stopped in front of the Tolliver Family Farm stand.

"Oops. Gotta go sell some trees now. But don't worry. I'll make sure Murphy knows I'll cover for him this weekend so you two can have a fun night out."

The couple spent forty-five minutes agonizing over whether a five-foot or six-foot tree would have the most impact in their high-ceilinged loft. "Get the six-footer," Kerry urged.

She gave them one of Jock's favorite lines. "If it's too tall you can always cut off a few inches — but I can't make it grow any taller." The woman laughed and her husband handed over the cash.

Customers arrived at a steady pace throughout the afternoon, picking up trees they'd reserved over the weekend, or choosing a tree for delivery, and she was relieved when Vic arrived on his bike, primed to start work.

"Man," he said, looking around at the replenished stand. "How are we gonna sell all these trees before Christmas?"

"Check the tags," Kerry said. "A lot of these are already paid for. And I've got an idea for a little promotion you can help me with, as soon as you come back from your delivery rounds."

She was jotting down her shopping list when Austin came skipping into the stand, followed by his father.

Austin was bundled up against the cold and cradling a book against his chest.

"Is that a book you're reading for school?" Kerry asked, after greeting the pair.

He grinned and shook his head. "Nope. Dad bought it for me at the bookstore. See?"

He thrust the book into her hands. "It's all about dragons."

The picture book was called *Dragons Love Tacos,* and Kerry smiled too, as she leafed through the pages with their whimsical illustrations and story of a taco-loving dragon who accidentally ingests an especially fiery salsa.

"Dragons, huh?" she said, handing the book back.

"He's suddenly obsessed with them. Been talking nonstop about dragons all morning," Patrick said. "He made me look up all the lyrics to 'Puff the Magic Dragon.' "

Kerry blushed.

He leaned down and whispered in her ear. "I guess that's gonna be our song now, huh?"

Austin was hopping up and down with barely contained excitement. "Kerry, do you think we could put some dragons in our story? That's why I love this book. I mean, it's kind of a baby book for a kid like me, who can read, but the dragon pictures are really cool."

"Definitely," Kerry replied, opening the book again to study the illustrations.

"Yeah. Our dragons could guard the gate to the forest," Austin said. "I bet that would scare off the bad guys."

She nodded and pulled her sketchbook out, turning to a fresh page. She quickly inked a dragon, giving it bat wings, a scaly body, spikes along its spine, a forked tail, feet that ended in fearsome claws, and an imposing head with powerful jaws and hooded eyes.

"Damn!" Patrick took a half step backward. "That dragon would definitely scare me if I were a bad guy."

Austin studied her drawing and tapped the dragon with his finger. "Our dragon is friendly when he wants to be, right, Kerry?"

"Of course," Kerry said. "But can we have one of the dragons be a girl?"

"I guess that would be okay," Austin said.

"Listen, I happen to know several girls who are dragons, especially in the morning," Patrick said.

"You mean, like Mom?"

"Only before she's had her coffee," Patrick said. "And you can never tell her I said that."

Kerry tapped the end of the pen on the paper for a moment, while she tried to imagine just what a girl dragon would look like. Hair bow? Pink sneakers? A bra? She gazed around at the street, hoping for some sort of inspiration.

Instead, she saw Heinz, slowly making his way across the street in her direction.

Queenie saw him too, and bounded out to meet the old man, tail wagging. She pushed her snout up against the pocket of his thick woolen coat.

"Oh, hello," Heinz said, his chuckle becoming a wheezy cough as he scratched the dog's ears and held out the treat he knew she was seeking.

"Are you all right?" Kerry inquired. Her friend's face was unusually pale, and as he leaned on his cane he seemed unsteady on his feet.

"I'm fine," Heinz said. "This very cold air, sometimes, it doesn't agree with me."

Kerry jumped to her feet. "Please sit. Can I get you some coffee, or some tea?"

"Nothing at all," he said, waving away her concern. He pointed down at the sketchbook. "What's this ferocious creature I'm seeing?"

"It's a dragon," Austin said. "To help guard the magical forest from the bad guys."

"Ohhhh," Heinz said, nodding slowly. "Yes, I think a dragon would be a very effective deterrent to bad guys."

"There should be two dragons, though," Austin said. "Kerry says one should be a girl."

"I agree."

"The problem is, I don't exactly know what a female dragon might look like," Kerry admitted.

"Perhaps I could try?" Heinz asked.

Kerry stood up. "Be my guest. I'm going to go get us something hot to drink. Which is it? Coffee, or tea?"

He sank down onto the chair. "Well, tea if you insist. Maybe with a drizzle of honey, if it's not too much bother."

"Kerry, look!" Austin called out to her as she returned to her post. She carefully placed the foam cups on the edge of the worktable, along with some chocolate-dipped biscotti.

Heinz had retrieved her colored pencils from her box of art supplies and had, in the space of ten short minutes, created a distinctively feminine-looking dragon, with long, fluttery eyelashes, and pink-painted claws. She looked fearsome, and yet adorable, if that was possible.

"Oh, Heinz, she's perfect," Kerry declared.

Heinz's chuckle turned into a spasm of coughing. His face reddened, and his chest heaved with the effort of breathing.

"Hey," Patrick said, alarmed. "Are you all right?"

"One moment," Heinz gasped, putting his hand to his chest. A minute later, his color returned to normal.

"I'm all right," he announced. "Just a silly cookie crumb went down the wrong way."

He managed to stand and reach for his

cane. "I really must be going."

"Let us walk you home," Patrick said. "You seem pretty winded."

"No, no," Heinz said. "That's kind of you, but I'm fine. Just old and foolish to eat sweets my doctor forbids me to have. I have errands and appointments."

"Please," Kerry said. "Let Patrick walk with you. You really don't seem well."

The old man's smile vanished. "I'm perfectly capable of taking care of myself." He nodded at Austin, patted Queenie's head, and slowly began hobbling away.

CHAPTER 35

Over the next few days, Kerry felt herself settling into the season. It snowed again, just enough to glaze the Christmas trees and the grass and shrubs in the pocket park with a thin layer of frost, and the sky was blue and cloudless. She had her own holiday playlist blaring and mulled cider heating up in a borrowed coffee urn, and she'd lit the fire in the oil barrel. She'd even donned a festive red-and-green felt elf's hat with tiny silver bells that jingled every time she moved her head.

Mariah Carey was just starting to belt "All I Want for Christmas Is You" when the trailer door flew open and Murphy stepped out with a murderous look in his eyes.

"What the actual hell?" he bellowed, glowering at his sister. "What's that racket?"

"It's called Christmas music," Kerry said calmly. "It gets people in a shopping mood."

"It gets me in a shitty mood," he said. His

hair was wild and unkempt, and it looked as though he'd slept in his clothes. He lifted his head and sniffed. "And what's that smell?"

"If you're referring to the delicious aroma of fall spices like cinnamon, nutmeg, and cloves, that's probably the mulled cider I'm planning on serving our customers today." She pointed at the urn, which she'd plugged into the extension cord running from Lombardi's.

"But that other rank smell? I'd say that's a disgusting elixir of unwashed socks and mountain man musk. And as we used to say when we were kids, the smeller is the feller."

He retreated back into the trailer, but a few moments later emerged with his shaving kit in one hand and a laundry bag slung over his shoulder, walking past her without a word.

Customers drifted in and out to purchase trees, but when business slowed after lunch, Kerry cranked up the volume of the music and went back to work crafting wreaths.

Murphy ventured out of the trailer around two. He nodded in her direction, then walked across the street and into Lombardi's. Half an hour later, he returned with a paper sack, which he handed her.

"The lunch special was meatball subs," he said. "Claudia thought you might be hungry."

"Thanks. I'm starved," Kerry said, unwrapping the sandwich that was oozing with spicy marinara sauce and melted mozzarella.

Murphy sat down at her worktable and poured himself a cup of the spiced cider. "How're we doing today?"

She dabbed at her mouth with a napkin. "Eight trees, and half a dozen wreaths."

He reached for his ever-present notebook. "Not bad. But we really need to put the pedal to the metal to sell all the rest of these trees."

"That's why I'm giving away cider and playing Christmas music, Captain Obvious," she said, trying not to show her annoyance. "Hey, since you're already up, can you watch the stand for a little while?"

"What for?"

"I'm almost out of materials for the wreaths. I'll just run over to the wholesale flower market and be right back."

"Guess that'll be okay." He turned and pointed at the pile of trees leaning up against the side of Spammy. "Are those all for deliveries?"

"Yeah," Kerry said. "They're all paid for

and I've tagged each one with the address." She frowned. "Vic should have been here by now."

"Forgot to tell you. He's not coming till after five. He's got a dentist's appointment."

"I wish I'd known that," Kerry said. "I promised the Fosters and the Carters that they'd have these trees this afternoon."

Murphy shrugged. "I'll deliver 'em while you're gone. Won't take long."

"You're gonna leave the stand un-manned?"

"Just for a few minutes," he said. "They're right here in the neighborhood. Don't worry about it. It's slow right now. Probably won't pick back up till five, when people are head-ing home for the night."

"But —" she started to protest, but he held up his hand, like a traffic cop.

"I been doing this for years without any help from you, okay? Leave it to me. I know what I'm doing."

She was still miffed at her brother's cavalier attitude when she returned to the Christmas tree stand an hour later and the CLOSED sign was strung across the entrance.

The pile of trees for delivery was definitely diminished. She unloaded her supplies and began tying bows and wiring holly bunches to the wreath forms she'd completed earlier in the day. The late-afternoon sky was gunmetal gray. The temperature had dropped and the wind kicked up bits of dried leaves and pine needles, blowing them around in the frigid winter air.

"Kerry?" Gretchen McCaleb hurried into the tree stand. She was wild-eyed, dressed in a ski jacket with a beanie pulled over unusually messy hair. "Have you seen Austin?"

"Not today," Kerry said. "Isn't he with his dad?"

"No. I promised to take him Christmas shopping. We got down to the lobby and I realized I'd left my phone in the apartment. I told him to wait right there in the lobby for me, but when I got downstairs, he was gone! I went back upstairs, thinking maybe he got tired of waiting, but he wasn't there. I've been all over the building, knocked on everybody's door, but nobody's seen him. Patrick is on his way over here now."

Gretchen's voice was brittle with anxiety. "I can't find my baby. I don't know what to do." She glanced around the stand. "Could he have gone someplace with your brother?"

"Maybe. I just got back here myself," Kerry said. "Murphy is out making deliveries. Maybe Austin went with him."

"Any word?" Patrick called as he double-parked his car at the curb. His face was etched with worry. "Has anyone seen him? Did you call the police?"

"I was just about to," Gretchen said. She reached for her phone, but Patrick put out a hand to stop her. "Look."

He pointed down the street. Heinz walked haltingly toward them, one hand on his cane, the other clasped firmly around Austin's arm. "Thank God," Patrick said softly.

Gretchen took off running, followed by Patrick. She fell to her knees in front of the boy, hugging him tightly to her chest. "Austin! Oh, Austin."

Heinz released the child's hand and now stood a few awkward inches away.

Gretchen looked up at the old man. "How could you do that? How could you take my boy? Do you know how frightened we've been?"

"Gretch!" Patrick said sharply.

"No, Mom!" Austin cried. "Don't yell at Mr. Heinz. Don't be mad at him. It's not his fault." He struggled to escape his mother's grasp.

"Austin?" Patrick said sternly. "What happened? Where did you go?"

"I found Murphy's bike! The one the bad guys stole," Austin said. "I was waiting in

251

the lobby, like Mom said, but then I saw him ride by the building on it. So I followed him. And I saw where he was hiding it."

"What's this about my bike?" Murphy asked as he joined the group.

"I found your bike!" Austin said proudly. "The bad guys took it."

Patrick looked up at Heinz. "Is this true?"

"Two blocks away," Heinz said. "On Hudson Street. I don't usually walk that way, but today, I needed my glasses repaired at a shop there. I was coming out when I saw our little friend here, peeking out from behind a telephone pole."

"The bad guy hid the bike under the stoop!" Austin said. "There's a little gate, and he put it there and locked it up. But I know right where it is now!"

"It does look like Murphy's bicycle. And the trailer is there too," Heinz said. He turned his head and coughed into a handkerchief.

"Who did you see with the bike? Which bad guy?" Murphy asked. "Do you mean one of those dudes selling Christmas trees over there?" He pointed toward the Brody brothers' hut.

"I, uh, I'm not sure. He had on a hoodie. Like the color army guys wear. And sunglasses. But I knew it was Murphy's bike because of the sign on the back. Tolliver Tree Farm. Right?"

Gretchen was still kneeling. She grasped her son's jacket by the collar. Tears streamed down her face. "Austin. You can't ever, ever do anything like that again. Little boys can't just wander around the streets of the city. There are some really bad people out there . . ."

"I'm almost six and a half! And I wasn't wandering," Austin said indignantly. "I was on the street where Dad and me get our hair cut. I was going to come home, as soon as I figured out how to get Murphy's bike back. And then Mr. Heinz saw me. And he's one of the good guys, right?"

"Okay, well, you're back safely now, and that's the most important thing," Patrick said. "And yes. Mr. Heinz is definitely a good guy. But your mom's right. You can never, ever do that again. If your mom or I tell you to stay someplace, you stay right there. No matter what. Right?"

"Yes, sir." Austin stared down at the toe of his boot. "But what about the bike?"

Murphy stared across the street. "Guess I'll go have a little chat with those two bozos to straighten out a few things. But first, I'm gonna get my bolt cutters out of the truck and reclaim my property."

"I'll go with you," Patrick said. "As wing-man."

"I can show you where the bike and trailer are hidden," Heinz said quietly.

"And I'll go too. Because I'm the one that found it," Austin said, puffing out his chest.

"Oh no," Gretchen said. "It's getting dark. You're coming home with me, young man."

She took Austin's hand and steered him homeward.

True to Murphy's prediction, traffic picked up considerably as daylight faded. Vic arrived and was quickly dispatched to deliver trees. Kerry watched anxiously for her brother's return.

Finally, nearly an hour later, Murphy came pedaling down the street with the trailer hitched to the back of his bike and the bolt cutters sticking out of the trailer.

"You did it!" Kerry said, as her brother dismounted from the bike.

"Went down slick," Murphy said, looking around the booth. "And looks like it's going good here too."

"The trees are really flying out of here now," Kerry said proudly. "Vic just took three more trees to deliver. But tell me about the great stolen bike caper."

"Not that much to tell. Heinz showed me

where the bike and trailer were, and like Austin said, they were in one of those gated areas under a front stoop, and the gate had a big ol' fairly new-looking chain and padlock on it. Which I cut off."

"Was anyone around? Weren't you afraid the cops might stop you?"

"Nah. The place where it was hidden is under construction. There was all this scaffolding out front. Anyway, this is the city, Kere. People mind their own business. Besides, whoever put it there was a thief."

Kerry looked past her brother.

"Patrick went home, if that's who you're looking for," Murphy said. "He told me to tell you he'll call you later."

"Oh, uh, no," she said, quickly trying to cover her tracks. "I was wondering about Heinz."

Murphy rolled his eyes. "Whatever. Heinz left. I don't think he's feeling too good."

"Yeah, I'm worried he's really sick," Kerry said. "All of a sudden, he looks so frail."

"Well, he's an old guy. Probably pushing ninety. Way older than Dad." He reached into a plastic sack and brought out a new bike chain, wheeled the bike over to the utility pole, and padlocked the bike and trailer to it. "That oughtta do the trick."

He straightened up, then grabbed the bolt cutters.

"What are you going to do with those?" she asked.

"Gonna go across the street and have a friendly conversation with the brothers, especially the clueless one who's now wearing the green hoodie Austin described to us."

"But you wouldn't actually . . . hurt anybody. Right?" Kerry asked uneasily.

"I wouldn't. But the Brody brothers don't know that."

CHAPTER 36

Thirty minutes later, Murphy was back. He had a darkening bruise beneath his left eye and a wad of blood-soaked paper towels wrapped around his right hand, which was clutching part of a six-pack of beer.

Kerry stared at her brother in horror. "Are you all right? What happened? I thought you said there wouldn't be any violence."

"Wasn't no violence," he said, his tone of voice matter-of-fact. "I told those boys I knew they stole my bike rig, they tried to deny it. But Duane, the dumbass, was wearing that green hoodie. We had words. He made the mistake of taking a swing at me, so I laid the bolt cutters upside his head. Just a little tap, to get his attention. Then Donny, he's the lardass, jumped me, and I had to explain things, mountain style."

Kerry pointed to his hand. "You're bleeding."

Murphy chuckled. "Just a scratch. Anyway,

it's all worked out now."

"Worked out how?"

"I told 'em I wouldn't call the cops about the bike, wouldn't show 'em the cell phone photos our witness took of Duane hiding my bike. And first thing tomorrow, they're gonna pack up the rest of their pitiful-looking trees and be out of our hair once and for all."

"That's great," Kerry said. "But couldn't you have done that without a beatdown?"

"That wasn't a beatdown," Murphy protested. "I just softened those boys up a little, and then they were ready to listen to reason."

He gave her a broad wink. "Really, I think that loud-ass Christmas music of yours is what drove 'em off. I mean, nobody can listen to Mariah Carey scream about all she wants for Christmas *that* many times."

She rolled her eyes and pointed to the six-pack. "What's with the beer?"

He wiped his hand on the seat of his jeans, leaving a bloody streak, then popped the top of one of the three remaining cans. "This here is diplomacy. After we got things settled, I bought us a round. Now it's all good."

Murphy pulled his lawn chair closer to the fire. "You wanna order some takeout from Red Dragon? I'm getting kind of hungry."

They sat by the fire for another couple hours, eating steamed pork buns and wonton soup. They sold four trees, and eventually, Murphy made a show of turning down the volume on the Christmas music.

Kerry made an effort not to look at her phone, but in between customers, and once, when her brother went to Lombardi's for a bathroom break, she sneaked a peek. But there was nothing from Patrick.

At ten, barely able to keep her eyes open, she got to her feet. "That's it for me. See you in the morning."

Murphy looked up from his notebook. "Hey, uh, Kere, you had a hell of a day today. The numbers are really good."

"I know."

"We've only got about thirty trees left. We should easily sell out by the weekend."

"You think?" Selling out would mean leaving the city. And Patrick. And Austin.

"Definitely. Thing is, I kind of promised Claudia I'd take her out Friday night."

"Oh?"

"Like out. On an actual date. Where we go to a restaurant besides Lombardi's."

"Sounds reasonable to me. Claudia's great. Really special."

"Yeah. But it would mean you working my shift that night," Murphy said.

"That's not a problem. I can work a double that day." Kerry looked her brother up and down. "What were you planning to wear on this big date night and where are you going?"

He tugged at his unkempt beard, then looked down at his current attire, which, besides the jeans, included his barn coat, muddy boots, and faded flannel shirt.

"Well, not this, obviously. I'm still figuring out the restaurant part."

"Did you pack any nice clothes at all? Do you even own a pair of shoes that aren't boots?" She shook her head. "Never mind, I already know the answer."

"Claudia knows how I dress. And she must like how I look." He smirked.

"Don't you want to take her out some-place really special? Get dressed up to show her that you care? I really think we're gonna have to buy you some decent new clothes."

"Dammit. I hate new clothes," he muttered.

CHAPTER 37

When she woke up Wednesday, Kerry reached for her phone. A text message from Patrick had come in around midnight, long after she'd fallen asleep.

Meet up for coffee in the morning?

She jumped out of bed and dressed hurriedly, pulling her hair into a ponytail, and it wasn't until she was about to step outside that she noticed Queenie asleep on Murphy's bunk.

"Be right back," she promised, giving the dog a pat on the head. She rushed over to Anna's to use the bathroom, passing Murphy, who was snoring away on the lawn chair near the oil barrel, wrapped in his sleeping bag and a quilt.

She hooked the leash to Queenie's collar. "Come on, girl. Let's go seize the day before the day seizes us."

The dog trotted over to a bush in the pocket park and relieved herself while Kerry texted Patrick back.

Coffee works. Just got up and gonna walk Queenie. Back here in ten.

As she was crossing the street she noticed with grim satisfaction that the Brody brothers' tree stand was no more. The only sign that they'd ever been there was a couple of desiccated Scotch pines and a pile of lumber from the dismantled hut that rested at the curb in front of the deli.

When she returned to the stand, Murphy had retreated to the camper and Taryn Kaplan greeted her. The twins were bundled up in their stroller. "You and Murphy will be heading south pretty soon, right? I bet you'll be glad to be back home, sleeping in your own bed, with real heat and plumbing."

"Um, yeah," Kerry said. She'd spotted Patrick emerging from Anna's with two foam cups and a white bakery bag.

Taryn must have noticed the grin that spread across Kerry's face as Patrick approached.

"But maybe our neighborhood holds other charms, right?"

Kerry blushed. "Something like that."

"Hi, Pat," Taryn called as her neighbor approached. "I heard you guys had quite a scare when Austin went missing the other day."

"We did," Patrick agreed, handing Kerry a coffee and the bakery bag. "But fortunately, Heinz brought him back to us."

"Gretchen must have been beside herself." Taryn looked down and saw that one of the twins had offered Queenie his pacifier, which the dog was now happily licking.

"Oh, Oscar." She took the pacifier and stuck it in the pocket of her jacket. "We better get moving, or we'll miss story time at the library." She looked over at Kerry. "If you want to shower and do some laundry today, be my guest. We won't be back till after lunch."

"I'll definitely take you up on that if there's a lull in business this morning," Kerry promised.

Patrick waited until Taryn and the twins had moved on. He handed her the bakery bag.

"Mmm," Kerry said, nibbling at a still-warm croissant. "You know how to spoil a girl, don't you?"

Patrick sipped his coffee. "I'm wondering if we can have that do-over I owe you. Thinking maybe Friday night? Gretchen and Austin are going upstate to visit family. We could go out, or stay in, and I could cook us a nice dinner. Your choice."

"You cook?"

"Is that so surprising?"

"None of the Tolliver men cook — aside from grilling burgers or smoking a pork butt."

"And you never dated a man who cooks?"

"My last boyfriend could make toast and scrambled eggs and that was it. Actually, his eggs tasted like rubber bands, but he was so proud of his effort I never had the heart to break it to him."

"I worked summers during college at my uncle's restaurant at the Jersey Shore, so yeah, I cook. I do a kick-ass mushroom-stuffed tenderloin. What about it? Dinner in or out?"

"Neither, I'm afraid. I promised my brother I'd cover for him Friday night. He's got big plans with Claudia."

Patrick's face fell so dramatically Kerry was tempted to laugh, but she fought the urge.

"Oh well. Damn."

"Miss?" A man's voice interrupted them. She turned to see an older couple, examining one of the last large trees.

CHAPTER 38

Hunger drove her to Lombardi's for a late lunch. She sat at the bar and chatted with Danny while waiting for her usual to-go order of minestrone.

"Hey, have you seen Heinz today?" she asked, as he polished glasses fresh from the dishwasher.

"Come to think of it, I haven't. Which is weird, because he missed Tuesday night, which is eggplant parm night, and Heinz never, ever misses his eggplant parm. You think he's okay?"

"I hope he is, but I'm starting to get worried. The last time I saw him was Monday night, when he found Austin after he went missing," Kerry said. "He had a terrible cough, and he looked so pale."

"Yeah, he was here for lunch Sunday and I noticed he didn't look so good. I shoulda known something was up when he didn't get the tiramisu. Old guy has a raging sweet tooth."

One of the busboys emerged with a paper bag with her order. "Here ya go," Danny said, handing it over. "Let me know what you find out about Heinz. I'll check around with some of our other regulars, to see if they've seen him."

"I'm guessing he lives in the neighborhood," Kerry said. "Maybe I should stop in and check on him? Do you know if he has family?"

"He's never mentioned family to me. He's a quiet guy. Doesn't talk that much. I assume he lives close by since he's here so often, but I got no clue exactly where. If you see him, let him know I saved him an order of eggplant parm, will ya?"

Murphy was awake and stoking the fire barrel when she returned to the Christmas tree stand. She sat down at her worktable and opened the still-steaming container of soup.

"Smells good," he said, sitting opposite her.

She held out the container. "Want some?"

"Nah. I, uh, listen, Kere, maybe I could use some help with figuring out what to wear Friday night."

She raised an eyebrow. "Oh really?"

"I went through my clothes a little while ago. They're, uh, kind of raggedy."

"Understatement of the year. Look, Murph. You're gonna need a decent pair of slacks, and a shirt, and probably some kind of sport coat."

"A sport coat?" he whined.

"You want my help or not?" she demanded.

He shrugged. "Whatever. Danny hooked me up with reservations at a little French place here in the neighborhood, so we're all set on that end."

"That's great," Kerry said. "Way to show some initiative. Now, are you going shopping, or am I?"

He recoiled as though she'd asked him to stick his hand in the fire. "Oh, hell no. I ain't shopping."

"Okay, fine. I already know your sizes. I've been helping Mom buy you clothes you hate since you were sixteen. But you'll have to buy your own big-boy shoes. Real leather. Think you can do that by yourself?"

"No problem," he said, rolling his eyes. "Just one thing. No pocket squares, and no ties."

Two hours later, Kerry returned to Spammy with a blue-gray Harris tweed sport coat and cashmere scarf from her now favorite vintage clothes dealer, and charcoal-gray slacks and a white dress shirt bought on sale at Bloomingdale's.

She unpacked her shopping bags for Murphy's inspection. He gingerly touched the fabric of the sport coat. "Not terrible," he said.

"Can I make one more teensy suggestion?" she asked.

"Hell no," he retorted. "I got trees to deliver. Mind the store while I'm gone."

As soon as Murphy pedaled the bike back into the stand, she pounced.

"You need a haircut," she said flatly. "The whole 'work up front, party in the back' mullet look is history."

"I was gonna cut my hair before Friday. I even sharpened my scissors."

"I'm talking about a real haircut. Also, your beard needs trimming. You look like a wooly mammoth."

Murphy recoiled in genuine horror. "You want me to let a stranger cut my hair and trim my beard?"

"News flash, big bro. There are professionals who do that for a living. And they don't use pruning shears."

"Nuh-uh. That's a slippery slope. Next thing I know, you'll be wanting me to get a manicure or something. There's no going back after that."

Kerry caught his big paw in hers. The skin was dry and calloused, the nails grimy, the cuticles cracked. "These look like the hands of a serial killer," she said.

He snatched his hand back. "Don't start."

She started anyway. "Get a haircut, dude."

"Fine," he said, with an exaggerated sigh. "I won't like it, but I'll do it."

She handed him a slip of paper with the name and address of the place Patrick had shared with her.

Murphy read it and scowled. "Salon Stephanie? Is this your idea of a joke? I'm not getting a haircut at some beauty parlor."

"It's Salon Stephanè. That's French for Stephen. Patrick gets his hair cut there. You've got an appointment at three Friday, and I prepaid a deposit, so don't even think of being a no-show."

CHAPTER 39

On Thursday, after a mostly sleepless night, Kerry woke up with a sense of dread — cold, gray, damp dread, a reflection of the weather outside the trailer.

Murphy was asleep, facedown in his bunk, but Vic arrived early, eager to make some extra Christmas money. She explained her mission and left him in charge of Queenie and the tree stand, while she set out to look for Heinz.

It had sleeted overnight and partially melted, and within fifteen minutes of sloshing through the melting muck, her shoes were soaked through to the skin.

Her first stop was at a liquor store just down the street. She'd made a sketch of Heinz, and slid it through a slot in the plexiglass window that separated the clerk from the customers.

"Have you seen him lately?"

"Old guy, wears a dusty coat and walks

with a cane? Don't think I seen him lately."

She ducked into the Red Dragon a few doors down. The girl at the counter had pixie-cut hair and bangs dyed bright blue. She studied the sketch. "I think my grandma knows this man. Hang on."

The shop's windows were steamed over with condensation and the place smelled heavenly, like roasting meats, ginger, and garlic.

A moment later, the girl was back with a wizened old woman dressed in a spotless long white apron. She spoke to the woman in what Kerry assumed was Chinese. The woman nodded and answered rapid-fire, finishing with a dramatic miming of coughs.

"She says this is Heinz," the girl translated. "Always gets the number three combo. Grandma says he was here Saturday, and he coughed a lot. She said you should tell him to come back and she will fix him her special broth."

Kerry got more discouraged with each stop. Either people didn't know Heinz, or they recognized him, but hadn't seen him in at least three days. It was sleeting again, and she pulled the hood of her jacket over her damp hair, shivering and imagining Heinz out in this weather.

Three blocks away, she spotted Salon

Stephanè, and an optician's shop, Owl Opticals, and remembered that Heinz had said he encountered Austin after getting his glasses repaired.

The bell on the door jingled to announce her arrival. The front counter was vacant, but soon a middle-aged man in a white lab coat came bustling from the back room. "Help you?"

"Hi," Kerry said. "This is going to maybe sound creepy, but I've been looking for a man I think might be one of your customers. His name is Heinz?" She produced her sketch.

"Heinz Schoenbaum? He was in here just the other day getting his glasses repaired."

Kerry felt a glimmer of hope. Now she even had a last name for her elusive friend. "Yes! He told me he'd been here. But I haven't seen him in a few days, and I'm getting worried."

The optician crossed his arms over his chest. He was tall and thin, with a shiny bald head, and stylish Elton John–inspired glasses with sparkly oversized frames.

"What's this all about?" he asked. "Not to be nosy, but what is Heinz to you?"

"He's a friend. My brother and I run the Christmas tree stand over by the park, and he stops by there every day. Without fail.

Until this week. The last time I saw him, he had a terrible cough, and he seemed really run-down."

"I noticed he seemed under the weather," the optician admitted.

"If I just knew where he lives, I could stop in and see if he's okay," Kerry said, her voice echoing her mounting desperation. "You must have an address for him, right?"

"Sorry, but no way I can share a patient's private information with you."

She'd expected that answer, but plunged ahead. "Do you know if he has family locally? Someone who's looking after him? I swear, I'm not a stalker."

The optician seemed to waver for a moment, but then shook his head. "All I can tell you is that he's never talked about family, but then, Heinz isn't much for idle chitchat."

Kerry felt like crying, and the optician must have sensed her despair. He stepped over to a desktop computer, muttering as he typed. "I could lose my license for this."

"I'll never say a word to anyone," she whispered. "Cross my heart."

"No good. The only address I have for Heinz Schoenbaum is a post office box," he reported, looking up from the computer. "But I *can* tell you he lives in the neighborhood. Once, after I'd dilated his eyes, I tried to call him a cab, but he wouldn't hear of it. Then I asked if I could call someone to walk him home, but he said he lived only a few blocks away."

"Doesn't really narrow it down," Kerry said. "Thanks, anyway." She turned to go.

"Hey, miss," he called out. "Can you let me know if he's okay? Heinz has been a customer here for decades. He was my dad's patient, before he retired."

"I promise I'll let you know," Kerry said.

Murphy and Austin were waiting when she got back to the tree stand.

"Hey, Austin," Kerry said, trying to sound cheerful when she felt anything but. "How's it going?"

"Not so good," Austin said, shaking his head.

"Austin here insisted to his mom that he needed to come down here to wait for Heinz," Murphy said. "So we've just been hanging out, talking about hot cocoa and stuff like that. Austin says marshmallows are excellent with hot chocolate, but I say they're garbage. Nothing but straight-up corn syrup. Nasty stuff. You agree with me, right?"

"I love marshmallows on hot chocolate,"

Kerry said, drawing closer to the fire barrel.

Austin turned puppy dog eyes to her. "Did you see Mr. Heinz?"

"No, buddy," Kerry admitted. "I couldn't find him. Maybe he's staying home, because the weather is so nasty."

"That's what I told him," Murphy said. "Or he went to visit family out of town. After all, it's almost Christmas."

"No way." Austin's chin was stubbornly set. "He wouldn't leave before we finish the story."

His face clouded over. "Maybe something bad happened." He pointed across the street, at the pile of debris where the Brody brothers had been. "Maybe the bad guys got him. Maybe they tied him up and put him in their truck and kidnapped him."

"No, no, no," Murphy said quickly. He squatted down on the pavement until he was at eye level with the boy.

"Me and the brothers patched things up. They told me they took my bike and trailer for kind of a joke. A not-funny joke. But we're cool now. They decided to sell the rest of their trees someplace else. That's all. They wouldn't actually hurt Heinz."

Austin shook his head. "I still think something bad happened. We need to find Mr. Heinz."

Murphy looked at Kerry, and then back at the little boy. "We're trying. Okay?"

Kerry took the child's hand in hers and squeezed it briefly, before releasing it. "You know what I think we should do? I think we should work on the story ourselves. Just you and me. As a surprise for Mr. Heinz." She was freezing and longed to get into dry clothes and out of the cold.

"We could work inside Spammy. At the table. And draw pictures. What do you say?"

"Nuh-uh," Austin said, shoving his mittened hands into his coat pocket.

"Austin?" Gretchen hurried up to the Christmas tree stand. "I'm sure Murphy and Kerry will let us know as soon as they find your friend. But we need to go home now and get ready to leave town in the morning." She reached for her son's hand, but he snatched it away.

"Mom! Noooo," Austin exclaimed. "I have to finish my story. I have to give my present to Mr. Heinz."

"Later," Gretchen said, grasping the boy's shoulders and turning him toward their building. "We have to go home. Right now."

"Nooooo," Austin wailed. He looked up at Kerry, his expression pleading. "Tell her. Tell her I have to stay."

"Enough!" Gretchen said sharply. "Do

you want me to tell Santa that you're misbe-having?"

"I don't care. I hate Santa Claus!" Austin exploded, windmilling at his mother with mittened fists. "And I hate you."

"Hey, now!" Murphy said sternly.

The child turned his tear-streaked face to Kerry's brother. "Tell her, Murphy. Tell her I need to stay here with you. And Kerry."

"You can't," Kerry said softly, feeling as though her heart were being ripped out of her chest. "Murphy and I have work to do now, so you need to do what your mom says. And as soon as we find Heinz, we'll let you know."

"Come on," Gretchen said, her voice softening. She leaned down and hefted the boy onto her hip. "We're going home now."

Brother and sister watched as Gretchen made her way back toward her building, with Austin sobbing and howling in protest. Murphy glanced over at Kerry. "Somehow, we gotta find that old man."

CHAPTER 40

Murphy visited the bodega and returned with beer and a bag of popcorn. Kerry helped herself to a handful of popcorn. "Don't tell me this's dinner."

"No, this is our starter course. The main course is being delivered. Pizza. No anchovies, since you hate them, and because I'm such a sweetheart of a brother."

Murphy threw more logs on the fire and sipped his beer. "You know, if we keep selling trees at this rate, I'm thinking we pack it up and head home on Saturday."

"Saturday?" Kerry nearly choked on a slice of pepperoni. "Why so early?"

"Why not? We'll easily sell out before then. What's the matter? You getting used to camping out in the cold, listening to me snore and peeing in strangers' houses?"

She leaned back in her rickety lawn chair and took in her surroundings. Their remaining trees were wrapped in twinkle lights, the shop windows were decorated for Christmas, and lights shone softly from the apartment buildings up and down the street. The temperature was below freezing, her feet were wet, and she was wrapped in a Big Bird sleeping bag that probably hadn't been washed since her kindergarten days, but even with the nagging worry about Heinz's welfare, somehow, a warm glow had settled over her. It dawned on her that in less than a month, these few crowded city blocks had become her home and these strangers now felt like neighbors.

And one of those neighbors was . . . something more.

"Kere?" Murphy was leaning forward, waiting for her reaction. "Look, if you're still worried about Heinz, don't be. We'll find him tomorrow. I promise."

"Okay," Kerry said, nodding. "I believe you."

The next day Kerry expanded her search by a couple blocks in each direction, only occasionally encountering someone who recognized Heinz. Unfortunately, none of them had seen him in recent days or knew where he lived.

Dejected, she trudged back to the stand, where she found Vic beaming with pride.

"I sold three trees, all at full price, including that last big tree some lady paid eight hundred bucks for," Vic said. He dug in the pocket of his jacket and brought out a thick roll of bills.

"Good work," Kerry said. "I'm gonna go grab some lunch. Do the trees need to be delivered?"

"Yeah, but I thought I'd wait until this afternoon."

"No, go ahead and load 'em onto the bike trailer. Let's get them delivered now, in case the weather turns nastier later."

"You want to leave the stand unattended?" Vic looked puzzled.

"Just for an hour or so," Kerry said. She stretched the bungee cord across the entryway and hung the CLOSED sign from it. "Go on. Scoot."

When she got back to the stand, Murphy was awake, showered, and officially annoyed.

"Where were you? And where's Vic? It's our last day here. We should have had all hands on deck, selling these last trees."

"Vic is delivering an eight-hundred-dollar tree he sold at full price," Kerry said. "I think we can afford to take a forty-five-minute lunch break."

"I told him to mark all the trees half off," Murphy said.

"And I told him we'll sell them at full price. You're the one who's been laying it on thick about how we need to make enough money on this trip to get the farm out of the red."

"We more than made our goal. You did great, Kerry. But our selling season is over. I don't wanna have to load up these last few trees tomorrow and haul 'em back home."

Kerry dug her hands in her jacket pockets to keep from smacking her brother in the nose. She had no intention of telling Murphy she wasn't ready to leave the city — and Patrick — yet. A lifetime of experience with the men of the Tolliver family had taught her that the best way to deal with them was passive resistance.

Instead she favored him with a sweet smile. "Don't you have a hair appointment to get to?"

Patrick dropped by shortly before five. The temperature had continued to drop, and she'd bundled herself in virtually every warm article of clothing she owned.

"Any news about Heinz?" he asked, dropping a casual kiss on her cheek that warmed Kerry from the inside out.

"None. I've asked everywhere. Nobody's seen him, and nobody can tell me where he lives. Should I maybe file a missing person report? Or call hospitals around here?"

"You could try," Patrick said. "But since you're not family, and the only thing we can tell anyone is his name, I doubt the police would take you seriously. Give it another day."

"I may not have another day," Kerry said, feeling even more dejected. "Murphy is dead set on heading for home tomorrow."

"But Christmas isn't until Monday. I thought . . . I mean, I hoped, you and I would have a couple more days to spend together."

"Me too. I've been doing everything I can to sabotage his plan, but if you know Murphy, you know once he gets his mind set on something, neither hell nor high water will stop him."

Patrick kicked at the fire barrel with the toe of his boot. "Just because Murphy's leaving tomorrow, that doesn't mean you have to. Right?"

She pointed at Spammy. "Even if I wanted to, I can't just keep camping out here, with no plumbing and no kitchen. For one thing, your neighborhood association won't let me. So yeah, I guess that means I'll be heading home too."

Patrick took a deep breath. "You said *if* you wanted to — do you? Do you want to stay here in the city? Or are you dead set on going back home to North Carolina?"

Kerry felt her cheeks go hot. Leaving here, going back to the small town where she'd always felt like an outsider, was the last thing she wanted. But what other options did she have?

Before she could try to answer Patrick's question, her brother pedaled up on his bike. At least, she thought it was Murphy.

CHAPTER 41

Murphy Tolliver was almost unrecognizable. The mullet was gone. His dark, unruly hair had been tamed, conditioned, and styled — combed back in waves from his broad forehead, with sharply razored sideburns. The bushy mountain-man beard was neatly trimmed, and for the first time since she could remember, Kerry could actually see the lower half of her brother's face, which, she had to admit, was pretty damn handsome. Without a droopy mustache obscuring his mouth, Murphy's broad smile was surprisingly warm. The resemblance to their father, down to his clear blue eyes and the touches of silver at his temples, was remarkable.

His ruddy, weather-beaten skin was now smooth, even glowing. Kerry couldn't help herself. She reached out and touched his face. "Bro? What all did they do to you at that salon?"

He batted her hand away. "After the guy cut my hair and trimmed my beard and my freaking eyebrows, they made me go into another room where they had candles burning and tinkly music playing and some lady dressed like a doctor came in and worked me over."

"That must have been Ninette," said Patrick. "She's the best esthetician in the city."

"She rubbed some kind of flowery-smelling lotion all over my cheeks and my forehead, and before I could stop her, she took kind of a belt sander to me. I dog-cussed her and told her I wasn't paying to have all the skin on my face blasted off, but she just laughed and said it was part of what she called 'the Salon Stephanè experience,' and I should just sit back and enjoy. Then she put a hot towel over my face, and I guess I must've dozed off, because the next thing I knew, she was shaking me awake and telling me it was time to pay up and go."

"Whatever they did, and whatever it cost, it was worth it," Kerry assured him. "You've been completely transformed. It's like 'My Fair Laddie.' "

"Shut up," Murphy growled, looking secretly pleased with himself. He glanced around the stand and abruptly changed the subject. "Doesn't look like you sold too many more trees while I was gone."

"It got super cold," Kerry protested. "And tomorrow's Saturday. According to your notebook, that should be our last, busiest day. Why not have a sell-out and then plan to leave Sunday? It'd be a Christmas gift to Dad."

"We leave tomorrow," Murphy said firmly. He chained and locked his bike to the light pole. "I gotta get dressed for dinner. In the meantime, if you want to give Dad a great Christmas gift, get busy and sell the rest of these trees tonight. I've got Vic lined up to help me knock down the stand first thing in the morning."

Patrick threw a couple logs on the fire. "So that's it? You're leaving town two days before Christmas? Austin is already upset about Heinz. He's going to be heartbroken when he finds out you're going home."

"What about Austin's dad?" Kerry asked softly.

Patrick gazed directly into her eyes. "Same. Only more so." He took her hand in his. "Is it selfish of me to ask you not to go?"

She let out a long sigh. "Be practical. What's here for me in the city?"

Instead of answering her question, he posed one of his own. "What's waiting for you back in North Carolina? You don't have a job, you've been living with your mom. I get that family ties mean a lot to you, but maybe those ties are more like that chain on Murphy's bike?"

"Are you suggesting I should up and move here? And live where? Patrick, it's sweet that you want me to stay, but do you know what graphic artists earn? I can't afford to live in New York." She gestured around at the manicured park and the distinguished-looking brownstones surrounding it. "Not this New York, anyway."

"Don't undersell yourself," Patrick said stubbornly. "I've seen your work, Kerry. You're an amazing creative force."

"Miss?" a woman's voice called out. Kerry turned to see the night cashier at Happy Days, the bodega across the street. She was hatless and wearing a lightweight jacket, blue jeans, and threadbare sneakers and was accompanied by a little girl of maybe four or five. The child wore jeans, a too-small pink puffy jacket, and Mary Jane shoes that had long ago lost most of their pink sparkle coating. She had a halo of tightly wrapped braids, each fastened with a tiny pink bead. The woman was pointing to the last tabletop tree in the stand.

"Is this the right price? Forty dollars for real?" Her accent had a lilting patois, maybe from the West Indies.

The little girl's dark eyes glowed with excitement as she touched the twinkling lights.

"Uh, no," Kerry said hastily. "I made a mistake. It should say twenty dollars."

"Oh." The woman's shoulders drooped. She looked down at the little girl. "We can't get this tree, baby. It's probably too big anyhow."

The child looked away, then nodded sadly. Apparently she was used to being told no.

Kerry did some quick backpedaling. "Actually, all these trees are marked on clearance tonight, because we have to leave tomorrow. So that tree would be two dollars."

The woman looked dubious, but she dug in the pocket of her coat and brought out a couple of crumpled dollar bills. "Two dollars? Is that right?"

The little girl tugged at the older woman's hand and stood on her tiptoes to whisper in her ear.

"My granddaughter wants to know how much for the lights."

"The lights are included," Kerry said.

"Tell the lady thank you, Babydoll," her grandmother prompted.

"Thank you, ma'am," the child whispered.

"You're very, very welcome," Kerry said.

They loaded the lit tree in a plastic trash bag, which the grandmother hefted over her shoulder. As they walked away, Babydoll turned and gave a shy wave.

"Merry Christmas," Kerry called.

She was struck by the mixed emotions she was experiencing. She was elated at being able to essentially give away a tree to a little girl and her grandmother. But one less tree meant they were that much closer to selling out — and closing the stand to head home.

When she turned around to explain her feelings to Patrick, she discovered he'd vanished. She glanced up and down the street, even checked inside Spammy, but he was gone. Just then, her phone dinged to signal an incoming text.

Didn't mean to ghost you. Gretchen called and Austin's sick. I'm going to meet her at Grand Central and bring him back to the apartment.

Kerry's fingers flew over her phone's keyboard.

Hope it's nothing serious.

His reply came a moment later.

Just a tummyache. I'll call you later and we can continue our convo. Stay warm.

She pulled up the collar of her coat and tugged down on the brim of her knit cap. It was going to be a long, cold night.

The trailer door opened and Murphy stepped out, dressed in his new finery.

"Well?"

Kerry gave a long, low wolf whistle, and her brother blushed.

"I feel weird. Like I'm walking around in someone else's skin." He tugged at the scarf around his neck.

"You look like a big, gorgeous stud-muffin," Kerry told him. "Claudia is the luckiest woman in New York tonight."

"I'm counting on me being the luckiest guy in the city tonight," her brother countered as he stood, looking across at Lombardi's.

CHAPTER 42

The first fat fluffy flakes of snow landed lightly on Kerry's eyelashes at precisely 10:05 on what had been an interminably long, cold, lonely night.

She'd sold three more trees for a combined total of sixty-three dollars — the odd number caused by her latest customer, a half-drunk college kid who swore he only had three bucks in cash and a Metro-Card on him. She'd handed over the tree, along with a candy cane, and he'd given her a boozy hug before strolling away, dragging a hundred-dollar tree behind him on the icy pavement.

At ten thirty, she texted Patrick.

How's the patient?

She stared down at the phone, watching the tiny text bubbles.

Sleeping, finally. Can you come up?

Could she? Kerry looked around. Four lonesome trees leaned against the railings of the Christmas tree stand. The snow was falling faster now and people spilled out of neighboring bars and restaurants, laughing and chattering in the chilly night air.

She whistled for Queenie, who, clever girl that she was, had burrowed into a couple of moving blankets beneath the worktable. The dog poked her nose out and looked at Kerry.

"Come on. Let's put you up for a while." Kerry led Queenie into the trailer, where she happily leapt atop Murphy's bunk before curling up on his pillow. Then Kerry closed and locked the trailer door.

Outside, she pulled the bungee cord across the entrance to the tree stand, hanging the CLOSED sign. She started to walk away, then changed her mind.

She took down the hand-painted price list, crossing through it with a bold red marker, writing across it in large letters:

FREE TREES! MERRY CHRISTMAS
FROM THE TOLLIVER FAMILY.

Patrick buzzed her into the lobby and met her in the hallway outside the apartment.

"Come on in." He gestured toward the

open door, and kissed her as she walked past.

"I'm so glad you texted," she whispered, as she tiptoed into the apartment. "I was freezing and dying of boredom down there."

"No need to whisper," he told her. "Austin is passed out in his room. A herd of elephants couldn't wake that kid when he's sick."

As Kerry stood looking out the window, watching the snow drift past, Patrick slid an arm around her waist and kissed her neck. "Can I get you a glass of wine?"

"That would be nice," she said, looking down at the street below. She saw a young couple holding hands, running gleefully into the Christmas tree stand, clapping their hands as they read the sign she'd left behind. The woman pointed at the largest of the remaining trees, one that had been priced at three hundred dollars a few hours earlier, and the man wrestled it out of the stand and began dragging it toward the sidewalk.

Patrick was back, handing her a wineglass. "Hey! They're stealing your trees. Want me to go down there and stop them?"

"They're not stealing. I'm giving them away."

"Why?"

"Why not? It's almost Christmas. Whether I leave tomorrow or the day after tomorrow, what's the difference?"

He touched her chin, swiveling her face until hers was inches from his.

"It makes a difference to me. I need more time with you. I'll take whatever I can get."

"Another reason to close down the stand and give away the rest of the trees. Instead of standing down there, miserable and cold, I can be up here with you, warm and —"

He was kissing her now, and she leaned into him, wrapping her arms around his neck.

"Dad?" A small, very familiar voice floated across the room. They both froze.

Austin stood in the doorway from the hall. His hair was mussed. He was dressed in rumpled red-and-green footie pajamas and clutched a stuffed dragon under his arm.

"Hi, Kerry," he said, yawning widely. "What are you doing here?"

She edged away from Patrick's embrace. "I wanted to check on you. How are you feeling?"

"I'm okay. My stomach hurted, but Dad gave me ginger ale and crackers, and now I'm all better."

"That's great news," Kerry said.

Austin pointed out the window, at the

snowflakes floating past.

"It's really, really snowing." He frowned. "Where's Queenie? Won't she be cold?"

Kerry laughed. "She's inside Spammy, snuggled up on Murphy's bunk."

He turned large, sorrowful eyes back to her. "Did you find Mr. Heinz yet?"

Patrick placed a hand on his son's shoulder. "We talked about this, Austin. Mr. Heinz is probably just staying home, because he has a cold, just like you had to stay inside today, because you had a stomachache."

Austin shook his head vehemently. "But I had you to take care of me. He doesn't have anybody. Tell him, Kerry. Tell him we need to find Mr. Heinz."

Kerry knelt down on the floor. "We tried, I promise. I looked, and Murphy looked, and we talked to a lot of the neighbors, but nobody knows where he lives. I bet, as soon as he feels better, you'll see Mr. Heinz walking around the neighborhood again, just like he always does."

Austin's gaze turned back to the window. "We should go look for him right now. We could ask all our neighbors. We could put up signs with Mr. Heinz's picture on them, like the Westons did when Dexter ran away. Remember? Someone saw the sign and they found Dexter hiding behind some trash cans in the alley, and he came home. Remember, Dad?"

"A stray cat isn't the same as a grown-up who can take care of himself," Patrick said. "We can't knock on people's doors this late. And we definitely aren't leaving this apartment tonight, especially since you're sick."

"I'm not sick!" Austin exclaimed, stomping his foot. "I just pretended. So mom wouldn't make me go with her. So I could stay here with you. And Kerry, and help you find Mr. Heinz."

"Austin?" Patrick's tone was stern. "What do you mean you pretended to be sick? Your mom said you were barfing. She saw you."

"Because I drank my chocolate milk really fast, then stuck my finger down my throat," Austin said proudly. "I faked her out."

"You lied to your mom? And me? Made us worry that you were sick when you really weren't? That isn't honest and it isn't right, and you know better."

"But Dad . . ."

Patrick pointed to the hallway. "Back to bed, young man. Right now. And in the morning, we're calling your mom and you're going to apologize for lying to her."

Austin's upper lip trembled and his eyes filled with tears. He shuffled slowly toward

his room, his stuffed toy dragging on the
floor.

CHAPTER 43

"Poor kid," Kerry murmured.

Patrick flopped down on the sofa and patted the cushion next to his. "Poor kid, nothing," he fumed. "I hate he played us like that."

Kerry sat down beside him. "I used to pull stunts like that when my folks split up. I guess it gave me a sense of power to manipulate them when everything else in my world seemed to have fallen apart."

Patrick picked up a remote control, clicked it, and flames magically appeared in the fireplace. He sipped his wine. "This is just so unlike Austin. He's usually a really honest kid."

"Well, he's worried about his friend. I love his empathy and sense of loyalty." Kerry took Patrick's hand in hers. "You and Gretchen are doing a great job navigating a divorce. I know firsthand how tough it can be on a family, so I really admire how you two have worked to keep from disrupting Austin's life."

"You seem to have survived coming from a broken home just fine," Patrick said, stroking her hair.

"Appearances can be deceiving," she admitted. "I love my dad, but looking back now, as an adult, on how he cheated on my mom, and seemed to have so little regret about splitting up our family, it's still hard for me to respect him. My mom, on the other hand, doesn't hold a grudge. She says that's just how he is. She's back at his place now, taking care of the old coot herself, because wife number three, who's younger than me, decided she wasn't cut out to be a nursemaid. Their relationship now is way better than it was when Murphy and I were kids."

"I think we're figuring things out a day at a time. Gretchen is apparently seeing someone seriously. Me? The divorce was final a year ago, but I still haven't had a real relationship with a woman. Until now."

Kerry chortled. "A hottie like you? I find that hard to believe."

"I'm not saying I haven't gone out. I tried the dating apps. Lots of first and second dates. But nothing clicked. Until now."

He held her face between the palms of his

hands. "I can't believe you really intend to leave tomorrow. Just when I've found you."

"Don't talk about it," Kerry begged. "It's too depressing."

"I won't." He pulled her onto his lap and kissed her, running his hands beneath her sweater, her T-shirt, and her thermal underwear top, finally finding and unfastening her bra. "No more talking."

She looked uneasily toward the hallway. "Um, is this a good idea?"

He was busy pulling her sweater over her head. "Best idea I've had all year."

Kerry chuckled but captured his hands in hers. "Are you forgetting something? Your six-year-old was standing right here ten minutes ago."

"I'm sure Austin is exhausted from faking his parents out. Fast asleep with visions of sugarplums and all that." He pushed her hands away and resumed his quest to undress her.

She giggled but eased herself off his lap, pulled her sweater back into place, and gave him a chaste kiss. "Hope this doesn't make me sound too slutty, but I want this as badly as you do, Patrick. What I *don't* want is to scar your kid for life by having him catch the nice Christmas tree lady naked with his daddy."

"Noooo," Patrick groaned. "Our last night together and you expect me to spend it, doing what? Toasting marshmallows on an open fire?"

"That's *roasting chestnuts* on an open fire," she corrected him. "Let's just make the most of the time we do have together, okay? Enjoy the fire, cuddle, listen to some Christmas music? Or watch a movie?"

"Let's compromise," he suggested. "I say we watch a movie in front of the fire *and* cuddle, only naked? I'll even let you pick the movie. I'm assuming your idea of a heartwarming Christmas flick is *Die Hard*?"

She raised an eyebrow and held out her empty glass. "Okay, you get to choose the movie, but I'm keeping my clothes on. More wine, please."

They stretched out the length of the sofa and settled in to watch Bruce Willis battle Hans Gruber and his band of terrorists. Kerry had never felt so content, so absolutely at home, as she did, enfolded in his arms. Of course, Patrick didn't keep his hands, or his lips, entirely to himself, but with a plaid wool blanket thrown over them, she wasn't overly worried about traumatizing Austin should he wander into the room. As soon as Hans Gruber was history and

Nakatomi Plaza was little more than a smoldering ruin, Kerry stretched and yawned. Patrick stood up. "Think I'll go check on Austin," he said, a little too casually.

Kerry stood too. "Can I ask for a favor?"

He wrapped his arms around her and kissed her neck. "Depends on what it is."

"I'd give anything for a long, hot shower before I have to leave. It's been two days and I've got a long drive ahead of me tomorrow."

"Deal. But only if I get to join you."

"Patrick . . ."

"We'll lock the bathroom door," he promised. He pulled down the waistband of his jeans, showing off the pattern of red and green reindeer. "See? Just for you."

When the hot water finally gave out and they were both pink and after-glowing, Patrick went to check on his son while Kerry got dressed. She tiptoed out of the bathroom and found him in the hallway, standing outside Austin's closed bedroom door.

"And to all a good night," he said. "This time, there's no faking it. He's fast asleep." Patrick caught her hand in his and led her to the darkened living room and the bank of windows. "Look at it out there."

What Kerry saw was a curtain of white. The outsides of the windowpanes were rimmed with ice, and below, in the park, the trees, cars, and even Spammy were covered in a thick blanket of snow. The multicolored lights shone through the snow shower. She shivered despite the layers of clothing she was wearing.

"I think you need to stay," he said. "It'll be totally innocent. I'll sleep on the sofa, you can have the bed, and in the morning, we'll explain to Austin that the weather was too nasty for you to leave."

"You sound like that pervvy old Christmas song, 'Baby It's Cold Outside,' " Kerry said. "I wish I could stay, but I can't. Queenie will need a walk, and Murphy has been very clear that we need to break down the stand and hit the road first thing in the morning."

"I'm not just talking about tomorrow," Patrick said. "Can we sit by the fire and talk before you rush off into a blizzard?"

"Just for a minute," Kerry conceded. She'd checked her phone. It was after one. She followed him to the fireplace and sat down on the sofa.

"We never finished discussing your long-term plans," Patrick said. "I know you're not looking forward to going back to North

Carolina, to moving in with your mom again. I'm not trying to put words in your mouth — or maybe I am, but it sounds to me like you were feeling stuck back there. And being here, in New York, could be a way to get unstuck. Creatively, and personally. And yeah, if you were here, I'd like to think we could be together."

"You're right, on all counts. But I have to be realistic. Even if my freelance career was flourishing, which it's not, let me remind you again, I can't afford to live in this city. Or anywhere near it."

"You could live with me," Patrick said. "My studio's not very big, but it's workable. And we'd be together."

"No thanks," she said firmly. "I appreciate the offer, but I won't move from sponging off my mom to sponging off you. Besides," she said, lightly touching his chin. "You've known me for less than a month. We haven't even had a real date yet. How do you know I'm not a psychopathic killer? Don't you think moving in together is a pretty big step?"

He shook his head stubbornly, and she saw where Austin got his obstinate streak. "Doesn't matter how long we've known each other. When it's right, it's right. We're good together. And I believe in you, Kerry, and in your talent. You can totally make a living with your art . . ."

She let out a long sigh. "This is a lot for me to think about."

"Yeah. It's called adulting. So what do you say?"

She jumped up from the sofa, grabbed her coat, and headed for the door. "I gotta go. Poor Queenie needs to be let out to pee. It's late . . ."

"Are you running away from me now?" Patrick asked.

"I . . . I . . . I'll call you in the morning," Kerry stammered, and she fled the apartment, as though she were being chased by Hans Gruber himself.

CHAPTER 44

"Kerry! Kerry!" Someone was pounding on the camper door. "Hey! Unlock the door!"

It was Murphy. She sat up, and Queenie, who'd burrowed under the covers beside her sometime during the night, gave a brief yelp of protest.

The temperature inside the trailer was like a deep freezer. Colder, if possible, than it had been when she'd returned there just a few hours earlier. She switched the tiny light sconce by her bunk, but nothing happened. She glanced at the woefully inadequate space heater she'd turned on the night before; it wasn't functioning. The power was off.

"Come on, Kere. I'm freezing. There must be a foot of snow out here."

She wrapped a sleeping bag around her shoulders and pulled on the door handle, but it didn't budge. She jiggled it furiously.

"I think the lock is frozen," she called.

"Well, unfreeze it. Use your hair dryer or something."

"Can't. I think the power's off. That's why the lock is frozen."

"Okay, now I see the issue. The extension cord was so loaded down with ice it broke. Dammit," Murphy muttered. "Be right back."

"Hurry," she called. "Queenie and I need to pee."

Ten minutes later, he was back. She heard a clicking noise and a moment later, the door opened as shards of ice fell to the ground.

Murphy held up a small butane lighter and offered a grim smile. "Come on out. Vic should be here soon. I'm gonna change, then I'll walk Queenie and we'll get ready to roll."

He climbed into the trailer and quickly started to strip out of his date-night finery. "Be careful. The sidewalk's like a skating rink. And bring me back some coffee."

She raced, breathless, into the bodega, and saw that the clerk was the grandmother to whom she'd sold the two-dollar Christmas tree. "Can I please use your bathroom?"

The woman smiled and pointed to a door

307

on the opposite wall, marked PRIVATE, KEEP OUT.

"Thanks," Kerry said, when she emerged. "Two large coffees, please."

The woman fixed her order and smiled as she handed them over. "On the house. From me and Babydoll."

When she got back to the trailer, Murphy was squatted down on the pavement next to Jock's truck. He stood up and wiped his hands on the back of his jeans. "Those sons of bitches. They slashed all four tires. On Spammy too."

"You think it was the brothers?" Kerry hadn't looked at the truck in at least two days, since the last time Murphy had moved it.

"Who else?"

"What do we do now?"

"I'll get new tires for Dad's truck, but it ain't worth spending the money on Spammy. At this point, just about the only thing holding her together is duct tape and prayers. Guess I'll have her hauled off to sell for scrap. In the meantime, Claudia just called. She's watching the Weather Channel, says the roads are iced over bad. No way we can leave today, even if the tires were okay. You can't be towing a trailer in these kinds of weather conditions."

Kerry didn't know whether to cheer or cry.

Murphy must have read her mind. "Looks like you get your wish. We stay another day. Claudia wants to fix us breakfast at her place. You in?"

Kerry's stomach rumbled on cue. "All the way in."

As they scurried across the street Kerry shot a sidelong glance at her brother. "How was last night?" And then she couldn't resist. "And this morning?"

His answer was a typical grunt. "Good."

"What did Claudia say about all your manscaping? And the new wardrobe? Did she approve?"

He shrugged. "She didn't have any complaints."

And that, she knew, was about as much as she would get from her uncommunicative big brother.

Claudia's apartment was in the same building as the restaurant, two floors up.

Her nest was small but undeniably feminine with pale Tiffany-blue walls, a rose velvet sofa, and floral chintz curtains at the windows overlooking the park. Bookshelves stuffed with romance novels, historical fiction, and cookbooks flanked the windows, and silver-framed family photos covered every flat surface. Murphy's head almost brushed the low ceiling, and he looked distinctly out of place as he ushered Queenie inside.

"Sorry, but we couldn't leave her in the trailer," he said, gesturing at the setter.

"It's okay. I locked the cat in my bedroom," Claudia said, waving them into the tiny kitchen, where they were greeted with the scent of bacon and frying onions. She was dressed in a blue velour tracksuit, and as always, her hair and makeup were freshly done. She'd set plates at a table in an alcove with bay windows. She glanced over at Kerry. "Wanna invite Patrick to join us? There's more than enough."

Kerry hesitated. "I guess I could ask."

She retreated to the living room and stared at her phone for a moment. She wanted to see him again, desperately, but hated the way she'd run out on him the night before. She was a loser, a chicken-shit, a coward, and worse. It would serve her right if he ghosted her the way she'd ghosted him.

He answered on the first ring. "Kerry? Where are you? I'm looking down at the tree stand from my window, but it doesn't look like anybody's around."

Kerry told him about the slashed tires and the bad roads and the resulting change of plans. "Claudia wants to know if you'd like to join us for breakfast at her place. And Austin too, of course."

There was a long pause at the other end of the line. "Is that what you want? After last night, I got the impression that you'd just as soon make a clean break and blow town."

She winced. "Guess I deserve that. Yes, I'd love it if you and Austin could come over for breakfast, and no, I don't want a clean break. I can't tell you what I do want. Because I'm that screwed up."

The five of them sat elbow-to-elbow around the breakfast table, passing platters of omelets, home fries, bacon, and slices of thick-sliced grilled country bread. The grown-ups had Bloody Marys, and Austin had coffee with milk.

"Miss Claudia," Austin said, heaping strawberry jam onto his toast, "can I come to your house for breakfast every day?"

Claudia winked at the child. "Well, honey, I mostly just have coffee in the morning, but the next time I do cook breakfast, I'll be sure and invite you over."

"Cool." Austin took a gulp of milk, then

turned to Patrick. "Since it's morning now, can we start putting up posters and knocking on doors? We gotta find Mr. Heinz."

Murphy raised an eyebrow. "Posters?"

"Austin wants to have posters made of the sketch Kerry made of Heinz," Patrick explained. "Since we don't know where he lives, he'd also like us to do a door-to-door canvass. I've tried to explain why that's not practical . . ."

The boy pulled a sheet of folded paper from his pocket and smoothed it out on the tabletop. Kerry stared, as she hadn't realized he had the sketch.

"Can I borrow a pen?" he asked their hostess.

"Yes, of course." Claudia turned to a small hutch behind her, opened a drawer, and brought out a pen.

Austin gave her a nod of thanks, then looked at Kerry. "How do you spell Heinz?"

"H-E-I-N-Z," Kerry said. The child laboriously penned the name in large block letters.

"I forget what you said his last name is," Austin said.

"I'm not really sure of the spelling, but I think it's S-C-H-O-E-N-B-A-U-M," Kerry said.

"Schoenbaum?" Claudia said, tilting her

head. "How did you figure that out?"

"The short version is, his optometrist recognized him from my description, and he told me Heinz's last name," Kerry answered.

Claudia stood up abruptly and left the room. When she came back, she had a file folder in hand. She extracted a piece of paper and handed it to Kerry. "This is our lease for the restaurant. And this apartment."

Kerry skimmed the document and looked up. "Schoenbaum Holdings. You think Heinz maybe owns this building?"

She shrugged. "It's not a common name. My granddad signed the original lease. I've never known who Schoenbaum is. If we have issues, we deal with Rex, the building manager, or Carlos, the superintendent."

"Does the lease have a mailing address?" Patrick asked, peering over Kerry's shoulder.

She shook her head. "Just a post office box. The optometrist did tell me the address he had for Heinz is a PO box."

Austin looked from his father to Kerry to Claudia. "Does this mean you know where Mr. Heinz lives?"

"Not necessarily," Patrick said.

Kerry was still looking at the lease. "Claudia, do you think the building manager could tell us where Schoenbaum Holdings is located?"

Claudia snorted. "Rex won't give us the time of day. He's a paper shuffler. But Carlos might know something."

"Can you ask him if he knows Mr. Heinz?" Austin asked. "Please?"

"Carlos isn't big on chitchat, but I'll call down and see if he'll come check on my kitchen sink, which is draining really slow," Claudia said. "And I'll bribe him with food. His wife doesn't really cook."

The building superintendent wore zip-front coveralls and a wary expression. Claudia showed him the sink, he poured drain cleaner in, and the problem was fixed. "Anything else?"

"Let me fix you a plate of food, since you're here," Claudia said, heaping eggs and bacon and toast onto a plate. "Coffee?"

Carlos looked at the group seated around the table. "I'm supposed to be on the clock."

"Understood," Claudia said, pouring him a mug and handing it to him. She pointed to her vacant chair. "Here, take a seat while you eat."

"Just for a minute," he said. He sat down, grabbed a shaker, and liberally coated the food with pepper before starting to enthusiastically shovel it into his face.

"Say, Carlos," Claudia said with a deliberately casual tone. "Do you know anyone from Schoenbaum Holdings?"

"The company that signs my paychecks? No. I just know they clear every week."

"Do you know if the owner's name is Heinz?"

Carlos speared a piece of bacon and chewed. "Like the ketchup?"

"Like this guy," Austin said, waving Kerry's drawing at the superintendent. "Mr. Heinz."

"Him?" Carlos took the sketch and studied it. "Yeah, sure, him I know."

"How do you know him?" Kerry asked eagerly.

"Old guy lives here. According to Rex, he's got a sweet apartment on the top floor, but he don't stay there. He stays in the basement. So, no way that guy owns this whole building."

"Can you take us to see him?" Austin asked. "Right now? Can you take us to see Mr. Heinz?"

"I don't know . . ." Carlos picked up his toast and dunked it in the mug of coffee. "He's a pretty private old guy. Never seen anybody coming or going from his place.

315

Don't think he'd appreciate some strangers showing up at his door."

"We're not strangers. We're his friends," Austin said indignantly.

"We're worried he might be really sick," Kerry explained. "Up until this past week, he came around our Christmas tree stand every day. And the last time we saw him he had a terrible cough and didn't seem himself."

"I don't know . . ." Carlos looked over at Claudia. "I could get in big trouble with Rex . . . It's kind of an invasion of privacy, isn't it?"

"You leave Rex to me," Claudia said briskly. "And you can look for something extra in your Christmas envelope this year. Now let's go."

CHAPTER 45

Carlos led the group — Kerry, Austin, and Patrick — down to the building's basement.
When the freight elevator doors opened and they stepped out, Austin was wide-eyed, taking in the dimly lit basement's cinderblock walls and cracked concrete flooring, low ceilings crisscrossed with innumerable exposed plumbing pipes and electrical wires, and the huge boiler hunkered in a far corner of the space.

"How come Mr. Heinz lives in a dungeon?" he whispered, clutching both Patrick and Kerry's hands.

"Don't know, buddy," Patrick said. "But you know, it might not even be him."

"It's gotta be him," Austin insisted as they picked their way past the clutter of paint cans, building supplies, and discarded plumbing fixtures.

"Over here," Carlos said, pointing to a door on the other side of a caged tenant storage area.

"I could lose my job if this gets back to my boss," Carlos fretted. "If anybody asks, you came down here on your own. I had nothing to do with it, right?"

"Absolutely," Kerry said. "And thanks."

She glanced uneasily over at Patrick and took a deep breath. "What now?"

But Austin had no such hesitation. He ineffectively pounded the heavy steel door with his fists. "Mr. Heinz? Are you at home, Mr. Heinz? It's me, Austin. And Kerry and my dad are here too. Can we come in and see you, Mr. Heinz?"

The boiler in the corner hissed and groaned, but the basement was otherwise silent.

"Maybe we should come back later," Kerry said.

"Nooooo," Austin howled.

"Let me try." Patrick looked around and found a short length of iron pipe. When he banged on the door the clanging echoed through the basement. "Heinz?" he called. "Are you there, Heinz? It's Patrick and Kerry. Are you all right?"

Kerry pressed her ear to the door. She heard a faint, almost inaudible wheezing sound.

"Heinz?" she shouted.

She put her ear to the door.

"Go away." The old man's voice was so weak she could barely make out the words. "I'm sick, and I don't want you to get sick."

Alarmed, she tried the knob. It turned easily. "We're coming in," she called, opening the door a fraction of an inch. "Just a welfare check."

"No, don't. Just leave me be."

"I'm sorry, but we can't do that," Kerry replied, opening the door wider.

It took a moment for her eyes to adjust to the darkness, but gradually the room came into focus. It was small and chilly, sparsely furnished, and smelled of damp and sickness.

Heinz was sitting in a chair near a tiny window that had been painted over. He seemed to have shrunk just since the last time she'd seen him. He was dressed in a tattered flannel bathrobe, his eyes sunken into his face, pale except for his cheeks, which were a bright scarlet. He held a crumpled handkerchief to his lips.

Austin approached his friend without trepidation. "Mr. Heinz, you don't look so good," the child said.

"Go . . . away," Heinz said feebly, waving his hands. "Shoo."

Kerry found herself moving forward. She touched the old man's forehead even as he recoiled at her touch.

"You've got a raging fever," she said. "Have you had any medicine? Eaten or had anything to drink?"

He gestured toward the other side of the room, which held a narrow iron bed and a small nightstand on which stood an empty cardboard ramen cup and a bottle of water.

"I'm fine," he rasped, before seizing up with a fit of hacking coughs that left him doubled over and gasping for breath.

Kerry looked over her shoulder at Patrick. "He needs a doctor."

"No, no," Heinz protested. "A little cold is all."

"Our neighbor, Abby Oliver, is a pediatrician," Patrick said. "She's Austin's doctor. I saw her this morning. Maybe she could . . ."

"Call her and ask her to come over, please," Kerry said. She noticed Austin, who was edging closer to his father, wanting to help, but clearly terrified at Heinz's state of distress.

"Better yet, why don't you and Austin go fetch her. I'll stay here with Heinz."

"No doctor," Heinz said. "I refuse."

"It's either that or I call nine-one-one and have you taken to the emergency room,"

320

Kerry said. "Have you ever been in an emergency room over the holidays? I have."

"Just leave me be," Heinz said wearily, closing his eyes and slumping back against the chair.

"I think he should be in bed. Don't you think he should be in bed?" Patrick asked. Without waiting for Kerry's reply, he reached down and gently helped the old man to his feet, and basically carried him over to the bed. He plumped up the single wafer-thin pillow, and pulled the sheet and blanket up, tucking them under Heinz's chin.

"He really feels hot," Patrick whispered as he passed Kerry. He held out his hand to his son. "C'mon, buddy. Let's go get Dr. Abby."

Kerry looked around the apartment. It was neat, with clothes hung on pegs, shoes tucked under the chair Heinz had just vacated, but otherwise totally devoid of personal effects. Her closet at home was bigger. There was a kitchenette, with a tiny two-burner electric stove, an under-counter refrigerator, a sink, and a cupboard. She found a canister of tea, and a mug, and set a kettle to boil on the stove.

In the bathroom, she found a bottle of

aspirin. She dampened a towel with cold water and placed it on Heinz's head and bullied him into swallowing the aspirin with some water. When the water was ready, she made tea in the single mug she found in the cupboard, stirring it with one of two spoons.

"Sip this, please," she told him. He sighed and turned his head away, but Kerry was undeterred. She reached for his wrist and examined his hand. The skin was pale and unusually shriveled. Her father's skin had looked the same, last winter, after a bout of flu, when she and Birdie had carted him off to his doctor, much to his displeasure.

"You're dehydrated," she said bluntly. "Drink the tea. Or would you prefer to be hooked up to a machine to get IV fluids?"

"You should mind your own business," he said, in between coughs. "I take care of myself. Nobody asked you to interfere."

"Why is it so cold in here?"

"Why are you so bossy?"

She spied a blanket folded on the back of the chair and tucked it around him. "Don't you have heat?"

"Not much insulation in these old walls. And I don't care to be hot."

Kerry dragged the chair over to the bed and sat down. "Keep drinking the tea. Do you have any crackers or anything like food in this place?"

"I eat out. Food brings bugs, and I despise bugs."

She circled the room, looking for a thermostat, and shivered when she found it was set at sixty-two degrees, even though the temperature in the apartment was probably hovering in the low forties.

Finally, she heard the clanking of the freight elevator, and a moment later, Patrick and a young woman dressed casually in yoga pants and a hoodie burst into the room. Kerry recognized her as someone she'd frequently noticed around the neighborhood.

Heinz, struggling to sit up, regarded the newcomer with undisguised disdain. "Who is this girl?"

"I'm Dr. Oliver," the woman said. She pulled a stethoscope from her jacket pocket, rubbed the stem in the palm of her hand to warm it up, and bent over the old man. "I'm a board-certified doctor, and I'm going to listen to your chest now." She pushed aside the fabric of his robe.

"Deep breaths," she said gently. "In and out."

Heinz complied, but his breath ended in a rattling cough.

"Again."

She sat him up and placed the scope on his back. "Breathe again, please."

That done, she took a digital thermometer from another pocket and placed the tip in Heinz's ear canal. When it beeped a second later, she frowned.

"One hundred two," she said, her voice stern. "Mr. Heinz, how long have you had this cough and fever?"

"I hear fine, no need to shout," he said fussily. "A little cold, that's all."

"No, sir. From the sound of your lungs, I'd say you have double pneumonia." Dr. Oliver shivered and pulled her jacket closer. "Why is it so cold in here?"

"He says he likes it like this," Kerry said.

"We need to get him somewhere warm, immediately. He's dehydrated too. He needs to be admitted to a hospital."

"No hospital," Heinz shot back, glaring at her. "You're not my doctor."

"True. I'm only here as a favor to Patrick. And Austin." She turned to Kerry. "If you're not his family, and he doesn't want to seek further treatment, there's not much I can do here." She turned back to the patient. "Do you have family, Mr. Heinz?"

"No. They are all gone."

Silence fell over the small, frigid room.

"What if we moved him someplace

warmer? And got him some antibiotics?" Kerry asked, desperate to find a solution. "I could stay and see that he's taking care of himself. See that he's eating and drinking and taking his meds."

"You're going to keep him in that camper in the park?" the doctor asked, not unkindly.

"Of course not." Kerry locked eyes with the old man. "Heinz, the superintendent tells us he thinks you have an apartment on the top floor of this building. Is that true?"

Heinz looked away. "I don't . . . I don't stay there." He abruptly rolled over and turned his back to these unwanted visitors who'd invaded his space.

"Heinz?" Kerry said.

His voice was muffled. "I live here now."

"Please don't do this. If something should happen to you, Austin would be heartbroken. And so would I."

"He wants to finish your story," Patrick put in. "And he says you're the only one who can do that."

Slowly, the old man turned to face them. "Go away and leave me in peace."

"I'm not leaving you," Kerry declared. "You can ignore me, or dog cuss me or whatever, but I'm staying right here."

She looked up at Patrick, who shrugged his agreement.

"He really should be in a hospital," Dr. Oliver repeated, shaking her head. "He needs fluids. See if you can get him to drink some Pedialyte, or even Gatorade."

She sat in the bedside chair. "Mr. Heinz, I know you can hear me. Are you allergic to any medications?"

"No."

"Any other health concerns? Heart disease, diabetes?"

"I'm old. That's my health concern."

The doctor chuckled. "At least he still has a sense of humor. Okay, I'll call in a prescription for some antibiotics. Get him warm, keep him quiet and rested. See if you can get some soup in him." She turned to Patrick. "Text me if you need me. Because of the weather, we're staying home over the holidays."

Patrick nodded his thanks, then turned to Kerry. "I hate to go, but I left Austin with Peg, my next-door neighbor."

"We'll be okay," Kerry said. "Can you let Murphy know where I am and what I'm doing? And thank Claudia for brunch?"

He looked at his watch. "As soon as Gretchen gets back, I'll pick up the prescription and everything else Abby says he needs."

"If I take the pills, will you go away?" Heinz

fixed Kerry with a baleful stare.

"No chance," she said.

"I could call the police, have you arrested for trespassing."

"You don't have a phone," Kerry pointed out.

He closed his eyes. End of discussion.

Kerry sat on the chair at his bedside and began scrolling the internet. A short while later, his breaths became steady. He was asleep. When her phone rang, she jumped up with a start and walked quickly outside the apartment.

CHAPTER 46

"Mom?" Kerry's heart pounded. "What's wrong? Is it Dad?"

"If you mean is it Jock making me want to set my hair on fire, then, yes, it's definitely your dad," Birdie retorted.

"But is he okay?"

"He's fine. He's like a cockroach. You can't kill that man. I just left him and he's walking around, issuing orders and generally being the same old pain in the ass he's always been."

"Really?" Kerry brightened. "But I thought the doctors said —"

"Those doctors don't know jack about Jock Tolliver. Anyway, he's healthy enough that I'm going back to my own house today and I'm going to sit down and drink a glass of wine without anybody whining my name and asking me to fetch something. Now, quit stalling and tell me what's going on with you up there."

"I've got some bad news about Christmas," Kerry said.

"Murphy called to tell us about what happened to the truck and to Spammy. I told him in no uncertain terms that he can't just have Spammy melted down for scrap metal, but of course, your daddy sided with your brother and now it's as good as done. I'm so mad at the two of them I could spit."

"Mom?" Kerry said, puzzled. "I had no idea Spammy meant that much to you."

Her mother's voice was tearful. "Maybe I'm being silly, but I loved that old tin can. And do you want to know why?"

"Yeah."

Birdie let out a long sigh. "I shouldn't tell you this, and you better never repeat it, but you were conceived in that doggone trailer."

Kerry didn't know whether to laugh or cry. "Seriously? In Spammy? When?"

"Do the math," Birdie said. "The week before Christmas 1988, right there at Abingdon Square. Your daddy got into the moonshine, but I can't remember what got into me." She giggled. "Well, that's not exactly true."

"Mooom," Kerry exclaimed. "Gross."

"Never mind," Birdie said briskly. "Either way, I don't think you need to worry about waiting on tires for the truck to head home.

Just get on a plane. I'll pay for your ticket."

Kerry bit her lip and blurted out the rest. "I can't come home. Not right away. I've sort of got a commitment up here."

"Ohhh." Birdie laughed. "Your brother mentioned there's a new man in the picture."

"Mom, he's close to ninety if he's a day," Kerry protested. "Has no family, lives alone in an almost unheated basement apartment, and he's got double pneumonia. Somebody has to look after him."

There was a long pause while her mother worked that out. "Well now, that's different. I guess you'd better do what you can for the poor soul."

"I'm sorry to spoil Christmas, but I can't just walk away and leave Heinz like this."

"I'd disown you if you did," Birdie said. "I guess Christmas can wait until we're all together again."

Kerry smiled. She should have known her unselfish mother would agree with her decision to stay in the city. "Love you, Mama Bear."

"Love you more, Baby Bear. Do you have enough clean underwear?"

"I'm thirty-four, Mom. But thanks."

Before Kerry could walk back into the

330

apartment, the freight elevator doors opened and Patrick stepped out, carrying two large shopping bags.

He hurried to her side and kissed her cheek. "Okay, I got the prescription and some Gatorade, and Claudia insisted on sending down a quart of soup and some crackers, and, oh yeah, I ran by the apartment and grabbed an electric blanket."

"You must have been a Boy Scout," Kerry said.

"Nah. We got one as a wedding gift, and I never liked the idea of sleeping under a live wire."

They went into the apartment. Patrick found an outlet and plugged in the blanket and spread it over the still-sleeping Heinz.

"Come outside," he whispered. "I have something else to show you."

As soon as they stepped into the basement, Patrick held up a key chain with a single key.

"This is the key to Heinz's apartment on the seventh floor."

Kerry took the key from him and turned it over and over. "This has to be illegal."

"Illegal would be letting that old man freeze to death in there, and you with him," Patrick countered.

"How did you even get this?"

"You can thank Claudia. She bribed the super with the promise of a month's worth of dinners on the house."

"Totally illegal. And unethical. And how do we even know that apartment is livable?"

"We won't. Until you go up and check it out. If it's okay with you, I'll stay here and watch the patient."

CHAPTER 47

She took the elevator to the seventh floor, found and unlocked the door, flipped a light switch, and found herself in a time capsule.

Apartment 708's front room was a large, dimly lit open-plan space furnished as a living room. She hurried to open the heavy drapes pulled tightly across a bank of windows like the ones in Claudia's unit. Light flooded the room, revealing a tufted Chesterfield sofa with dusty black upholstery facing a small fireplace with gas logs. A Lucite-and-brass coffee table held yellowing newspapers, a stack of unopened mail, and a mug with a spoon balanced on a plate that held what looked like a fossilized Little Debbie snack cake. A glance at the front page of the newspaper on top showed a date of August 23, 1992.

Everything was coated with a fine layer of dust. Delicate cobwebs dangled from the chrome-colored sputnik chandelier and stretched across the filmy, dust-caked windows.

"Oh my," Kerry whispered, turning in tight circles to take it all in. The walls of the apartment were painted a deep, chocolate brown and everywhere, there was art. Over the fireplace mantel, on all the walls of the living room, art was hung floor to ceiling, gallery style, and more canvases leaned in stacks against the wall and tabletops.

It was an eclectic collection, featuring landscapes, collages, still lifes, pen-and-ink drawings, charcoal sketches, watercolors, and oils. Kerry recognized the artist's work immediately.

She stepped up to the largest, most arresting work in the room. It was a sensitively drawn portrait, the only one in the room. The sitter was a young man, olive-skinned with large, liquid dark eyes, chiseled cheekbones, and a high forehead. A fringe of dark hair fell over one eye, and he had a dreamy, faraway half-smile.

The portrait had been done in chalk, on what looked like a recycled brown paper grocery sack, but it was mounted in a chippy gold Renaissance-style formal frame.

Kerry stood in front of the picture, studying it for a long time. In lieu of a signature in the lower right corner there was a tiny black silhouette of a tree. She moved around the room and saw that all of the other pieces had the same marking.

She took a quick tour of the apartment. In the bedroom, the bed was unmade, the covers flung aside as if the last occupant had just awakened.

A toothbrush rested on the edge of the bathroom sink, alongside a razor and a can of shaving cream. Another toothbrush was slotted into a wall-mounted toothbrush holder.

The kitchen counter held a Mr. Coffee machine with a half-full pot of blackened sludge alongside a container of dried-up half-and-half.

A narrow door on the far kitchen wall was locked. Kerry jiggled the door handle, her curiosity piqued. She was about to attempt to jimmy the lock when she spotted a single key, dangling from an under-counter mug hook.

The door opened into a smaller room that had obviously been used as a painting studio. The only furniture consisted of a large wooden easel and backless iron stool and a worktable covered with jars of brushes, boxes of watercolors, pastel crayons, and pencils. The rough-planked wooden floor and the walls were spattered with paint. Blank and half-finished canvases were stacked in a crude wall-mounted rack.

Kerry walked around the room, batting away the cobwebs covering everything, touching the canvases and trying to imagine why Heinz would have abandoned this space to move into what Austin had correctly termed a dungeon. She opened another door and discovered it held a tiny bathroom with an old-fashioned claw-foot tub, pedestal sink, and high-backed commode.

She went back to the living area, searching for a source of heat and feeling relief at the sight of a thermostat on the wall near the front door. She slid a knob and was gladdened at the resulting whoosh of power.

Her mind was made up. Somehow, she would have to boss, and yes, bully, Heinz into moving back into this apartment.

CHAPTER 48

The old man was too weak to put up much of a defense. He leaned heavily on Patrick's arm as he was walked into the seventh-floor apartment. He gazed around the living room and his eyes rested briefly on the portrait that had caught Kerry's eye, then quickly looked away.

"The bedroom's this way," Kerry told Patrick, pointing to the open door. Together, they managed to trundle Heinz into the bed, which Kerry had made up with clean sheets.

Heinz sank back against the pillows, sniffed, and made a face. "What is that awful odor?"

"That's the smell of Pine-Sol, plus the blood, sweat, and tears I expended scrubbing and disinfecting this place," Kerry said, holding out her work-reddened hands. "You could at least pretend to be grateful."

"For what?" Heinz rasped. "For being

force-marched back into a past I want to forget?"

His face crumpled as he looked around the room, his eyes focusing on the small framed black-and-white photograph Kerry had discovered while cleaning. He closed his eyes as an act of dismissal. "I'm tired. Will you please, for God's sake, leave me alone in peace?"

"Afraid not," Patrick said. "We can't leave you alone until you're over this pneumonia."

"I'm going to sleep on the sofa out there," Kerry told him. "And make sure you eat properly and take your meds."

Heinz's eyes flew open again. "Who invited you to move in here? Go away and sell your Christmas trees and sleep in your trailer."

"It's me or the hospital," Kerry said, unimpressed with his acting. "Besides, Murphy had Spammy towed away to the scrapyard today, so now I'm officially homeless. You wouldn't turn away a homeless friend at Christmas, would you?"

"Is it really Christmas already?" His voice faltered as he rubbed a hand across his chin, bristly with a five days' growth of snow-white beard. "I must have lost track of time."

"Tomorrow is Christmas Eve," Kerry said.

"Time for you to go back home to the mountains," Heinz said. "To your family."

"Not until you're better," Kerry said firmly. She patted his shoulder. "Now rest."

Kerry and Patrick tiptoed out of the bedroom, leaving the door ajar.

"This place is . . . something else," Patrick said, looking around the living area. "I know this city is full of eccentrics, but how do you suppose someone like Heinz, whom I always just assumed was borderline homeless, came to own an apartment like this, in this neighborhood?"

"Don't forget he apparently owns the whole building," Kerry said.

"Maybe he inherited it?" He gestured at the art that surrounded them. "Along with all these paintings?"

"Don't think so," Kerry said slowly. "Most of these paintings are the work of the same person, a fairly famous artist who suddenly, inexplicably, stopped painting back in the early nineties, and dropped out of sight."

"Heinz? What makes you think that?"

She led him by the hand to a large landscape painting of a verdant forest, and pointed to the bottom left corner, to the tiny imprint of a tree. "That's his signature."

"Huh?"

"The artist who painted most of these works never signed them with his name, just this little dingbat. As soon as I saw this painting, in particular, I knew. The brushwork, the intricate detailing, I recognized it from the illustrations Heinz has been doing for Austin's story."

"What's the deal with the tree then?"

"Heinz's last name. Schoenbaum. I looked it up. It means 'beautiful tree' in German. I did a Google search and found an old article from *New York* magazine about an artist who was the darling of the New York art scene in the eighties and nineties. His work was being exhibited nationally, even internationally, and regularly selling for high six figures. And then, in 1992, he just dropped out of sight."

"You're talking about Heinz?" Patrick asked.

"Let me show you something," Kerry said. She led him to the small bedroom off the kitchen that she'd discovered earlier.

"So, this is where he painted," Patrick said. "What else did that article say about Heinz?"

"He grew up here in the city, studied art at the Pratt Institute on the GI Bill, bounced around at different jobs, always painting on the side, until he was part of a small group exhibit held in a warehouse in the Meat-packing District, where one of his paintings caught the eye of a wealthy collector. That painting sold, and the collector's friends started buying his work too. Pretty soon, he was able to support himself with his art."

"If he bought this building, I'd say he did pretty well for himself," Patrick commented.

"He was at the top of his game, and then, bam. He apparently just vanished," Kerry said. "I couldn't find any other mentions of him on my Google search, other than auctions listing resale prices of his work, after that '92 article."

Patrick followed her back to the living room, where she dropped down onto the sofa by the fireplace.

"So, his paintings still sell?" he asked, sitting beside her.

"Definitely. The collector I told you about? She passed away last year, and her estate sold one of Heinz's paintings, a nude done in oil on board, for one point two million."

"Wow." Patrick gestured at the art-filled walls surrounding them. "There's probably a small fortune just hanging in this living room, huh?"

"Not so small a fortune," Kerry corrected him.

"Hey." Patrick put his hand over hers.

"Kerry, did you mean what you told Heinz? That you'd stay here until he's better?"

She nodded. "Unless he calls the cops and has me evicted."

"Will Murphy be able to make it home for Christmas?"

"Doubtful," Kerry said. "He's been watching the weather apps, and the interstate is still like an ice rink. He'll stay at Claudia's place until the roads are in better shape. In fact, he's supposed to bring me my clothes as soon as he finishes breaking down the tree stand."

"Won't your mom be disappointed about both of you missing Christmas?"

"We talked. Murphy had already called to tell her and Dad about Spammy. And about Heinz. She understands. Like she said, we can have Christmas anytime."

"Your mom sounds like a good sport," Patrick said.

Kerry leaned her head back against the sofa cushions. "I feel bad now, because I basically accused her of being a doormat for taking care of my dad after his heart attack."

"She has a good heart. Like her daughter."

"It was Austin who wouldn't let us rest until we found Heinz," she reminded him. "So give yourself some credit here too, pal, for raising a child with such a strong sense of compassion."

"My little weirdo," Patrick said, shaking his head. "He does have friends his own age, but ever since he could talk, Austin's just seemed to relate more to adults. I know he's a great judge of character, because he fell in love with you at first sight. And so did his old man."

Kerry sank back into the sofa cushions and studied his face. "Don't do this," she pleaded.

His smile came easily, spreading across his lips like warm honey. "Too late. You can't run away like you did last night. No place left to hide."

"What you're asking me to do — move up here, with no job, no place to live, no prospects, is just plain crazy. Even if I wanted to . . ."

He cocked an eyebrow. "Do you? Do you want to be with me? That's what it comes down to, Kerry. Everything else, we can figure out. Together. If that's what you want."

"I'm scared." The words were rushed and squeaky, as though an anvil rested on her chest.

"Scared of what?" He picked up her hand, kissed the back of it, turned it over and kissed the palm.

"I don't know. Of doing the wrong thing. Of trying and failing. I got fired from my last job, you know. Rationally, I know it wasn't my fault. But emotionally? It makes you doubt yourself. Your work. Your worth."

"That's ridiculous. I've seen your drawings. Those dog portraits? The illustrations for Austin's story? You're a natural talent."

Kerry shook her head. "Thanks, but you don't know what the art world is like. It's totally subjective, and there are a million people out there trying to do what I dream of doing. People with more talent, more smarts, more connections."

She looked away, but then when she turned back to him, her eyes glittered with unshed tears. "But mostly, I'm afraid of failing you, and Austin. I know what it's like to have your family fall apart. I don't want that to happen to him, again."

Patrick guffawed. "You couldn't fail us, even if you tried. I don't know what went on in your parents' marriage, but I do know that we are different. Look. I'm not perfect, but I'd never walk away from you. Even when it was obvious that Gretchen wanted out of our marriage, I tried to make it work. For Austin. We did couples counseling, I went to therapy solo . . . finally, one night, when I was putting him to bed, he looked up at me and sighed and said, 'Daddy, I don't think you and Mommy should be married anymore.' Talk about ripping your heart out."

"Oh God," Kerry whispered.

"Turns out, even a five-year-old could see what I couldn't," Patrick said with a shrug.

CHAPTER 49

After she'd sent Patrick away without the answer he wanted but she couldn't give, Kerry felt at loose ends. She leafed idly through some thirty-year-old magazines, thought about reading one of the dense-looking novels on Heinz's bookshelves, and finally went to the kitchen and fixed herself a cup of tea from the small stash of groceries Patrick had brought.

She was startled by the doorbell ringing. When she opened it, her brother was standing in the hallway.

He thrust a large white paper sack into her hands. "From Mrs. Lee, at the Red Dragon. Somehow, everybody in the neighborhood heard Heinz is sick, and they're all worried about the old dude. According to the granddaughter, Mrs. Lee says her soup is Chinese penicillin, and you should make sure he drinks every drop. She put some dumplings and potstickers in there for you, too."

"Thanks," Kerry said, holding the door open wider. "Wanna come in? Heinz is sleeping."

Murphy stuck his head inside the door. "Wow. Cool place. Lotta art, huh?"

"Most of it was done by Heinz," Kerry told him. "Come on in. He won't care."

"Nah. I better go. Still gotta finish breaking down the rest of the stand, then I'm having Dad's truck towed to a storage facility until you can drive it back home."

"Was it sad, watching Spammy get hauled away to the junkyard?"

"Sad? It's a fifty-two-year-old trailer, Kere, not your grandma. With all the trees we sold this year, Dad can afford to buy a new trailer. One with working taillights and plumbing. Mom was pretty pissed at me, but she'll get over it."

Kerry nodded. Her brother and father were definitely cut from the same cloth — only sentimental about their dogs and guns. In that order. "Where's Queenie?"

"Vic's watching her for now, then I gotta figure out something else until we head home. Claudia's cat is not a fan."

"Bring her up here to me," Kerry said impulsively.

347

"Really?"

"I don't think Heinz will mind. I get the impression he likes dogs better than people."

"Sweet. I'll bring Queenie tonight when I drop off your clothes." He hesitated, then leaned in and gave her a quick peck on the cheek. "Thanks, sis."

She cracked the door of Heinz's bedroom and studied the patient. He was snoring softly. His color had improved, and he wasn't coughing.

Finally, she gave in to the urge she'd been fighting since she'd arrived in the apartment. She took her mug of tea and went into the studio.

Surveying all the colorful art materials, she felt like a kid in a candy store. She found a new oversized sketch pad on a table near the window, opened it, and placed it on the easel. The tubes of oil and acrylic paints were long since dried out, but she reached into a Folger's coffee can and pulled out some colored pencils.

Humming, she started doodling. Thumbnail sketches of the dogs she'd met in the neighborhood, then sketches of their owners.

She flipped the page and began drawing

the Tolliver Family Christmas tree stand, with Spammy in the foreground. She imbued the battered and rusty vintage camper with a charm and personality it didn't actually possess in real life, round porthole windows that resembled eyes, a trailer hitch that could be interpreted as a button nose, and an oversized bumper that looked like a slightly upturned smile. Maybe Murphy wasn't sentimental about the old girl, but Kerry discovered that she was already recalling fond memories of the weeks she and her family had spent in the little canned-ham camper of her childhood.

As she colored in the details, adding rows of Fraser firs criss-crossed with colored lights, wreaths hanging on hooks, and customers (and their dogs) browsing for trees, she began thinking of a story of her own.

The whimsical story of a spunky little vintage camper who leaves her tiny mountain town for an exciting adventure in the big city. A camper named Spammy.

Her tea grew cold and the minutes flew by as she filled the pages of the book with her story and illustrations.

When she looked up from the easel she glanced at her phone and realized that three hours had passed. Night had fallen, and it was time to check on Heinz.

She heated up the soup Mrs. Lee had sent, pouring it into a thick china mug, and placed it on a tray, along with a glass of water and the medicine the pediatrician had prescribed.

Heinz was sitting up in bed, yawning. He scowled when he saw her. "Don't tell me you're still here."

"Afraid so," she said, resting the tray on his lap. She pointed to the soup. "Mrs. Lee at the Red Dragon sent that over for you. She says you're to eat every last drop."

He took a sip and grimaced. "Gaaaah. Terrible."

"It smells okay to me. What's it taste like?"

"Ginger. Garlic. Fish paste. Something fetid and stagnant. Fermented ditch water." He took another sip and shuddered.

"My grandma would say if it don't kill you it's sure to cure you." Kerry handed him his antibiotics. "Drink it down and then take these."

Heinz dutifully finished the soup and swallowed his meds, placing the empty mug on the tray.

"I do feel slightly better," he admitted. "So I suppose I should thank you for that."

"It's my pleasure," Kerry said. "You really had us all very worried when you disappeared like that. Austin was beside himself. We were ready to post Wanted posters with your picture on them all over the West Village."

Heinz reached for his glasses from the nightstand, put them on, adjusted them, and gazed at her. "I don't quite understand why you would choose to stay here and play nursemaid to a virtual stranger, when you could be home, celebrating Christmas with your family."

His question gave her pause. "We're not strangers," she said. "We're friends. You, me, Austin, Patrick, Murphy, and Claudia. What's that saying? Friends are the family you choose? I guess we've chosen you. Whether you like it or not."

He fiddled with his glasses again and took a sip of water. "Friendship is not something that comes easily to me. I'm not used to being taken care of," he said matter-of-factly. "As you can tell by all this . . ." He gestured around at the room and the apartment beyond. "I've been alone for a very long time. By choice."

Kerry chose her next question carefully. "But you weren't always alone, right?" She glanced at the nightstand and noticed that Heinz had placed the framed photograph upright again.

"No." The way he said it told Kerry the topic was closed. For now.

"I hope you don't mind, but I thought, as long as I was invading your home, I might as well trespass on your studio. I'm afraid I borrowed some of your art supplies. It's an amazing space. I really got inspired, working there."

He shrugged. "I'm not really in a position to stop you now, am I?"

"Is it all right? That I used your studio?"

"It's fine," he said, waving his hand in dismissal. "Tell me what you're working on."

"Better yet, I'll show you."

Heinz studied the first page of the story. He tapped the sketch of the happy camper, with its smiley bumper and porthole windows, pressed his lips together, and nodded. He turned the pages slowly, reading the text aloud.

Kerry squirmed self-consciously as she heard him murmuring the words she'd dashed off in a sort of hypnotic frenzy of creativity, and she had to force herself not to flee from the room, and the stinging criticism she was sure Heinz would direct her way.

When he'd read through all the pages, he turned back to the beginning and went more slowly over each page. "Bring me a pencil," he told Kerry. "And an eraser."

She did as requested, and he spent another thirty minutes jotting notes in the tiniest block print, on each page. It was torture, sitting by silently and watching him dissect her work.

Finally, he handed the sketchbook back to her, along with the pencil and the eraser.

"Well?" She was holding her breath, waiting for the worst.

"This is actually quite good."

"It is?" She exhaled slowly.

"Your work is much improved since we first met. Looser, with a real personality. The story has humor and charm, and somehow, you had even me caring about the fate of that dreadful camper of yours."

"It's meant to be a children's picture book, so I couldn't draw something as awful as the reality of Spammy being hauled away to a junkyard," Kerry explained.

"No. That would be too cruel, even for me," Heinz agreed. He handed her the sketchbook. "You can see I made some suggestions. Places where the perspective could be altered, or the composition reworked. Of course, I'm no expert on children, or the kind of books they like, but I think your story has real potential."

353

Kerry found herself beaming. "I don't know what came over me. This story and the illustrations came pouring out of me while I was in your studio. It felt like something I'd had bottled up inside me for a long, long time." She clutched the sketch pad to her chest.

"Is that what creating something new felt like to you? Back when you were still painting?" she asked.

"I don't remember."

"And I don't believe you. Heinz, I looked you up. You're famous. An art world sensation. Did you know that the nude painting of yours that Della Lowell bought back in the eighties sold last year, at auction, for one point two million?"

"Ridiculous," he said. "Why would she sell the thing, anyway?"

"Her estate sold it. She died two years ago."

Heinz recoiled, as though he'd been slapped.

"I'm sorry. I thought you knew. The article I read said she was in her late nineties. Her stepchildren apparently weren't the artsy kind."

He ran his hand over his chin. "I had no idea. Of course she died. Everyone does, and she was a very old, very grand lady.

Della was a tastemaker. After she bought that nude, everything changed. My career took off. She took me to lunch one day. At a restaurant where that bodega is now. Pointed across the street, at this building, and suggested, no, insisted, I should invest in real estate. Her husband owned one of the biggest brokerages in the city. He arranged everything, managed for me to buy it at an unheard-of price. George and I, we couldn't believe our good fortune."

Kerry picked up the black-and-white photo from the nightstand. "George?"

Heinz nodded. "My dealer, my muse, my partner in all things. We'd been living in a hovel, really, but it was near his gallery. We had three good years here. Only three. And then, he was gone."

There was so much she wanted to ask Heinz, the questions tumbled over themselves in her mind.

The doorbell rang. Heinz raised an eyebrow.

"It's probably just Murphy. Bringing me my clothes and things from the trailer. Oh, and I told him I thought it would be all right if he brought Queenie here too, because he's staying at Claudia's and she's got a cat . . ."

"Fine, fine," Heinz muttered. "Bring all the strays. I'm too old and sick to stop you."

CHAPTER 50

As soon as Kerry opened the door Queenie gave a short, happy bark of recognition, then went bounding through the apartment, straight for Heinz's bedroom.

Murphy had Kerry's overflowing duffel bag slung over one shoulder, and a plastic trash bag stuffed with what she assumed was the rest of her belongings. Behind him, in the hallway, lay a smallish, forlorn-looking Christmas tree.

He set the baggage down inside the living room, turned, and dragged the tree inside. "This was Austin's idea," he said sheepishly. "Vic had to leave early, so Patrick brought him down to help me take apart the rest of the stand. This was the last tree. I guess it was so ugly nobody even wanted it for free."

"Let me guess. Austin insisted Mr. Heinz had to have a Christmas tree," Kerry said. She pointed to a spot in the corner of the room. "Put it over there. Heinz has already had to get used to the idea of a squatter, and now a dog. This might just put him over the edge. Or not. Did you bring a stand for it?"

"We sold 'em all," Murphy said. "How about I just kind of lean it against the wall?"

"Why not? In the meantime, I'll go check to see how Heinz is getting along with your dog."

To Kerry's amazement, Heinz was sitting up in the chair beside the bed, with Queenie sprawled across his lap, gazing up at him adoringly and licking his chin.

"Poor girl," she heard Heinz murmur as he stroked the dog's silky ears. "Did the bad people leave you all alone out there in that cold and snow?"

"Poor girl, my aunt Fannie," Kerry retorted. "I gather you're feeling better?"

The old man shrugged. "Mrs. Lee might be right about that soup of hers. But I don't think I could survive a second dose."

"Murphy is here. He brought you a, um, surprise. Do you feel well enough to walk into the living room to see what it is?"

"Not another guest, I hope," Heinz said, slowly standing and tightening the belt of his bathrobe. "This isn't Bethlehem. The inn is full and I don't have a stable."

He took one wobbly step and Kerry hurried to his side. "Put your arm around my shoulder and lean on me," she instructed. "Let's take it nice and slow."

By the time they reached the living room, Murphy had managed to prop the Christmas tree up by wedging it between stacks of thick, leatherbound books. He was standing back, admiring his handiwork.

"Good God, man," Heinz exclaimed, sinking down onto an armchair. "Those are extremely rare first editions you're using as ballast."

"They work good, don't they?" Murphy asked. "A lot classier looking than your run-of-the-mill stand."

"I suppose." Queenie jumped onto Heinz's lap and wagged her tail appreciatively. He buried his nose in the fur of her head. "Do you know? This dog smells like Christmas trees."

"She oughtta. That's what pays for her room and board and vet bills," Murphy said, heading for the door. "I better get going, but thanks again, Heinz, for letting my girl stay here with you."

"Which girl is that?" Heinz asked, with a hint of a smile. "Kerry, or Queenie?"

"Both," Murphy said. "As far as I know, they're both house-trained."

■ ■ ■ ■

Heinz leaned back in his chair and gazed around the living room. "It's been so long," he said haltingly, "since I sat in this room. So many memories . . ."

"Good ones, I hope?" Kerry said.

"Mainly. George was an extrovert and enjoyed entertaining. We would have parties after an exhibit opening. Champagne, caviar. Jelly beans. George loved jelly beans. He loved having people around. Me? Not so much. I suppose I was a lone wolf until we met."

"And how did you meet?"

"Art school. I was just out of the navy, just back from Vietnam, coming to terms with who I was and what I wanted from life. I signed up for a life-drawing class at Pratt. He was our model one night. A group was going out for drinks afterward. The others dragged me along."

"And you clicked?"

"Oh no, no, no," Heinz said, his chuckle devolving into a cough. "We argued. That night and every other time we were together. About politics, art, the war, everything. But he was so passionate. And funny." His eyes strayed to the portrait on the wall. "And beautiful. George had a beautiful soul."

"That really comes through in your painting," Kerry said.

"We fought about that portrait, of course. George hated it. He kept trying to sell it. Every time I'd come back from an out-of-town trip, he'd have it turned facing the wall, or draped in a dirty T-shirt. One time I found it in our basement storage area."

"How did he come to be your art dealer?" Kerry asked.

"Nobody else wanted to represent me," Heinz said. "George was always more interested in commerce than art. He knew about a storefront in the Meatpacking District. The place was a disaster. But he could afford the rent. His family had money, unlike mine, and also unlike mine, they didn't care that he was gay. He sweet-talked me and some of our friends into being part of a group show. That space became his gallery, and I was the first artist he signed."

"And then Della Lowell discovered you?"

"She showed up at the gallery out of the blue. She'd seen a flyer somewhere about the show, and that nude caught her eye. She paid three thousand seven hundred dollars for it, as I recall, and at the time, I told George he was out of his mind to put that high a price tag on a work by an unknown artist. It was more money than I'd ever dreamt of."

Kerry walked slowly around the room, surveying the canvases hanging on the walls and stacked on the floor. She sat down again, in the chair opposite Heinz's.

"Can I ask? Why did you stop painting? Why did you walk away from this apartment, from your career, everything?"

"George. One minute he was here, in that chair you're sitting in now, making outrageous jokes about something, then the next minute, he said he had a crushing headache and a minute after that he was gone. A cerebral hemorrhage. He was forty-two."

"I'm so, so sorry," Kerry said.

"I didn't know who I was without George. Without him goading me, bullying me, encouraging me. I couldn't paint. Couldn't stand to be here . . . without him. I was lost. I asked the building superintendent to clean out that space where I live now, and I locked this door. Today was the first time in . . . I don't know how many years since I was here last."

"I wish I had known that," Kerry said. "I had no idea being in this apartment would be so painful for you. But you were so sick, are still so sick . . . I was afraid you'd die down there, alone in that freezing cubbyhole, and I just couldn't let that happen."

"Are you in the habit of saving people's lives, even if they don't want them saved?" he asked.

Her eyes widened. "Are you saying you *wanted* to die?"

"Doesn't everyone, after they reach a certain age, think they want to die at some point in their life?"

Kerry stayed quiet.

"I suppose I didn't want to die," Heinz confided. "But after I got sick, I couldn't really think of any particular reason to keep living."

"You mentioned family a moment ago. Don't you have any family?"

"Not in a long time. My people were very conservative, very religious. I think they always suspected what I was and they were deeply ashamed of me. My parents are long dead. I had two brothers, both older than me, who let me know they didn't approve of my lifestyle. They said I was a disgrace to the family name. My little sister Geneva, bless her, was always my champion. She passed shortly after my parents."

Kerry got up and looked at the large landscape painting nearest her. "Is that why you sign your paintings with the tree icon? Schoenbaum, beautiful tree?"

362

"You figured that out, did you?"

"With help from Google," she admitted. "Seriously, Heinz, if being here really is unbearable for you, maybe we can figure out someplace else for you to convalesce. I mean, you own this whole building, so forgive me but I can't think that money is an issue. Maybe there's another apartment available?"

He continued to stroke the top of Queenie's head. The setter's muzzle rested on his leg and her eyes were closed. She was asleep, her body shuddering with every snore.

"I think . . ." he said slowly. "I think it will be all right. Somehow, the painful memories, most of them, have been banished. Now I have only one serious problem."

"What's that?" She jumped up and went to his side. "Is the fever back?"

"No. I'm feeling slightly better. But how do I manage to get out of this chair and back to bed without disturbing our girl here?" He gazed down at the slumbering dog.

"Queenie!" Kerry said. The dog raised her head. "Come!" She took a cushion from the sofa and placed it on the floor. "Here."

The dog jumped down and splayed out

on the cushion and almost instantaneously went back to sleep.

"Marvelous," Heinz said, rising slowly from his seat. "If only I could fall asleep that quickly. We had a dog, George and I. A beautiful wirehaired dachshund named Pablito. He was such a good boy."

The old man's eyes glistened. "I haven't thought of Pablito in years and years. I painted him several times. One of those canvases must still be around here."

He clutched the back of the sofa with both hands. "Kerry?"

"Yes?"

"Thank you for caring for me. And about me."

"You're quite welcome."

"I'm going to sleep now. I'm sure while you were pillaging my home, you found the linen closet? With sheets and blankets and pillows?"

"I did."

"But I'll bet you didn't find the Murphy bed in the studio, did you?"

"No. I was planning on sleeping on the sofa out here."

"The Murphy bed should be quite comfortable. Good night."

CHAPTER 51

The shock of chilly air that met Kerry as she left Heinz's building the next morning felt like a slap in the face. It was bitterly cold and snowflakes swirled around in the gray skies. The sidewalks were still icy, and crowded with people out doing last-minute shopping and errands, so she led Queenie carefully but quickly through the park for her morning bathroom break.

All signs of the Tolliver Family Christmas tree stand were gone. She felt a sharp pang of sadness, thinking of Spammy's fate, but a moment later, Queenie was barking and tugging at the leash, because she'd spotted Murphy standing in the doorway at Anna's.

"How'd she do last night?" Murphy asked, scratching the dog's head.

"She was perfect. Slept on a pillow in the living room. I slept on a pull-out bed in the studio. Best night of sleep I've had since I got here."

"How's the old man feeling?"

"A little better. He's still asleep."

A cab pulled up to the curb and deposited Patrick and Austin, both of them loaded down with shopping bags.

"Kerry, Kerry," Austin greeted her. "Just one more sleep and Christmas will be here." He was hopping up and down with excitement. Suddenly, he stood very still.

"Where's Spammy?"

Kerry and Patrick exchanged a worried glance.

Murphy searched for a palatable answer. "Somebody took a razor and slashed all Spammy's tires," he said.

"Those bad guys?" Austin exclaimed. "I knew it!"

"I can't prove it was them, but the tires were ruined. They're expensive to replace, and it would have cost more money to fix the camper than she was worth. So we, uh, had Spammy taken to a place where old cars and campers go. Kinda like a nursing home."

"Oh. But where will you guys live now?" Austin asked.

"As soon as this weather clears up, I'll drive back home to the mountains in North Carolina, where I have a real house, with heat and running water," Murphy told him.

"But until then, Miss Claudia is letting me stay at her apartment."

"And I'm staying at Heinz's apartment, so I can help take care of him," Kerry volunteered. "Queenie's staying there too."

"That's good, I guess. Hey, Kerry. Me and Dad got you a Christmas present. You wanna know what it —"

"Whoa!" Patrick laughed as he clamped his hand across his son's face. "Christmas gifts are supposed to be a surprise, remember?"

Austin pushed his father's hand away. "Oh yeah," he giggled. "But wait until you see how cool this present is."

Kerry felt her face grow hot despite the icy temperature. "I don't . . . have any presents for anyone. I didn't know I'd still be here today."

"Don't give it another thought," Patrick said quickly. "We got you something small and inexpensive. We don't expect anything in return."

"But Dad," Austin protested, shaking the shopping bag he held.

"We'd better get home," Patrick said, cutting him short. "Kerry, do you think Heinz would mind some company this evening? We won't stay long, I promise."

"I think he'd like that," Kerry said.

"Dr. Oliver told me to tell you she's going to drop by and check on him later this morning."

The door of the bakery opened again, and Lidia stepped out holding a white paper sack. "Your brother says Heinz is sick. Just a few cannoli and biscotti and amaretti for him. And the little wedding cookies he likes."

"Oh, Lidia . . ."

Before she could say anything else, the clerk from the bodega came bustling up with a plastic grocery bag. "This is for the old man," she said, pressing the bag into Kerry's hands. "Ginger tea. My auntie sends it from home. The very best for a head cold. And some lemon throat lozenges. You tell him to get better quick, you hear?"

"I will," Kerry said. "Thanks so much."

Abby Oliver tucked her stethoscope into the jacket pocket of her running suit and removed the pulse oximeter from the patient's fingertip. "Your chest sounds clearer this morning, Mr. Schoenbaum, and your oxygen saturation looks good."

"It's Heinz. No one calls me Mr. Schoenbaum."

"Okay, Heinz. Well, no fever today, and your color is better. I'd say the meds are working. How did you sleep last night?"

"Fine, fine," he said. "But too many people fussing over me. Eat this. Take that. Drink this."

"Sounds as though you have friends who care about you. You can never have enough of those," Dr. Oliver said. "Just stay warm and keep doing what you're doing. Also, if you're not too weak, it's good to get up and walk around every so often."

Heinz found Kerry in the studio with a lukewarm cup of tea in one hand and a sketch pad in the other. He lowered himself carefully onto a wooden chair and peered over her shoulder.

"What's this?"

"I've been trying to come up with an idea for a Christmas gift for Austin. It's Christmas Eve, and he and Patrick are going to come over to see you tonight, and I have nothing for them."

"And what is that supposed to be?" Heinz asked, pointing at the sketch while simultaneously trying and failing at diplomacy.

"Trying to draw a picture of Spammy. And Queenie, of course. Something to remember us by," she said.

"It's so serious-looking," Heinz said. "Dark. Even brooding. Why not draw it the way you did with your little storybook?"

She considered the sketch. Ripped it from the pad, wadded it up, and tossed it in the trash.

"I think I'm stuck. I've been sitting here for ninety minutes, trying to come up with something that will be meaningful to a little boy."

Heinz cocked an eyebrow. "And his father?"

"Am I that transparent?"

"You must be. I'm not a very astute judge of people's emotions, but even I can see the attraction between you and Patrick."

"He wants me to stay here. In the city."

"And what do you say to that?"

"It's impossible, of course. I have no job. No place to live, almost no money. And we've only known each other for three weeks. Like it or not, I've got to go home after the holidays, try to reboot my career."

"That's what your rational self is telling you. Now, what about your soul? What does your soul tell you?"

Kerry bit her lip. "I think . . . I know, that Patrick is the one. The kindest, most decent man I've ever met. I feel like me — my truest, most authentic self — when I'm around him."

"Right." Heinz clapped his hands. "There

is your answer. Everything else is . . . details."

"Having a way to support myself and a place to live is not just a detail," she countered.

"Your art, that's how you will support yourself. You are very talented, Kerry. This picture book you created yesterday — this is a book that can be published. And the story that we drew with Austin. Also a book."

"I don't know . . ."

"Here is what George taught me all those years ago," Heinz interrupted. "Your potential as an artist will never be achieved until you believe in yourself. Nobody else's opinion matters, unless you honestly believe you are making good art. Do you believe that?"

Kerry looked down at the sketch pad. "Yes," she whispered.

"Good. Now, get out of your own way. If you have a dream to make art for a living, do that. With all the passion and energy you possess. Everything else will follow."

"How? I don't know anybody in the children's book world."

"We knock on doors," Heinz said. "Many people in this neighborhood work in creative fields. Someone we know knows someone who can help."

"Who is we?"

He ignored the question. "Next. A place to live. Simple. You live here."

"No," she said quickly. "This is only until you're back on your feet and feeling better."

"I meant in this building. There is a very small studio unit that has been vacant for some time. The building manager's son was living there and paying next to nothing in rent because it has never been modernized, but he has moved on. If you like, it can be yours."

Kerry was dumbstruck by his offer. "I couldn't possibly accept an offer like that. It's incredibly kind, but no."

"This isn't charity," Heinz said sternly. "You will pay rent, of course. And you will need a job, and I have an idea about that."

She shook her head. "You and Patrick act as though it's a simple thing — to just pick up my life and move it to the city."

"Have you never lived anyplace besides your home in the mountains?"

"Well, yes. I lived in Raleigh for a few years after college, and then I moved to Charlotte. But that was different. I had a job, and I knew people there."

Heinz threw his hands in the air in disgust. "I give up. Such a stubborn girl."

"Takes one to know one," Kerry pointed out.

With effort, he managed to heave himself up. He stood with his hands clamped on the back of the chair, his breathing labored. "Go home then. Give up on a good man who could bring you happiness. Give up on your art. Give up on your dreams. Live a small life in a small town. And spend the rest of your life wondering 'what if?' "

He picked up his cane and walked unsteadily out of the room.

CHAPTER 52

Kerry gazed down at the drawing of the camper and smiled ruefully, thinking about the secret Birdie had shared with her. The old man was right, of course. About a lot of things. She flipped back through the pages of the sketchbook, until she came to Austin's unfinished story.

The little boy had been so eager to have the story finished, the last chapter written, before she and Murphy returned home. But she'd put that off, just as she'd put off giving Patrick answers, because, as usual, she was overthinking things. What was it Heinz had accused her of? Getting in her own way?

She picked up a handful of colored pencils, fanning them out in one hand, like a beautiful bouquet. A bouquet of possibilities.

Pencil met paper. She paused, picked up an eraser, then shook her head. No more erasing. No more second-guessing.

Two hours later, she walked out of the studio, to stretch her legs and check on Heinz. The apartment was quiet, the door to his bedroom closed. She tapped on the door. "Heinz? Are you okay? Is Queenie in there with you? I need to take her out for a walk."

A moment later, she heard the slow tap-tapping of his cane. The door opened. To her surprise, the old man was dressed, and it was apparent from his still-damp white hair that he'd showered and shaved.

"Can I get you something to eat or drink before I take Queenie out? I've been working on Austin's story and I guess I lost track of time."

He coughed slightly and nodded. "Food would be good. And tea."

"I'll just heat up some soup. And maybe some cheese and crackers? I'll bring it with your meds."

"Your doctor friend said I should get up and walk around, so I'll come in the dining room and eat like a civilized adult," Heinz said, giving her a slight smile. He turned to the dog, who was right at his heels. "Come, Queenie. Lunch."

The dining room featured an oval white marble-top table surrounded by six chairs of a similar design. Kerry set a plate in front of Heinz, with the bowl of soup and the cheese and crackers. When she returned to the table with her own plate, he gestured for her to join him.

"Claudia's famous minestrone?" he asked, dipping a spoon into the thick broth.

"My favorite," Kerry said. "I'm going to have to beg her for the recipe." She pointed at the table. "Heinz, is this a real Saarinen tulip table and chairs?"

He ate his soup and nodded. "Yes. We bought it after my second successful exhibit. I didn't know much about contemporary design. I'd studied Saarinen in art school, of course, but as I said, George came from money, and he was used to nice things. Everything you see in this apartment, we chose together."

"It's all so beautiful. Like what I always pictured an apartment in New York City would look like," Kerry said wistfully. She added, after a moment, "Now, I guess I can begin to understand why being here, with so many memories of him, was so painful for you."

Heinz looked away, then went back to eating his soup. Kerry realized she was ravenously hungry and did the same. When she was finished, she took their dishes into the kitchen, and, mindful of the old man's aversion to bugs, washed the dishes and set them to dry on a tea towel.

"You've been very quiet this afternoon," Heinz said, when she returned to the dining room. "Did you finish the boy's drawing?"

"Something like that," Kerry said. She picked up Queenie's leash, and a plastic bag. "C'mon, girl, let's go brave the elements."

"Could I see what you've done?" Heinz asked.

"I'd love that. In fact, I think the last bit could use something from you?"

"Oh?"

She went into the studio, got her jacket, hat, and gloves, and the sketchbook, which she placed on the table near the old man. "I'll be anxious to hear your thoughts."

The streets outside were eerily quiet. Traffic noise from passing cars and buses was muted. More snow had fallen overnight and everything in the pocket park was blanketed in a thick white frosting. She greeted Taryn, who was watching as her husband helped the twins build a snowman. Queenie gave a short happy bark of recognition at the sight of the boys.

"You're still here!" Taryn exclaimed. "I saw that your tree stand had been taken down and the camper was gone, so I just assumed you guys had headed for home."

Kerry explained about the slashed tires and the impassable roads and Heinz's health scare.

"I'm sorry about Spammy, and Heinz's illness, but selfishly, I'm glad you're still here. I'll bet Austin and Patrick are glad too."

"I think they are," Kerry said.

"Will we be seeing you at all after Christmas?"

Kerry hesitated.

"Never mind," Taryn said. "I am a hopeless romantic." She gave Kerry a quick hug. "Merry Christmas, Kerry. I hope you and Patrick find a way to be together, no matter what."

"I gotta go," Kerry said, blushing. "Queenie and I have been cooped up inside all day. We both need to stretch our legs."

When she returned to the apartment she found Heinz in the studio. He was bent over the easel, paintbrush in hand, but when she walked in, he quickly threw a cloth over whatever he'd been working on.

"You're painting?" she asked.

"Dabbling. Sit, please."

She did as he asked and he pointed to the

sketchbook. "Kerry, I must apologize. You are an adult and you are perfectly capable of deciding how you want to live your life and pursue your art. I had no right to speak to you the way I did."

"Sure you did," Kerry said. "After all, I broke into your home, forced you to let me and our dog stay here, forced you to accept medical treatment. I'd say you have every right to speak your mind. Besides, you were absolutely right."

"Is this where I say I told you so?" He smiled and tapped the sketchbook. "I saw that you left the last chapter of Austin's story unfinished. So I took the liberty of assuming you meant for us to write the ending together?"

"Exactly," Kerry said. She pulled the chair closer to the table and Heinz opened the sketchbook to show her what he'd drawn.

"It's perfect," she declared. "Except for one thing I think we need to add."

CHAPTER 53

The doorbell rang shortly after six and before Kerry could answer, Austin burst into the apartment, followed closely by Patrick, Murphy, and Claudia, all of them loaded down with shopping bags.

"Merry Christmas, Kerry," Austin called out. "Guess what? We brought lights for the Christmas tree. And presents. And pie!"

"And dinner," Claudia said, standing in the middle of the living room taking in the view of the apartment. "Wow. What a place. Now, where's the kitchen?"

"Oh my." Heinz looked at the faces gathered around his dining room table, at the remnants of the four-course feast Claudia had provided, and his own half-finished dish of tiramisu.

"I am . . . overwhelmed," he admitted.

"I know, I know. Too much rich food. My mom always did the same thing. Blame it on me coming from a restaurant family," Claudia said. "But you hardly ate anything, Heinz."

"This is the most food I've eaten in a very long time, and what I did eat was delicious," he said. "No, what I meant was, I'm overwhelmed, at all of you — for your kindness, for caring for me." He tossed Kerry a knowing look. "For rescuing me despite myself."

"You were really, really sick," Austin said, scraping the last bit of whipped cream from his dish. "But you look a lot better now."

"I feel better," Heinz admitted.

Austin looked around at the apartment. "Are you mad at us?"

"Me? No, why would I be mad at you?"

"Because Kerry and my dad made you move out of that dungeon. How come you wanted to live down there instead of up here?" Austin asked. "That place was dark and creepy and cold, but this place is nice and warm and it has big windows and a sofa and room for your friends."

"Austin!" Patrick's voice held a sharp note.

Heinz took a sip of water. "That's a very good question, my young friend. And the answer is that a long time ago, when I was living here, I lost someone I loved."

The boy's eyes widened. "Where did your

381

friend go? How did he get lost?"

"He died," Heinz said, choosing his words carefully. "This person was my whole world. And after he died, I couldn't bear to live here, with all the happy memories this place held for us. Everything here reminded me of him, and it made me very, very sad. So I decided I would live someplace else, where I wouldn't always be thinking about him."

"Oh." Austin seemed to be turning Heinz's rationale over and over in his mind as the adults exchanged anxious glances.

"Okay," Patrick said, a little too heartily. "Who's ready to open some Christmas gifts and drink some hot chocolate?"

"Me!" Austin said.

"But first some wine," Claudia said, jumping to her feet.

"Do you like the tree, Mr. Heinz?" Austin asked. "It was all my idea. And me and my dad bought the lights."

"It's beautiful," Heinz said. He was sitting in an armchair beside the tree, with a mug of tea clasped between his hands. "How did you know this is always where we used to have our tree when George was alive?"

"Who was George?" Austin asked. "Why did he die?"

"Austin . . ." Patrick started.

"It's all right," Heinz said. He pointed to the portrait above the fireplace. "That was George. He died very suddenly. It was a huge shock."

"He looks nice. Did you paint that picture?"

"George was very nice. Much nicer than me, and yes, I did paint that picture."

Austin stood up to examine the portrait closer, then pointed to the rest of the paintings in the room. "Did you paint *all* of these pictures?"

"Most of them," Heinz said. "Some were done by other artist friends."

"Did they all die too?"

An awkward silence fell over the room.

"I think some Christmas music would be great right now," Claudia said. She pointed at the sleek modernist stereo console under one of the windows. "Heinz, does the stereo still work?"

"I suppose so," Heinz said. "George was the music lover. I think there are some Christmas albums in the cabinet there."

"I'll help you look," Murphy volunteered. The two of them rifled through the stacks of albums on the console's shelves.

"Wow, talk about a blast from the past," Murphy said, holding up a pair of albums. "Look at all this cool old vinyl. Perry Como!

And Frank Sinatra. Look how swinging Frank looks in this fedora on the cover."

"The Beach Boys did a Christmas album?" Claudia asked. She dusted the album cover with the sleeve of her sweater, held it up, and read the liner notes. "In 1964! Wow. And here's Elvis's Christmas Album from 1957. George had great taste."

Murphy picked up another album. "Oh man, *A Christmas Gift for You from Phil Spector.* From 1963. I think my dad had the eight-track tape of this."

Claudia held up an album with Bing Crosby sporting a fur-trimmed Santa hat on the cover. "Okay, this is the one. *White Christmas.* We used to listen to this at my nonna's house every Christmas Eve. And it even has the Andrews Sisters. Okay if we play this one, Heinz?"

"You can try," Heinz said. He seemed amused by her enthusiasm for the vintage albums.

Claudia lifted the lid of the console and turned a dial. "It lights up," she reported. She slid the record from the album and dropped it onto the turntable.

Austin peered down into the cabinet. "How does it work?"

"Kids!" Claudia said with a snort. She picked up the tone arm and dropped it onto the vinyl. "See, Austin. There's a needle at the end of this arm, and it slips into a groove on the record, and then the music comes out of the speakers."

A second later the mellow sounds of Bing Crosby crooning "White Christmas" came floating through the speakers.

"Seems appropriate," Murphy murmured, pointing to the window, where white flakes were floating past outside.

"*Now* can we open presents?" Austin pleaded.

"On Christmas Eve?" Heinz frowned. "Is that permissible?"

"Austin is going to Gretchen's parents' house tomorrow morning, so the rule is, he gets to open one gift tonight," Patrick said.

The boy sprawled out on the floor at the base of the tree and retrieved a lumpy gold foil package that had been wrapped with yards of cellophane tape and multiple colors of ribbons as well as dragon stickers.

"The oldest person in the room opens the first present," Austin declared, handing the gift to Heinz.

"For me?" Heinz's hands trembled slightly as he slowly removed the tape and paper and ribbon.

"Hurry up!" Austin urged, standing at the old man's shoulder.

Finally, the paper fell away, revealing a clay creature with scales running down its back, a long, forked tail, and a cartoonish head with fangs.

"It's a dragon," Heinz said, turning the creature back and forth.

"I made it myself. But I'm not such a good draw-er as you and Kerry," Austin said.

"It's marvelous," Heinz said. "It's the best present anyone has ever given me."

Austin's face was wreathed in smiles. "Really?"

"Absolutely," the old man assured him. "Thank you, young friend."

Austin plucked a small box from beneath the tree. "Murphy, you go next cuz I think you're the next oldest."

"Actually, I'm two years older than him," Claudia said with a chuckle. "But go ahead and open it, anyway."

Murphy slit the tape on the box with a penknife, opened it, and lifted out a single key with a golden tassel attached. He glanced over at Claudia, who shot him a knowing smile, then he wordlessly tucked the key into the breast pocket of his flannel shirt.

"You're next," he told her, pointing to a wooden cigar box tied with a red satin bow.

Claudia unfastened the bow, opened the box, and lifted out a small carved wooden figure, about six inches tall, nestled in tissue paper.

"It's Santa," Austin said.

"Look closer," Murphy advised.

The figure had a dark, raggedy beard and a riot of untamed hair. He wore a red-and-black-checked shirt, jeans, and hunting boots. But the giveaway was the Christmas tree slung over his shoulder.

"No way! It's Murphy," Austin crowed.

Claudia threw her arms around Murphy's neck and kissed him soundly. "It's perfect! Did you carve it yourself?"

"It's nothing much, really," Murphy said, blushing. "I had time on my hands while I was sitting around the stand at night, so I kinda just started whittling on a chunk of cedar. I used Kerry's markers to color it with. Just something to remember me by after I've gone back south."

"As if I could ever forget Murphy Tolliver," Claudia said, kissing him again.

"There's another gift under the tree there for Murphy." Heinz pointed to a flat rectangular package wrapped in brown paper.

"For me?" Murphy looked genuinely surprised. "I don't have anything for you, Heinz."

The old man patted his clay dragon. "I have enough gifts. More than I've gotten in thirty years, now that I think of it."

When the brown paper was ripped away, Heinz's guests "ooohed" in unison as the gift was revealed — a watercolor portrait of Queenie. The dog's large dark eyes seemed to shine out from her face, and her muzzle, complete with the heart-shaped patch of brown fur, curved into something almost like a smile with just the tip of her pink tongue exposed.

"Don't touch the paper," Heinz urged. "The paint isn't quite dry. I had very little time to work on it, so it's not as detailed —"

"This is amazing," Murphy said, holding the edge of the portrait's frame. "You really captured her soul."

"She's a very soulful dog," Heinz said. "And excellent company. I'm going to miss her when she's gone."

"Why do Queenie and Murphy have to go? Why can't they just stay here with us?" Austin asked plaintively.

"We gotta go home and get busy growing Christmas trees so they'll be ready when we come back here to sell them next year," Murphy said gently. "Me and Queenie, we're from the country. We do okay in the big city for a month, but after that, we need to get back to the mountains and roam around in the woods where we belong. Just like you belong here in the city with your dad."

The boy's lower lip trembled.

"Austin, don't forget, you've got a gift for Kerry, don't you?" Patrick reminded him, pointing to the tree, where only two more gifts remained.

Austin retrieved a box wrapped in shiny red paper embossed with green Christmas trees and placed it in Kerry's lap.

"I love it already," Kerry said. "It's too pretty to unwrap."

"Wait until you see what's inside," Austin said.

Kerry ripped the paper away and opened the box, lifting out a snow globe. Pictured inside the glass orb, in exquisite detail, was a miniature three-dimensional scene of a small city park surrounded by distinguished brownstones.

"Oh my gosh," Kerry exclaimed. "It's Abingdon Square. Right here." She shook the globe and watched while the delicate flakes of white drifted to the base of the globe. She turned to Patrick. "I absolutely love it."

"Austin saw it in a shop window over on

Greenwich Avenue," Patrick said. "We wanted you to have something to remember us after you go home."

Kerry hugged the boy tightly. "Thank you, Austin," she whispered. "Now, there's one more present under that tree, and since you're the youngest, I think it must be for you."

The child had to crawl beneath the tree to grab the last gift. It was flat and wrapped in brown paper decorated with hand-drawn Santas, reindeers, and elves done in Kerry's distinctive drawing style.

He unceremoniously tore the paper off, then held the gift between both hands.

"It's our story!" He looked from Heinz to Kerry. "You made it into a book."

"Your story," Kerry corrected him. "We only had time to staple it together for now, but after Christmas, we'll have it printed and bound between real covers for you."

"Dad, it's my book," Austin said, balancing himself on Patrick's knee.

"You should open it and take a look," Heinz advised.

Austin leafed through the pages, pointing out the illustrations he'd dictated to the two artists. "Those are the bad guys that Mr. Heinz drew," he told his father. "And here's the owl that Kerry did." He stabbed the drawing of the boy and girl dragons. "Mr. Heinz made the lady dragon."

He kept flipping pages, but stopped suddenly, looking from Kerry to the old man. "You finished it. You finished the story."

CHAPTER 54

Austin stared down at the last page. The illustration showed three backlit figures. The gates to the forest were unlocked and flung open and a young boy, an old man with a cane, and a woman, all of them holding hands and accompanied by an alert, trusting dog, stood looking at the forest. In the distance could be seen a police cruiser, with two villains hanging out the back window.

"It's us!" the boy exclaimed, stabbing the drawing with his finger. "Me, Mr. Heinz, and Kerry. And Queenie. And there's the bad guys, going to jail, right, Kerry?"

"Being hauled off to the hoosegow," Kerry agreed.

"Do you like it?" Heinz asked, almost shyly.

"It's the best book I ever read," Austin said. "Right, Dad?"

"Look at the cover again," Kerry urged. Austin turned the book over and grinned.

"It's by me! Austin McCaleb, with illustrations by Heinz . . . I can't say that last name, and Kerry Tolliver. I wrote a whole book. I bet nobody else in my class has ever wrote a whole book."

"Written. And you did have some help," Patrick reminded him. "But yes, it's quite an accomplishment. I'm proud of you. And Kerry and Mr. Heinz, too."

"This was an awesome Christmas Eve," Austin said. "Can we have more dessert now? Like Miss Claudia's pie? Please?"

"Wait a minute. I think I see one more gift under that tree," Patrick said. "It's actually *in* the tree."

Austin walked completely around the tree until he saw a bright red envelope tucked among the fir's branches. He plucked it out and handed it to Kerry. "This one says it's for you." Kerry was taken aback. It was the first time she'd seen the envelope. She slit the flap with her fingernail and slid out a sheet of paper that held an out-of-focus photograph of a vintage camper.

"Is this Spammy?" She looked around the room, her eyes finally lighting on Patrick, who was trying hard not to grin. "What's this supposed to mean?"

Austin was hanging over her shoulder

examining the photo. "Yeah, Dad. What's it mean?"

"When Murphy told me he was selling Spammy for scrap, I had a crazy idea. I decided to buy it and have it restored. We're going to fix up the camper as good as new — better than new, with a real working bathroom and heat."

"Yayyyy!" Austin was jumping up and down with excitement.

"But why?" Kerry asked.

"Austin has always wanted to go camping in the woods, and well, I was thinking, maybe in the spring, when Spammy is all fixed up, we'll trailer down to North Carolina to visit you. And Queenie. If that's okay."

"In the spring? Sorry, but I won't be there then. I'll be here in the city," she said casually.

"What?" Murphy and Patrick asked at the same time.

"But, I thought . . ." Patrick started. "You said . . ."

Kerry's eyes sparkled with barely contained excitement. "A very good friend has offered me an opportunity that's too good to pass up. A job and a reasonably priced lease on an apartment right in this neighborhood."

Claudia rolled her eyes. "Reasonable? In this neighborhood? Did you find yourself a sugar daddy?"

"What's a sugar daddy?" Austin asked.

"Never mind," Patrick said. "Are you serious, Kerry? You're going to stay in the city? I mean, it's great, but just last night you said it was impossible. What's changed?"

Kerry and Heinz exchanged a knowing glance.

"Heinz gave me a stern talking-to," Kerry admitted. "Basically, he told me to get over myself. He pointed out that I'll never know if I can make it as an artist unless I try. He made me understand that I was being paralyzed, creatively, by my fear of failure."

"In turn, Kerry opened my eyes too." Heinz gestured around the room. "Thirty years ago, I left this place. I locked myself into, as my young friend here says, a dungeon. The past was too painful, so I let myself become a prisoner to my grief."

He clasped his hands around the mug of tea. "But then something mystical happened, right out there, in that park. A dog wagged her tail when she saw me, and a boy convinced me to draw him a picture. When I got sick, Kerry insisted on rescuing me. So annoying, this girl!"

That got a laugh from all of them.

"Kerry and Patrick and Austin dragged me back here, to this place of sadness, and forced medicine down my throat. I got better, and I looked around and suddenly, I realized, the present isn't such a bad place to be. George is gone, yes, but he left me with all this . . . beauty, and memories. Nothing can take that from me. I sat in my studio yesterday, and I picked up a paintbrush, and I felt . . . joy. I saw the future, and possibilities. And Kerry, and all of you, my friends, made that happen."

Kerry's throat tightened with emotion at the old man's unexpected declaration of cheer. "You made the impossible, possible," she told him.

"Heinz has asked me to work on organizing and cataloging his paintings," Kerry explained. "When that's done, we'll plan an exhibit and sale. But we're not sure how long that will take, because there are a couple hundred pieces here in the apartment and studio."

"And I lose track of how many more paintings I have in storage," Heinz said. "The job could take months. Years, possibly. I need an assistant I can trust, someone with youth and taste and energy. And selfishly, I need that assistant to live close by. As it happens, there is a long-vacant unit here in the building."

"Where?" Claudia asked, obviously dubious. "I know all the tenants here. There hasn't been a vacancy in years."

"It's the ground-floor efficiency formerly rented by Rex's son, who moved out several years ago," Heinz said.

"I remember that unit. You expect her to live in that dump?" Claudia asked.

Kerry's enthusiasm was undeterred. "It's tiny, and from the look of it, was last cleaned and painted during the Nixon administration, but it has a window with decent light, and the most revolting bathroom I've ever seen, and I can't wait to make it mine."

"We'll be neighbors!" Claudia said. "Fortunately for you, I love to paint. Walls, that is. It's my Zen."

Murphy thumped the coffee table with his fist. "Kere, I think this is great. You've obviously been miserable living back at home these past few months. What a cool opportunity."

"Thanks, Murph," she said. "I'm a little worried about hurting Mom's feelings . . ."

"She'll be fine with it," her brother assured her. "More than fine."

Kerry had been watching Patrick's expression as she unveiled her grand scheme, but to her dismay, his face had remained impassive. Her cheeks burned with embarrassment and she was suddenly stricken with panic. Maybe she'd misjudged him. Maybe he'd regained his sanity.

He stood abruptly and began gathering up empty wineglasses. "More dessert, anyone? Kerry, could you come out to the kitchen to give me a hand?"

As soon as the swinging door to the kitchen had closed, Patrick swept her up into his arms, literally lifting her from her feet into his embrace.

"You're really doing this? It's really going to happen?"

"Yes, you idiot," she exclaimed when she could catch her breath. "But you just gave me the fright of my life! I saw your face out there when I said I was staying. Everyone else was so excited. Even Murphy, who never gets excited about anything. But you didn't say a word. I was terrified you'd changed your mind. About me. About us."

"Never," he said, taking her face gently between both hands. "I will never change my mind about you. Or about us. I love you, Kerry Tolliver. Austin adores you. Apparently, everyone in this nutty neighborhood — even the biggest grump of an old man on the block loves you. But nobody, I promise, will ever love you as much as I do. Do you believe me?"

She wrapped her arms around his neck. Her lips met his, and he had his answer.

ACKNOWLEDGMENTS

So many kindnesses were showered upon me as I worked on this novel, to count them all would take more pages than I'm allotted. But, in short, research thanks go to my literary agent, Stuart Krichevsky, who fact-checked this Southern girl's New York City references, and who accompanied me on my scouting trips to the West Village, where I placed the fictional Tolliver Family Christmas Tree Farm stand. Thanks to Billy Romp and family, from Vermont, whose real-life tree-selling experiences in Greenwich Village loosely inspired my story. Thanks also to Doug Munroe, of West Jefferson, North Carolina, who shared his knowledge of Christmas tree farming, and for my sister from another mother, Beth Fleishman, and her long-suffering husband, Richard Boyette, who opened their mountain house in West Jeffie, as they call it, for a research trip. My publishing team at St. Martin's Press is simply the best, and I am beyond thankful to their leader, my amazing publisher and editor, Jennifer Enderlin, for her wisdom and guidance for this, our fifteenth book together. Fifteen books! Rounding out the team are the invaluable Alexandra Hoopes, Anne Marie Tallberg, Brant Janeway, Christina Lopez, Drew Kilman, Emily Dyer, Erica Martirano, Erik Platt, Jeff Dodes, Jessica Zimmerman, Kejana Ayala, Lisa Senz, Mike Storrings, and Tracey Guest.

Meg Walker of Tandem Literary has been my marketing whiz, sob sister, and constant friend for sixteen years, and I can't imagine publishing and marketing (and touring) a book without her at my side.

My Friends and Fiction sisters, *New York Times* bestselling novelists all: Kristin Harmel, Kristy Woodson Harvey, and Patti Callahan Henry, along with our AV Nerd/ Cabana Boy Shaun Henninger, and librarian extraordinaire Ron Block make work seem like fun, and I know I speak for all of them in thanking our 150,000 Friends and Fiction Facebook Group members for their support and love of books.

Stuart Krichevsky is still and forever the best damn agent in the business, and Paige Turner and I will always be grateful for that long-ago writer's conference prank that cemented our working relationship.

Never last and never least, I thank my family; husband, Tom, who is the wind beneath my wings; son, Andrew, and his love, Meg; son-in-law, Mark; and my fabulous grandchildren, Molly and Griffin, who are my anchor, my heart, my loves.

ABOUT THE AUTHOR

Mary Kay Andrews is the *New York Times* bestselling author of *The Homewreckers; The Santa Suit; The Newcomer; Hello, Summer; Sunset Beach; The High Tide Club; The Beach House Cookbook; The Weekenders; Beach Town; Save the Date; Ladies' Night; Christmas Bliss; Spring Fever; Summer Rental; The Fixer Upper; Deep Dish; Blue Christmas; Savannah Breeze; Hissy Fit; Little Bitty Lies;* and *Savannah Blues.* Andrews is a former journalist for *The Atlanta Journal-Constitution* and she lives in Atlanta, Georgia.

The employees of Thorndike Press hope you have enjoyed this Large Print book. All our Thorndike Large Print titles are designed for easy reading, and all our books are made to last. Other Thorndike Press Large Print books are available at your library, through selected bookstores, or directly from us.

For information about titles, please call:
  (800) 223-1244

or visit our website at:
  gale.com/thorndike